THE BONE CHURCH

THE BONE CHURCH

A NOVEL

VICTORIA DOUGHERTY

ISBN-10: 061598052X
ISBN-13: 9780615980522

For Dale

CHAPTER ONE
VATICAN CITY: MARCH 11, 1956

The viscount with the dense, copper hair rocked back and forth in the front pew. He whispered to the man next to him.

Felix pretended not to notice the disturbance. He unlocked the tabernacle and retrieved a gold chalice, pyx, paten, and crucifix from its purple silk interior, then arranged them on the altar before the Cardinal. A sweet, breathy gust of air blew in from the only open window in the chapel, making Felix's cassock flutter against his legs. It felt good – almost like the touch of a woman's fingertips.

"In nomine Patris, et Filii, et Spiritus Sancti. Amen," the Cardinal said, making the sign of the cross over his head and breast.

At long last, the viscount looked up from his rocking and whispering. He folded his hands and consigned them to his lap, where Felix could still see on the man's middle finger the shiny indentation where a bulbous emerald ring had rested until a few weeks ago. It had come time to pay off the Romanian attaché and his pet border guard in exchange for a wispy woman with an advanced case of Parkinson's disease.

"But what wouldn't a man do for his mother?" The viscount had said upon their last meeting. *Plenty,* Felix had thought. He'd once watched a man shoot his mother in the face for a single gold tooth rolled in a piece of blood-stained suede. Of course, the attaché had failed to disclose that the viscount's mother – in addition to her Parkinson's – was also in the late stages of dementia, soiling herself and exhibiting a total vocabulary of five words: "Paris, last Christmas" and "hideous curtains!"

Still, the viscount appeared grateful for her safe recovery. He'd even remarked that she was eating better.

"Judica me deus, et discerne causam meam de gente non sancta: ab homine iniquo; et doloso erue me."

Psalm 42. Felix recited it in tandem with the Cardinal. *Judge me, O God, distinguish my cause from the nation that is not holy; deliver me from the unjust and deceitful man.*

Mass was brief – twenty-five minutes start to finish – and Felix was glad of it. Cardinal Carlo Merillini's obligation to the row of elegant gentlemen bowed in the front pew was fulfilled. The Cardinal now stood in the back of the nave with Primo, his valet, while Felix collected the tithes and thanked the visitors: an Argentine cattleman, an American steel magnate, a Polish-born hotelier, the viscount, and a handful of other influential Catholics.

"Envy and death, Father," muttered the cattleman.

"I'm sorry?"

"It's all they know." He was a little man, fully bald.

"Yes."

The cattleman spoke lovingly of his Lithuanian wife. Pretty woman. Felix had met her before.

"Envy and death," the cattleman repeated.

The cattleman's sister-in-law and young niece had been killed by a Russian soldier at the end of the War. Raped on a bed of horse dung in their stables, then bludgeoned with a bottle of cheap brown vodka. Only his wife's daughter from a first marriage had survived the incident, hiding behind a bushel of hay and biting a salt lick to keep quiet. The cattleman mouthed the girl's name.

It was just the year before last when Felix had finally been able to arrange passage for the girl. Already sixteen by then, she'd been instructed to dress as a prostitute – presumably for one of the port guards – but was instead folded into the bowels of a sofa and smuggled over the Baltic Sea into Sweden.

"She still hates horses," the man said. "And she hates her mother." The cattleman tapped Felix's forehead with his index finger. "Poisoned her mind."

Felix looked the man in the eye and clasped his hand. He then took the cattleman's envelope and handed it to Primo.

"And this is the acquaintance I wrote to you about." The cattleman tugged at Felix's cassock.

Felix nodded at the Polish hotelier, though they hadn't been officially introduced. The man took Felix's hand and squeezed, bringing it to his lips and rubbing his twice shaved cheek over the priest's knuckles.

"A tragic story if I ever heard one," the cattleman said.

The Pole began to sob.

Felix put his hand on the Pole's head and assured him that he would speak to the Cardinal on his behalf. "These matters take time," he explained.

He didn't have the heart to tell the man how far down in the queue he was – how many dozens had come before him begging about a wife, a husband, a son or daughter, a brother, a lover. And how Felix, too, had begged and prayed until finally his turn had come.

St. Peter's Square was already awash in gold when Felix emerged from the Vatican's private visitors' chapel. For a moment, he watched the sun teeter at the top of the basilica's spire.

Cardinal Merillini stood at the entrance to Bernini's Colonnade with Primo at his side.

"Your Excellency." Felix bowed, kissing the Cardinal's ring.

"Liebermann has a contact in Prague," the Cardinal began. His voice was slow and deliberate, as if he had just awakened from a long sleep. "This man wants no help from our German friend – only as a point man on the inside. Distrusts Germans. But he claims he can deliver the woman by the end of the month."

He waved Primo ahead and the two men began their walk through the Colonnade.

"It's a man in Czech intelligence – a comer, not some flak in charge of tampering with the mail."

"What would a man like that want with us?" Felix asked.

"He wants to be paid, of course."

It was unlike the Cardinal to be so direct about their extra-vocational endeavors. The Cardinal was by nature an eloquent man who preferred the realm of ideas to the details of their realization.

"She has a son, you know," the Cardinal said. "The husband – this man Melan – was executed in 1952. He was one of the defendants in the Slanský show trials."

4

The Cardinal cleared his throat, but his voice remained rough, like a mortar and pestle grinding seed. "Pitiful turn of events," he continued. "Fourteen men. All of them Jewish, all of them innocent. Forced to confess to concocted acts of treason – and for what? For being intellectuals instead of blunt instruments."

Felix had never met Antonin Melan personally, but had heard he was a decent fellow, an ideologue who believed communism would save the world after the ravages of the Second World War. His only crime had been to trust the wrong people. And to be a true believer instead of a mere apparatchik.

Any records of Melan's immediate family – his wife, Magdalena, and the son, Ales, had been hidden or destroyed by the Soviets. For years Felix had searched, but was unable to find a trace of any Melan – either alive or dead. It wasn't as if Antonin Melan's family had disappeared, but rather had never existed – a not uncommon fate for those refusing to denounce a disgraced relative.

Until last month.

Magdalena Melan's name had resurfaced in Czechoslovakia as a foreign agent – a ludicrous charge if there ever was one. She was now, officially, an Enemy of the State rather than just a nuisance who needed to quietly go away.

"Does he have a name?" Felix asked.

"Who?"

"This contact – the man from Czech intelligence."

The Cardinal tipped his chin up, his lips forming a short, puckered line. "You know better than to ask." The Cardinal reached into his vestment and retrieved a large folder from under his arm. He handed it to Felix, contemplating the Czech Jesuit, who sifted through its contents.

Cardinal Merillini had hoped to dissuade Felix from any involvement beyond the strategic on this assignment, but forbidding him to go would've only invited disobedience. And once a priest flagrantly disobeyed an order, it wasn't long before he disavowed his robe.

"Thank you." Felix bowed his head, and the Cardinal led the way into an early Renaissance building, its interior decked in blue-veined marble. The Cardinal's office was perched on the third floor corner, one of many rooms that comprised his suite of apartments.

For Felix, visiting the Cardinal's apartments was a bit like coming home. The artists whose work his father had so admired from a distance – Caravaggio, Pisanello, Daret – were mounted in heavy gold frames. Michelangelo had painted images of the apostles on the wall alongside the banister, one of the few artifacts left unmolested during a seventeenth-century renovation.

Felix's first glimpse of those same apostles hadn't been in the books of his father's study or on his initial visit to the Cardinal's office some years before, however. It had been in his mind's eye when he was little more than a child – a reverie that he'd tried to convince himself was the result of an overactive imagination. Felix was a boy of nine and skating alone on a pond in the Blansko forest, when a still, mental image of Simon the Zealot, disciple of Jesus, avenging priest of the temple, appeared before him. Felix mistook him for a neighbor at first and began skating towards the figure when St. Bartholomew emerged from the snow. As Simon whispered into Bartholomew's ear, they faded away into a jumble of tree roots.

Back then, Felix had explained away every prescient dream and strange, wakeful image, the way a dweller in an old house might justify the creak of footsteps when he knew no one else was home.

"God's delays are not God's denials," the Cardinal rasped.

Felix looked up.

His Excellency wasn't referring to Michelangelo or the apostles, but had turned to face a painting that hung high behind his desk. It was an eighteenth century depiction of Lady Polyxena of Lobkowicz presenting the Infant of Prague sculpture to the Carmelites. A new addition to the Cardinal's collection, it had been loaned to him indefinitely by the Bishop of Verona.

The chandelier above them flickered, but the Cardinal ignored it. He placed his spectacles on his nose and squinted through the thick glass, studying the Infant's rosebud lips. He bit down, exposing his teeth as he noticed an irregular brushstroke in the painting – an unforgivable error made by a careless restorer.

"Hmm," he lamented. His thumb and index finger rode the links on a platinum chain strung around his neck, until they landed on a tiny replica of the Infant of Prague. The Cardinal picked up the holy relic, kissed it and made the sign of the cross before letting it dangle over his heart again.

The lights flickered once more, and this time they went out. A moment later, Felix heard the handle of the Cardinal's office door jiggle as his secretary, Francesco, entered. The young priest carried with him an arabesque lantern, the oil's acrid aroma saturating the room.

"*Buona sera*, Your Excellency," the Cardinal's secretary bid. His engorged eyeballs glowed in the dim lighting.

He explained that an electrical shortage had been causing problems for hours. It appeared to stem from the Cardinal's apartments – most likely in the western corner – and he begged permission to enter his superior's private quarters. The Cardinal agreed.

"It smells strangely of ...it's sweet, isn't it?" Felix observed, as they padded over the silk carpets in the Cardinal's living room. A low mist of smoke, barely visible in the glimmer of the lone oil lamp, hovered amidst the Cardinal's Baroque furniture.

Francesco led the way into the Cardinal's bath, illuminating a carved oval sink resembling a birdbath – all gold and trimmed in gemstones. A bidet, shrouded by red velvet curtains, hugged the southern-most wall. They could hear a faint drip.

"I bathed in the Sistine apartments today," the Cardinal said. "Not here."

Francesco opened the stained glass entry surrounding the bathtub. "Mercy," the young priest gasped.

Inside the glazed marble tub – his body splayed and rigid and his mouth open wide like a snake hole – lay Father Duch, an accountant to the Vienna Diocese. The towel warmer, still spitting an occasional spark, was partly submerged in the bathwater and discreetly covered the Father's genitals.

CHAPTER TWO
KLOBUKY, CZECHOSLOVAKIA:
SAME DAY

Magdalena Melan watched her son from the bedside window as he carried their last container of kerosene from the outhouse to the front door step. He set it down next to a row of three lamps in need of refilling and fiddled with the cap. The cold spell had come late and then lingered, prolonging an already bitter winter and crusting the snow with a layer of ice thick enough to support the trudges of an eleven-year-old boy without leaving so much as a footprint.

"Ales!" Magdalena furrowed her brow and tapped on the window pane.

He'd spilled some of the kerosene on his shoe and she was afraid he might try to light the lamps before unlacing it and putting it at some distance from him. He'd destroyed one of their good blankets that way just after they'd moved in, and was lucky to have only singed his hair.

She gestured to Ales and he nodded.

He screwed the cap back on the kerosene container and stood, massaging his right hand with his left. He was too frozen to fill the lamps right then anyway – his hands stiff

9

and numb – so he left the lamps and kerosene where they were and let himself back inside. There, he set his sights on an early dinner. There was soup to be warmed and a fire to be lit. The lamps could wait for another hour.

Magdalena hated being a burden to her young son, even if she was proud of the way he went about their business. At times, despite his shaggy bangs and shapeless trousers, she could see in him the man he would one day be. The man his father had been when she knew him. But the pleasure she took in Ales's maturity couldn't compete with the shame that overwhelmed her when he hunched down to hack fiercely into the crook of his elbow.

Ales had been suffering from a wet cough throughout much of the winter, and despite Magdalena's own waning health, she had done her best to lug herself out of bed the previous day to insulate their drafty windows with some old army blankets she had stolen.

"Come here, Ales," Magdalena tendered, as she watched her son shuffle around their hotplate with a hodge-podge of worn blankets wrapped around him. She wanted to warm his face and run her fingers through his honeyed hair.

"I'm making your soup," he said. "It's tripe – you like it."

"Soup, soup, soup," she sang, but her son was in no mood for her teasing. He appraised her sunken cheeks with a shake of his head. Her raven hair had lost its sheen and she smelled like a sick old woman.

"You have to eat," he told her. "You promised."

A knock sounded at the door, and Ales stepped off his stool. He listened, then looked through a crack in the door jam. Ales found he was looking at a stranger – a man in a heavy woolen coat, with a hat, scarf, and gloves. The man looked very warm indeed. Ales backed up with slow steps at first, and then ran over to his mother, getting under the covers with her.

The stranger opened the door and stepped in. He smiled at Ales, giving him a salute, before closing the door behind him. The squalling winds from outside rattled the little cabin, sweeping easily through its poor insulation.

"Who are you?" Magdalena demanded.

"I've come to help you."

The man took off his hat revealing a tuft of wispy hair on his head – like a baby's. He had a pale face and a sparse, blonde goatee.

"I don't know you," she said.

The man took a couple of steps forward in an official manner. With a simple, careless motion, he lit a cigarette and inhaled, taking no pleasure from it.

"Your boy looks ashen and thin. Not at all how a young boy should look. I have a son about his age and he's plump and rosy-cheeked. He loves to play soccer, and he's quite good."

"What do you want?"

"It's not what I want. It's what you want. Nutritious food. A decent place to live. A job. Wouldn't you like your son to have enough to eat? Warm clothes. To go to school?"

Ales hadn't been to school in well over a month, but Magdalena couldn't bear to send him there. She feared another man with foreign cigarettes would come and take her away while he was gone. Last time she'd only been in custody for a few days, but the time before that, they'd kept her for nine weeks.

Magdalena was afraid she'd be taken away, but also afraid for when she came back – always thinner than before, with shaking hands and an angry pitch to her voice that made Ales feel like he'd done something wrong.

"As you can see, Mr....?"

"I'm a friend, as I told you."

"Mr. Friend, we haven't had much choice in the matter."

"No, I suppose not, but I'm giving you a choice now." The man glanced once at Ales and flipped his ash, rubbing it into the doormat with the tip of his shoe.

"What kind of choice?"

"The choice to do the right thing for you and your son."

He stepped carefully over the newspapers and magazines Magdalena had laid over missing tiles, and appraised the crumbling hearth clogged with years of soot.

"I can take the boy to Prague today," he offered. "There, I'll make sure he's given a decent place to stay, good clothes, and plenty of food."

Magdalena looked into the man's eyes – a stone blue with flecks of white that looked like snow. Her stomach cramped and she dry-heaved onto her pillow.

"Are you alright, Mrs. Melan?" The man produced his handkerchief and blotted her lips and chin with it. "It was Meinl, wasn't it? Before your husband's grandfather changed it to Melan? I don't blame him for not wanting a Jewish name – even in those carefree days. I understand that bit of social climbing saved your husband's life during Hitler's time. That and some clever documents, of course." The man's teeth glowed in the fading daylight like sweet water pearls that had been strung loosely through his gums.

"My husband means nothing to me."

"Or to me!" Ales grunted, and the man forced a chuckle.

"That's not what you said during your questioning."

"I didn't say anything," Magdalena insisted.

"Then perhaps it was what you *didn't* say."

He lifted one of the green army blankets Magdalena had tacked over the windows and looked out onto a stretch of forest that separated the cabin from the next village over. Magdalena's eyes followed his and rested on the passenger door of his black Skoda. He'd come alone.

"I have no intention of taking Ales from you," he continued. "It's only temporary – until you can join him."

"Join him where?"

"A warm place, as I said. Certainly a place that's clean and has more than one room. I can understand why you left your State-issued flat, but this place is hardly any better."

Magdalena dug her fingers into her son's arm and held him close.

"There are no problems here," Friend assured. "Only solutions."

The pot trembled as the soup began a fierce boil. Friend moved to turn off the hotplate, inhaling the aroma of cream, tripe, and tomatoes. He picked up the stirring spoon, blowing on the soup before tasting it. It was as good as his grandmother's, he told her. Friend set the pot on Magdalena's night table and sat down on the edge of her bed. He leaned in closer and patted her hand.

"I truly want to help you do your part, but you have to help me. We have mutual friends, you and I, and we really can get you the things you need. But what I need from you is a little bit of faith. Mrs. Melan, if you don't do as I say, you'll die here. Maybe not this winter, but then there's the next, and then another."

Friend picked up her hand and kissed it, holding her fingers in his like a lover.

"I want to go with Ales today," she whispered.

"You'll join him within the week. You have my word. I'm not a murderer, you know. I wouldn't send you back to the apartment you were assigned to – it's a wonder you didn't come down with tuberculosis living there. And I certainly don't want you and the boy to be stuck here without any means of survival."

Friend rose from the bed and went to the small, wooden table next to the door. "Until then, you have to get your strength up. I'll leave some money for you here. It should be enough to keep you well fed until we meet again."

Magdalena watched him remove a fifty-crown note from his wallet and place it on the table underneath the red clay ashtray Ales had sculpted for her.

"No," she said.

"Come now, Mrs. Melan," Friend chided. "I hope this isn't pride talking. In a collective society, my money is your money, isn't that right? Think of it as a fair trade. I will care for your son until you can better care for him, and in return you will give me your trust. Trust is, after all, the foundation of any successful venture."

Magdalena lifted her son's head, touching her nose to his. She knew Friend's offer was not a request.

"He was going back to school on Monday. I swear it," she said.

Friend put his hands in his pant pockets and nodded his head. "I'm sure he was."

"And he hasn't any good shoes."

He lifted the blanket and wrinkled his nose at the boy's torn Oxfords.

"Getting a new pair should be the first order of the day, then," he said. "Young Ales, why don't you take your things and come with me? I have some gingerbread cookies in the car for you."

Ales buried his face under his mother's ear. "You can shove your cookies," he growled, but Magdalena shushed him. She stroked his hair and neck like she had when he was a baby.

"Please, comrade," Magdalena begged. "You can come for us both next week. We'll be ready. I'll buy Ales some new things."

Friend stepped closer and laid his palm on the boy's head. It was a definitive gesture, claiming the boy as if he were a tennis ball or a coconut.

"But I've come today."

Magdalena watched a sliver of moonlight creep in from under the door. Her hands still held the memory of Ales's supple face, and Magdalena caressed her arms, belly, and neck with them – the way her mother used to when Magdalena had trouble falling asleep. She knew how quickly the sense of a touch could be forgotten. How suddenly a week could seem like a year.

Though it had been nearly thirteen years since her mother's death, there were still nights Magdalena would try to recall her caress as she lay on the brink of sleep. Her hands had always been soft and moist from her lilies of the valley skin lotion. Yet it wasn't her mother's touch, but her smell Magdalena missed most – a mixture of soap and cigarette smoke that reminded her of a campfire in the woods after a light rain. It was a perfume that had permeated the cellar room they'd shared during the war – at least until her mother's body had begun to turn on itself.

She would've done anything to have her mother with her today. Her mother would've known what to do. She had always been so good at finding opportunities to play to people's vanity, to their secret desires. Mama might have looked at Friend and known if he was truly alone, sent by "mutual friends," as he said, or just another one of them. Cast to finally take away the only thing she was sure she loved.

Perhaps they expected her to kill herself now.

Magdalena sat up – abruptly – with more strength than she knew she had, and inhaled deeply through her nostrils. She put her heels down on the floor and stood, dragging a blanket with her. She sniffed her mattress, the air, the army blankets serving as curtains.

"I'm going crazy," she said aloud. The smell of her mother had gone as suddenly as it had come – a physical expression of memory, like a phantom itch on a severed limb.

Her mind had only tricked her like this one other time. On the day she found out what had happened to her husband's remains. The authorities had refused to give her Antonin's ashes after he was hanged, but an anonymous letter had informed her they had been mixed in with cement – along with the ashes of the other defendants from his trial – and used to fill a series of potholes on the road from Prague to Slaný.

Casually, she had thrown the letter into the fire, excused herself, and gone to the toilet. She hadn't wanted Ales to hear her sobs, and was glad to have to leave their flat in order to visit the facilities they shared with two other families. As she sat in the water closet with her face buried in her knees, a brief whiff of her mother had come through a cracked window that opened to a weed-infested courtyard.

It was a fragrance that almost spoke to her, saying, "Yes, it was an unjust end to the life of a good man." One who had accepted gratitude in the place of love, and who knew Magdalena's heart would always remain with Ales's father.

Magdalena sat down on her bed again and let the blanket fall to her waist. She murmured her son's father's name and ran her fingers along her neck the way he used to – using the nail of her index finger to simulate the scratch of his callus.

CHAPTER THREE
THE CZECHOSLOVAK BORDER: MARCH 21

A hiss came from the underbelly of the train. It issued a pant – guttural – like the final breath before a soul leaves its body. The kind of breath Father Duch had been denied due to what had been described at his funeral mass as "an unspeakable accident."

This hiss, becoming a screech as their train glided into the border gates between Austria and Czechoslovakia, gave Felix a piercing headache. The extra padding in his business suit, making him look fifty pounds heavier, made him sweat also.

Hans Liebermann looked up from his copy of *Der Spiegel* and mouthed, "Welcome home." He seemed terribly amused by that and repeated it to himself as he continued to read an article about a bribery scandal in the West German parliament.

Felix had been back in his birth country for twelve minutes, after having fled nearly a decade before. From his compartment window, the rural villages looked to have changed very little, but they *felt* different. During the reign of the

Nazis there had at least been a sense of urgency, but now, as he looked out onto the church steeples and small seas of red roof tiles marred by negligence, he saw only inertia goading them forward.

Felix reached up and opened the window in their train compartment. Liebermann had dozed off, briefly, and snorted awake at the sound of the wheezing wind.

"Aye, aye, aye," the German sighed. "*Dann mal los.*"

Felix folded his hands together and rested his forehead on the tips of his knuckles. He wasn't praying, but listening to his own breath, clearing his thoughts, and concentrating on the days that lay ahead.

In his lap lay the eggshell envelope Cardinal Merillini had given him. He opened it and pulled out a passport, driver's license, and marriage certificate – all well-worn with soft edges and various ochre stains. The name "Conrad Horst" was registered along with Hans Liebermann's on a business license more than five years old, and a piece of onion skin stationary had been slipped into its fold. *While you are a soldier of God*, it read, *you are not, in effect, a soldier.* It was written in the Cardinal's small, upright cursive.

"I spoke to the Pilsen brewmaster yesterday," Liebermann yawned. "He is an artist, always looking for a new canvas to paint on. And like any self-respecting brewer, he would love the prospect of introducing another Czech masterpiece to more discriminating palates. I've even secured a beer truck. Much better than a train, don't you think?"

Felix lowered his voice and spoke directly into the German's face. "So long as that canvas can fit a woman inside of it, I don't care if it's made of plywood."

"Are you speaking as my assistant?" Liebermann jibed.

"I'm speaking as the man who pays you."

Liebermann huffed and pulled a fresh cigarette from an ostrich leather case. He offered one to Felix. "I could use a cognac, couldn't you?"

Felix shook his head.

"Come on, it's not so early," the German prodded. "Not for my good friend Conrad, anyway."

The border guard entered their compartment and Felix produced Conrad Horst's documents. The guard lingered over his photograph before looking carefully at Felix's face.

"Everyone has a double," the border guard told him.

"*Was?*" Felix asked in German.

"*Einen doppelt,*" the guard enunciated. "You look like a hockey player from the '36 Olympics." The guard mimed holding a hockey stick and hitting a puck.

Felix swallowed and smiled. He knew he was breathing too hard and tried to hold his breath for a few moments – as if he had indigestion. The guard narrowed his eyes and threw Conrad Horst's passport into Felix's lap.

"Oh, forget it," the guard grumbled. "Fat kraut."

Felix gestured in the direction of the toilet and the guard nodded. Inside the tiny latrine, he took a couple of pain killers and sat down. An old injury in his shoulder was giving him trouble. Felix's legs shook and he leaned forward, steadying them with his elbows. He splashed his face with cold, non-potable water, fixed the glue under his mustache, and forced himself back to his compartment. The shuffling was starting up again beneath his feet, and the train began to move sluggishly away from the border gates.

"My friend, I told you not to eat the steak tartar," Liebermann blustered. He slapped Felix on the back and started to read his magazine again.

"Will she be with him?" Felix asked.

Leibermann turned the page. "Yes, of course."

"And you believe this man?"

"Believe?" Liebermann said. "I don't believe anyone. And this man doesn't believe us, I can tell you that. Imagine – he said he doesn't like my kind. And I said, 'Catholics?'" Liebermann hooted and stomped his foot.

It didn't matter if Liebermann believed him or not, Felix supposed. Liebermann's contacts were always dubious, everyone's were. Liebermann was, after all, his man – the Cardinal's man. A man who only a dozen years earlier had been one of the SS and would've shot Felix no sooner than hearing his name. Liebermann didn't know Felix's real name, and the Jesuit often imagined the look on Liebermann's face if he knew.

That was you? He might say. Perhaps at this point he would laugh.

"This woman, the political widow – who is she to you?" The German asked.

Everything, Felix could've answered. "An old family friend."

Liebermann smiled. "*Freundin, meine freundin,*" he hummed, putting his hat on and tipping it up, like Frank Sinatra. He stubbed out his cigarette and lit up a big, Cuban cigar. He tossed his magazine to the side. "That's better," he said.

Felix sat back, sinking into the warped metal coils undergirding his bench seat. He reached into his breast pocket, removing the photograph again. It was taken during the war, and was of a couple standing outside of a pub belonging to a small pensione called *The Shackles*.

The crude wedding photo flattered Magdalena's long, raven curls, taming them and making them appear glamorous. It couldn't do justice to her face, though, which stared impassively into the lens. Magdalena had never trusted the camera and wouldn't surrender to its seduction.

"Did you know that my father was born in this region?" Felix whispered, tucking the photograph back into his pocket. The train glided through a thick blanket of trees. On the other side of the modest forest was a town called Skornice, which translated to "almost nothing." It was an appropriate name, as the town was no bigger than a thumb-nail sketch – an appendage to Český Krumlov.

"My wife and I had a house in the Sudetenland near Zittau," Liebermann mused. "We were forced to leave it at the end of the war and left everything there as it was. I drove by it last time I was here on business. There was a young *hausfrau* hanging laundry over where my wife's garden used to be."

"Hans, tell me, how is it that you can have business in a socialist economy?"

Liebermann laughed and Felix looked out the window, watching his country slip by window by windowpane, until he recognized the approaching landmarks that signaled an entry into Prague. The Castle Sverak came up on their right, still lording over the countryside as it had since the time of King Otokar I; still keeping watch over the deepest part of the Vltava River.

Felix peered down to the water as the train slowed to cross the high bridge. Murky and green, the Vltava was the color of a cheap gem and hardly looked as if it sustained a world beneath its surface. It hadn't seemed that way years earlier, when Felix had last stood on the riverbank below him. The Vltava had been teeming with life then, even if made inhospitable by a long winter. And on that night, it had also welcomed death into its depths.

CHAPTER FOUR
THE OUTSKIRTS OF PRAGUE:
DECEMBER 18, 1943

" She hated the cold," Magdalena murmured as Felix cast Vera's body into the Vltava River. Its frozen surface shattered and Magdalena watched her mother's foot kick up like a showgirl's before her body dipped beneath the surface.

Vera had also hated lipstick, marzipan and Lutherans – excluding her husband, but not her late mother-in-law. Most of all, she hated being governed by anyone or anything.

Magdalena believed – despite her mother's cancer-eaten body – that Vera would find the strength to cast off the stones used to weigh her down. She would let her body rise to the surface, if only to be rotted by the sun rather than the water, and be pointed at by horrified village children as she floated through the countryside.

But for now, the great, the formidable Vera Ruza was lying at the bottom of the Vltava with only the carp to keep her company.

Magdalena pinched off her gloves and squatted down, sliding a postcard from her brassiere. On the front was a garland of skulls draped over a heavy set of doors that opened to a stack of human bones. On the bottom of the card, printed in small, black letters: *Ossuary at Sedlec – The Bone Church of Kutna Hora.* The postmark was dated 1932, and when Magdalena flipped it over she touched the faint imprint of her Aunt Sarah's handwriting. *"Would you EVER be entombed here?"* Sarah had written so many years ago. Vera, with her weak, shaky script, had replied only days before, *"It's as good a place as any."*

Magdalena laid the postcard on the ground, securing it with two rocks. "It's hardly a tombstone," she lamented, but Felix wasn't listening to her. His eyes were fixed on the river and he was whispering the Kaddish Vera had requested.

Magdalena reached into Felix's coat pocket and retrieved her silver hairbrush, clogged with tangles of black hair. It was one of only two heirlooms Magdalena had taken into hiding. She and Vera had used it every night in their cellar room, taking turns brushing each other's curls.

Magdalena kissed the bristles, a knot of she and her mother's entwined hair tickling her lips the way her father's mustache used to. Vera's hair had always been beautiful. She'd groomed it every day until that morning, even though she barely had the strength to raise the brush to her head.

"Mother to daughter and daughter to God," Magdalena said as she flung the hairbrush into the ripple that marked her mother's descent into the river. Her mother's charm bracelet – Magdalena's only other heirloom – clattered as she stuffed her hands back into her gloves.

"You must be freezing," she said, rising to Felix as she drew his coat more snuggly around her shoulders. An icy rain had begun to fall. She rubbed his forearms and put her chin to his shoulder, stroking her cheek against the worn, brown cotton of his shirt. He'd been quiet throughout their makeshift ceremony and Magdalena wondered if he was angry with her. She'd insisted on driving out with him despite the recent clamp-down on curfew violators and the increase in random document checks.

She reached up and dusted the raindrops out of his hair. It was the color of honey and sandalwood, and curled at the temples when wet. Magdalena smoothed it down and tucked it behind his ears.

"I'm fine," Felix mumbled.

He stared into the slabs of broken ice floating above Vera's grave. Magdalena hated it when he drifted off like this.

She didn't know that Felix was still conferring with her mother, continuing the conversation they had started less than an hour before her death. Nor did she know that his eyes had followed the current and traced her hairbrush as it sunk deep into the muddy water and settled into a craw at the river bottom, next to Vera Ruza's ribcage. The river's flow stirred Vera's hand. With each wave of the undercurrent, her hand drew it closer, until she was snuggling the hairbrush like an infant. Her eyes opened and she lifted the brush to her hair, stroking the bristles across her scalp and down the long tendrils that floated above her sunken cheeks.

In the coming days and weeks, Vera knew her skin would bloat and disintegrate, breaking away from her skeleton and providing food for the river's organisms. She whispered through the undercurrent, telling Felix and a lone trout that fluttered past her that she would be waiting, perhaps indefinitely, for any opportunity to find a better place to rest her bones.

CHAPTER FIVE
PRAGUE: NEXT MORNING

The rippled pages of Vera Ruza's journal stunk of talcum powder and ammonia. The camel binding, blotched with skin oils, looked a hundred years old. Magdalena was holding the tattered volume in her lap along with a prayer lantern, rereading a quote her mother had jotted down from Felix's copy of the Gnostic Gospel of St. Thomas.

"If you bring forth what is within you, what you bring forth will save you. If you do not bring forth what is within you, what you do not bring forth will destroy you."

Felix looked down at the shaky scrawl of handwriting, the ink smeared diagonally as Vera's left hand had dragged her pen across the page. In good health, Vera Ruza had denied both the God of her parents, Yahweh; and the God of her husband, Christ. Yet Vera's last written words were the ruminations of a saint.

"What if what you bring forth destroys you?" Felix whispered into Magdalena's hair.

He wanted to tell Magdalena about the way her mother's soul had lingered at her gravesite – pulling him with her down to the river bottom – but Magdalena snapped the journal shut and tossed it onto the plank-wood floor of his father's study. It smacked the surface hard, and a bust of the poet Svatopluk Čech shimmied on his pedestal.

"Don't bring it forth," she said.

She took Felix's hand from her waist, slipping it under the flap of her downy robe onto her breast. A near-empty bottle of slivovice dangled between his fingertips and she guided it to her mouth, and gulped down the few remaining sips of the plum brandy.

"Not your typical breakfast," Felix remarked.

Magdalena tipped her head up and put her tongue to his lips.

"Not your typical night."

They sunk further into the bedroom comfort of the worn, needlepoint sofa, letting the dying fire flicker over them. On the ebony mantle, a wedding portrait of Felix's late mother reflected a man standing in the doorway.

Marek Andel had a feline step that could pass through the house no louder than a sigh. He stood at his bookshelves, re-lighting a half-smoked cigarette that had been extinguished by the rain.

"Freezing out there," Marek said, resting a hand on his potbelly.

Magdalena jumped to her feet, and started to mutter an apology. She knocked the lantern off her lap, but Marek captured it in one sweep, putting a hand on her shoulder. He strode past them and sat at his writing table, lowering himself into his leather chair as if he was about to compose a letter he'd been putting off.

Magdalena put her fingers to her lips. She could smell the liquor on her breath as she backed up towards the doorway.

"Stay," Felix tendered, but Magdalena scampered out of the study and shut herself behind the hidden panel in the kitchen, sliding the lock closed before descending into the cellar. She couldn't look at the assemblage of books and magazines strewn about her mother's side of the bed – one of them, *Praguer*, still open to an article about local spots for mushroom picking – and crept into the far corner of the room, hoping to overhear what was being said upstairs.

"I walked from the train station," Marek chuckled. "Fell on my backside." He brushed his fingers through his sparse, wet hair and leaned back. A glimmer of lamplight fluttered across his face. "It was snowing in Kutna Hora when I left. Beautiful. I suppose I could've gotten a ride from the old Oberfuhrer from down the street, but well, you know. I told him to keep his driver home. My boy was picking me up."

Felix had forgotten his father was coming home a day ahead of schedule.

"Vera's dead," he murmured. He reached into his pocket and placed the keys to his father's car on the desk. "We took her to the ruins of Castle Sverak. River's deep there."

Marek removed a porcelain figurine from his breast pocket and set it next to his keys. It had once been lacquered in gold and royal purple but was now worn, the paint all but chipped away. Still, the miniature copy of the Infant of Prague – the Christ Child – retained its dignity with a strict posture and a hand poised in a gesture of peace, as if ready to wave and perform another miracle.

"I'd asked Him for relief from her suffering," Marek said, running a finger across the Infant's once-gilded crown.

Felix glanced down at the little statue. A family legacy, he hadn't seen the Infant talisman in years. Lately, however, it had begun popping up all over the house, his father moving it from room to room like a garland of garlic meant to ward off vampires.

Felix didn't care much for the Infant replicas. They used to be given by the Archbishop to only the Infant's most faithful adherents – like his father. Now, they were sold at every kiosk in town, reducing the Infant of Prague to a level of kitsch on par with a lucky rabbit's foot.

Felix imagined the throngs of pilgrims who came from all over the world to see the real Infant statue and the looks on their faces when they stepped off their train cars. Next to the snack bar at the main terminal was a new trinket booth where an image of the holy icon stared mutely at them from behind a window that also offered gargoyles and wind-up ladybugs. He wondered how the pilgrims could fall to their knees after that and plead into the genuine Infant's eyes the way Felix's father was pleading into the one blue gemstone left on his Infant replica's face.

Marek Andel looked up from the figurine and smiled. He put his hand on his son's cheek, his eyes wandering over Felix's features, taking in the remnants of his late wife – perfectly coiled ears and grass-green eyes. He then reached into his portfolio and slid an Argentine passport across his desk. Felix turned the cover to reveal Magdalena's picture pasted next to a row of small type font describing a Maria Ciccia – twenty-two years old, like Magdalena, and of Dutch-Italian descent.

"Where did you get that?" Felix asked.

"It's far too long a story for a morning like this." A plume of curled smoke floated above his nostrils.

Marek shuffled to his bookshelves and removed eight volumes of post-Renaissance Czech history, revealing a safe the size of a letterbox. He opened it, and grabbed several bundles of five-hundred-crown notes, stacking them on his desk. Then, opening his pen drawer, he reached inside and

VICTORIA DOUGHERTY

dealt two one-way tickets to Bratislava as if they were trump
cards in a game of Blackjack.

"You have to go," Marek whispered.

"You think someone knows about her?"

Marek shook his head.

He cracked the window and took a fresh cigarette out
of an old Bombay spice ewer. The freezing rain chattered
along the window sill; an occasional, grating drop pelting
the copper flower box.

"In Bratislava the stores are full," Marek said. "They have
butter."

"Of course they have butter. They're collaborators."

"Yes," Marek agreed. "But they haven't even begun any
massive deportations. Life in Slovakia is still good. Things
are relatively normal there."

"For a fascist country."

"You'll be training there, anyway, in a matter of weeks,"
Marek insisted. "Some of your teammates have already sent
their wives and children ahead."

Marek folded his hands, digging his fingernails into his
knuckles. "Magdalena will have a gentile's passport – it's a good
copy – and we can get her work papers and racial purity documents with that." Marek Andel looked up at his son and smiled.
"Maybe then you can marry and live some kind of a real life."

"Papa," Felix said. "I've never known you to be a
dreamer."

"And I've just hired an assistant for you down there,"
Marek continued. "She's young – a Hungarian born in the
Tatras – but would make an excellent nanny when the time
comes."

"We're not going to Bratislava!" Felix said. "At least, not
yet."

Marek plucked his cigarette from the ashtray and put it to his lips. The smell of his tobacco – cedar and burnt acacia leaves – infused the room. He pulled the tickets to Bratislava out of the pile of money and slapped them down, taking his son's shoulders in his hands and squeezing them. "I wouldn't have gotten that passport if it wasn't the only way right now. I'm doing the best I can and it isn't easy under these circumstances."

"What circumstances exactly?"

"Our responsibilities lie with that young woman downstairs," Marek said. "I made a promise to her mother, and I intend to keep it. You made a promise to Magdalena."

Marek picked up the Infant of Prague figurine and closed his son's fingers around its porcelain body.

"This is all we have left in helping to win this war," he said. "Take it with you to Bratislava and keep it in the pocket closest to your heart. God willing, I can come down and visit you soon. Perhaps even before Christmas."

Felix looked down at his father's hands, wrapped tightly around his own. The Infant of Prague was buried under their mound of skin and bones. "You've got to be joking."

Felix placed the figurine back onto the desk and turned away from his father. He stooped down next to the sofa, picked up Vera Ruza's journal, and tucked it underneath his arm.

"Everything has been too easy for you," Marek told him. "University. Big shot hockey player. It's all just fallen into your hands and you think no matter what you do, things will work out. The real world doesn't operate that way, son."

Felix held up Vera's journal – stained from her night sweats. "I think I have a pretty good idea of the way the real world works."

He pitched the journal onto the coffee table and wrenched the handle to the French doors, inviting a gust of wind and freezing rain into his father's study. "What have you gotten us into now?" he said.

Felix stepped out onto the portico and the wind slammed the doors shut behind him. He resisted his inclination to turn back. Instead, he looked out onto his father's yard, admiring his late mother's handiwork. Though the sun had been up for an hour, the grim sky gave the illusion of a permanent night. Still, Felix could see the squared-off bushes and neat rows of soil once brimming with flowers, herbs and vegetables. A painted wooden mermaid lazed near the cellar doors surrounded by rosemary bushes. She was the only non-living ornament that his mother would tolerate in her green space, and she sat beaming at Felix like an adoring sister.

"Bratislava," he whispered to her.

The frozen rain was turning harder and colder. Past the bushes and the stone boundary wall separating his father's yard from the next, Felix saw a twinkle of light near their neighbor's gazebo. He crept closer, the grass of the side garden crunching beneath his feet. But the light had disappeared, or perhaps, he realized, it had been a figment of his imagination, like so many things lately.

Felix closed his eyes and ran his fingers over the once jagged stones in the wall. They had been made smooth by time and weather, *like your father's belly,* his mother had said. He smiled at her memory.

"You have an amazing tolerance for the cold, my boy." The voice came out of nowhere and the face popped through the shards of rain. Felix blinked his eyes open. "Svoboda," the face reminded him.

"Yes, of course, I'm sorry, Mr. Svoboda," Felix said.

His neighbor's face opened into a wide, wet smile.

"Not at all, son. You're away an awful lot and I only moved back to my city house a couple of years ago."

Svoboda's body came into view, wrapped in two thick bathrobes with a trench coat slung over his shoulders. He motioned for Felix to follow him and he did, jumping the boundary wall and tracking the faint outline of Svoboda's coat as it twisted in the wind.

"I never used to like being in Prague – no," Svoboda continued. "I only came for an exhibit, or if my wife and daughter got bored."

He opened the door to his glass gazebo and ushered Felix inside, guiding him to a stone bench sculpted into a naked woman – her long back offering itself as a perch.

"One of yours?" Felix asked.

"My tax collectress," he chuckled. "Or at least she was."

The gazebo wasn't much warmer than the yard, but it was dry. The walls were thick with condensation, pearls of water rolling down the fogged glass. Svoboda had installed a small camping stove in the corner and the tang of grog stung Felix's nostrils.

"This'll keep you cheery," he said, ladling the brew into a clay herb pot. He raised his eyebrows and passed the potion as if he were inducting Felix into a secret society.

"Do you always come out here during foul weather?" Felix asked.

Svoboda slapped his knee. "A man of the outdoors – whether country mouse or city mouse," he laughed.

Though he was a half-head shorter than Felix, Svoboda seemed to grow taller as the hot grog flooded his system. His shoulders fell an inch or two and his neck stretched, giving him back his firm chin.

"Your father!" he exclaimed, startling Felix into dropping the pot. Grog splashed their shoes and clay triangles scattered over the gazebo floor.

"I'm sorry." Felix bent down to pick up the broken pieces, but Svoboda just kicked them aside.

"Don't mind those; I have one hundred and two of them in my garage."

Svoboda ladled more grog – this time into the tin water bowl that used to belong to his poodle. "I'm the fool who startled you, anyway. You want to come in the house for a moment? I've got an invitation for your father. Got it by mistake in the mail some days ago, but it won't take long to find."

Felix glanced back at the house and thought of Magdalena. She would be waiting for him – alone on the mattress she used to share with her mother. He wanted to crawl back down into the cellar and hum Gershwin into her ear until she was able to sleep.

"I could stop by for it tomorrow. Or Father. He got back from Kutna Hora a little while ago," Felix said.

Svoboda squinted past the foggy glass and into Marek Andel's yard, his lips tightening over his teeth. "Came back early, didn't he?"

Felix nodded.

"I'd love for you to come in, young man. Heard a lot about you. Besides, the liquor in the house is far better than the liquor out here." Svoboda hushed his voice into a whisper. "But don't tell anybody."

Felix set the bowl down and shook his head. The ice storm was mellowing into a light snow and the gazebo was losing its charm.

"I've stayed too long already," he said. "I do appreciate the grog, though."

The whites of Svoboda's eyes swelled and the sculptor cupped his cold hand over Felix's. "Can't I please nudge you to change your mind?"

"Another time," Felix assured him.

Svoboda rolled his mug of grog between his palms and exhaled. Artists were a strange lot, Felix thought. Emotional – like his mother had been. "Walk back very slowly," Svoboda cautioned. "Nothing's worth a broken bone."

Felix stepped out of the gazebo and promptly slipped on a footstone.

"Some ice skater," Svoboda chortled.

After ten careful paces, Felix turned back to wave at his neighbor, but Svoboda was gone.

The dim glow of the prayer lantern still seeped from his father's study as Felix crept closer to the house. Svoboda's gazebo rattled in the gust and Felix glanced back at the sculptor's Cubist mansion. It posed at the front right of his property like a piece of art in and of itself and was as dark as the decaying Castle Sverak had been when he'd put Vera Ruza to rest the night before.

When the wind settled, Felix heard a voice. It wasn't his father's, or Svoboda's. Felix's eyes darted around the yard – towards the front gate, the garden shed, and the cellar doors – until he realized the voice had come from inside. It had drifted – faint and barely intelligible – from the cracked window in his father's study.

"What are you planning here?" The voice sputtered. "A trip or something? I thought you only just returned from one."

"Quick business – that's all," Marek Andel explained. "I sold a property in Kutna Hora."

Felix glided down the concrete walkway and inched his way towards the study, keeping his back flat against the house. He craned his neck and peeked into the study with one eye. A dark silhouette of a man sat in the club chair near the bookshelves – leaning into the back cushion, as if having a snooze. He was holding Felix's tickets to Bratislava in his hand, along with one of the wads of cash Marek had retrieved from his safe. The other five bundles of hundred-crown bills remained in a pile on the desk top.

"Kutna Hora," the voice repeated. "Isn't that where the Boogeyman lives? In that church made of human bones."

"I wouldn't know." Marek shrugged. He turned to the mantel and tapped the toe of his shoe into the cold ashes of the hearth – quietly brushing the pale cinder dust over the exposed corner of Magdalena's new passport.

"I'm afraid I've been foolish," Marek said. "But only because I wanted to ensure that Herr Doktor's investment was safe."

The stranger spoke again. Felix struggled to make out his words as a shower of ice pebbles blew off the roof, but the man spoke at such a low decibel that none of his syllables could break through the clamor.

"He doesn't come home at all during hockey season," Marek was explaining as the noise cleared. "I'm only hoping he makes it for Christmas. My son is quite famous, you know. I'm afraid it's gone to his head. He scarcely even bothers with his old man anymore."

The stranger let the tickets fall to the floor and tucked the bundle of cash into his breast pocket.

"I never liked hockey," he said, wiping his palms on his trousers. "Soccer. Soccer's for me."

Marek Andel faced the stranger, planting his hands at his sides and exhaling deeply.

"If I could talk to Herr Doctor, Mr. Krev," he said, "I'm sure we could get all of this straightened out."

The man his father called Krev stood up from the chair and made his way closer to the lantern. It was then that Felix could see that he was hardly a man at all and certainly not someone a gentleman of his father's age and stature would be calling Mister. Krev was younger than Felix by at least five years and had a round face as fair as sour cream. A thin coat of blond, wispy hair covered his head and he sported a downy patch of fur on his upper lip that he'd probably been at pains to grow. The swastika band around his left arm seemed a poor attempt at adding authority to his lumpy tweed coat.

"Perhaps, Mr. Krev, as one Czech to another...?" Marek lifted another Infant of Prague figurine out of his pant pocket and held it out to Krev. It was brand new, painted in bright yellow vestments with a perfect gold crown. "If he won't speak to me, won't *you* please tell Herr Doktor that I didn't mean for there to be a misunderstanding? I can promise that next time, I'll follow his wishes to the letter."

Krev fidgeted, his eyes darting around the window and French doors. He took the figurine and shook it by his ear. He heard a rattle inside it, and smiled, plunging the new Infant into his ragged coat pocket.

"Herr Doktor certainly hopes you'll have better luck next time," he said, thrusting his small chin forward. "But not with his money, and not in this lifetime."

Krev's hand emerged from his pocket wrapped in a leather glove and clutching a long wire he slung around Marek Andel's neck, dragging him close to his chest. Marek's arms flailed and Krev dropped him – losing his grip on the wire and nearly stumbling to his knees.

"*Kurva!*" Krev grunted.

Felix dashed over the icy walk way, tripping over an upturned stone and slicing his hand on a rusted sickle the gardener had abandoned in the grass. He bit down and scrambled back onto his feet, but before he could reach the doors to his father's study, he heard a shot. Through the window, he saw his father on the floor – Marek Andel's arm twisted into an awkward V – with Krev standing above him. The boy was huffing and holding his gun at his groin.

Bile flooded Felix's throat as he turned from the window and squatted down. He swallowed it, punching his fist through a frozen puddle that had formed beneath a drainpipe. The bile came up again, and this time Felix couldn't stop it from streaming out of his mouth. He let it flow onto his shoes and seep into the frozen lawn.

He heard the click of the handle and saw Krev step out of the French doors, heaving a breath. Krev struggled to don his gloves, but his hands were trembling and he ultimately gave up on the task, shoving the gloves into his coat pocket. Felix started towards him, but a car pulled up to the gate, honking. He leaned behind the chimney pillar and watched Krev totter along the icy footpath until he grabbed the bars of the front gate and let himself out.

Krev had left the French doors open and Felix scurried through them, staying low to the ground. Although he knew his father was dead, Felix crawled to him and put his lips to his forehead.

Marek Andel's blood spilled out of his heart chamber onto the old, Turkish prayer rug he'd refused to replace despite its tattered edges and pet stains.

"Papa?" Felix implored, but Marek's eyes – wide and still as pond water – continued gazing out into the garden at the frosty bed where his late wife's ruby-orange tulip bulbs awaited spring.

There was a distinctive stink in the room coming from a puddle of urine that marked where Krev had stood. It was soaking into the rug at a slow and steady pace, letting its odor mingle with the musty smell of old books.

On the street, Felix heard a man curse in German and skid onto his ass.

"*Die Eisschicht!*" The German grumbled. More boot steps followed, hobbling clumsily towards the house – half sliding and half walking.

Felix could feel droplets of sweat forming on his back. The Germans were ruthlessly clear about consequences. His father's house would be searched and his belongings confiscated, while Felix would be left to explain Magdalena and the secret cellar room. Whatever crime against the Reich his father had committed was now Felix's crime as well.

He searched his father's jacket, but the keys to his car were gone, as was the money. They were spoils for his father's killer. Only the tickets to Bratislava remained and Magdalena's new passport – hidden in the hearth. Felix slipped his hands into the cool ash heap, gripping the edge of the passport and drawing it out. Ashes blew in swirls as he fanned soot off the document, and he caught a glimpse of what looked like the top of a porcelain thimble sticking out from under the charred remains of a fire log. He lifted the log, pulling his father's worn Infant of Prague out of the ashes. He looked into its one good eye and shook the figurine, but unlike the glossy new one his father had given Krev, it was empty. Felix then stuffed the Infant into his pocket, picked up the tickets and bolted to the cellar to collect Magdalena.

CHAPTER SIX

CESKÝ KRUMLOV: THAT
EVENING

Felix traced his fingers over his father's Infant figurine. As their train shuffled into Cesky Krumlov, he looked up at the stone walls of the Schwarzenberg castle. Carved high into the hill like a piece of sculpture, it lay just under the moon, tucked into a swaddling of rock, brick and lazy river. Its craggy, western façade loomed over them, but its eastern face looked down on the farm, nearly fifteen kilometers away, where Marek Andel was born. Felix had spent every summer of his youth there, running rough through the sloping countryside and picking wild mushrooms with his father in the forest adjoining their property.

"Only one night," he whispered to Magdalena, kissing her temple.

A painted tin sign with a prominent exclamation point welcomed German tourists, and Felix regretted taking the long way to Bratislava. An express train would've gotten them there in time for a late dinner, but Felix yearned to see his father's ancestral home one last time. It was only the morning train – the slow train – that passed by the family farm.

Reckless. Indulgent, he thought.

"Perhaps some stores will still be open when we arrive," Felix said. It was a ridiculous thing to say, but he wanted to appear normal. If the police ended up questioning their fellow passengers, he and Magdalena, or rather, Maria, would appear oblivious to the horrible events in Prague. "They were talking about shopping," the handsome woman sitting across from them might testify, making it look as if Felix and his new fiancé had left before any trouble began. He smiled at the woman and passed her a newspaper he'd pretended to read. She dipped her head, the feather in her hunter green hat twirling like a fairy as the train rolled to a stop.

Felix pulled Magdalena onto the train platform and rushed them out of the station. The cobblestone maze that made up the town center was just a few steps away.

"Maybe we should sleep at the station?" Magdalena said. "I bet lots of people stretch out on the benches there."

Felix slid his father's Infant into his breast pocket. "Lots of police, too."

"Police are everywhere," she said.

Felix looked down onto the river he'd learned to skate on: The same river that led back to Prague, and to Vera's grave, and to his father's body. Its surface gleamed like a glass eye.

"I want a good meal with some wine and a bed," he told her. Felix held up his wrist watch and removed from his little finger the ring bearing his family's crest. They had twenty-four crowns in addition to his father's wedding ring and platinum watch chain. He glanced at Magdalena's charm bracelet and she jerked her arm behind her back.

"We're going to need these things in Bratislava!" she insisted.

Felix held the watch up in the moonlight, polishing its crystal face with his coat sleeve. His mother had given it to him three years earlier for his twenty-first birthday.

"It's Patek Philippe," he said. "Should make a nice gift for someone."

Magdalena snatched the watch out of his palm and turned her back to him. "It's worth at least hundreds of crowns!"

"It's worth nothing," he said. "I'd give it away." Felix put his hands on her shoulders, his lips into her hair. "A few crowns aren't going to help us."

"Then what will?" Magdalena wrested herself from him. She stomped off the footbridge, onto a gas-lit lane dotted with restaurants and drinking holes. Her eyes flitted from pub to pub, scrutinizing the patrons – legitimate people with more than a half-baked passport – as they huddled in conversation. They were people with problems, living in uncertainty, but they had good papers and work permits. Magdalena watched a young man refill his wife's wine goblet, chinking his to hers, and was suddenly filled with an irrational jealousy.

"Do you really think things will be different in Bratislava?" she said. "What will they say when the Prague police come calling for us?"

"It's not as if the Prague and Bratislava police are such good friends," Felix said. "And my father's name is on a list that grows longer every day."

"Felix, you're not just any old Novák. Everybody knows you!"

Felix shrugged. It was true; he knew it. But he could do nothing about his face or his occupation. He stepped closer, wrapping his arms around her again. "Hopefully an athlete and his fiancée won't be worth the trouble."

Magdalena let him hold her this time. She dropped the watch into his coat pocket and eyed the little lane and each of its establishments. They were old and charming – set pieces from a Renaissance comedy.

"That one," she said, pointing at a small stone pub with an inn on its two upper floors. "The Shackles. That's where I want to have my dinner and sleep on a comfortable bed. Even if it's my last comfortable bed."

The pub looked more like a wine cellar with an arched ceiling trapping clouds of cigarette smoke. It was torch-lit and had a fire pit in the center, surrounded by regulars ogling three piglets, pierced nose to backside, as they spun on a spit. The piglets had died during birth, putting them into a legal no man's land, unaffected by the strict wartime laws that regulated slaughter. The owner of The Inn at the Shackles, also Krumlov's mayor, sharpened his knives behind the bar, as he offered tiny Tiso, Benito, and Adolf to the highest bidder.

"Not fair!" A local woodworker snarled as Felix tucked his handsome watch into the mayor's waistband.

"Big shots are always welcome in my place," the mayor laughed. He waved a miniature Czech flag and his patrons clapped. Felix held up a ten crown note and called for a round for the entire house.

"Give him the whole pig!" the bartender hollered.

The mayor raised his knives like a conductor and sliced off Benito's backside, laying it on a flower-trimmed plate, complete with a wedge of rye bread and a dollop of pickled cabbage. He leaned over the piglet's head and cut off his ear – the gold heart charm he'd pricked into the piglet's ear-flap glittering amongst the fatty juices. It was a pretty thing, if totally worthless, and Magdalena saw it as a good omen – a lucky charm.

"It's fool's gold," the mayor said, bending down and kissing Magdalena's knuckle. He put the plate in front of her and began carving the rest of the piglet for Felix. The woodworker pounded his fists on his table and began reciting garbled hunting poetry about the glories of fresh pork. He was stinking drunk.

"You have to stay," the mayor said. "Mine is a simple country inn, but I serve free shots of slivovice with every bed."

Felix clasped his hand and shook it, the pig fat dripping off the mayor's carving knife like melted wax. "How can we turn down free slivovice?"

"*Na Zdravi!*" the mayor cheered. "But what are we celebrating?"

Felix lifted his glass and glanced down at Magdalena. She was extricating the little heart charm from the piglet's tough skin.

"Our parents," he said. "Without whom we wouldn't be here."

The mayor roared and swung back his plum brandy. He rang the bell for last call and poured himself another while they ate.

When the last few stragglers finally slid off their bar stools, he led Felix and Magdalena into the kitchen and sat them at a butcher's table.

"My wife will kill me when she finds out you were here," he said. "She's at her sister's for the night playing midwife."

"Your wife likes hockey?" Felix said.

The mayor pulled back a lace curtain, revealing a wall tacked with nineteen years' worth of hockey memorabilia – newspaper clippings curled at the edges, ticket stubs, team flags and photographs all overlapped in a floor-to-ceiling collage.

Magdalena pointed to a photo of Felix with a black eye and two missing teeth.

"You'd better get used to it, my dear," the mayor said. "Your husband will get uglier every season."

"I might have to reconsider his proposal," she countered.

The mayor stopped laughing and crossed his arms, appraising them as he combed his mustache with two fingers.

"You're not married?" He gave a constipated smile and stared down at his brown woolen slippers.

The mayor didn't accept unmarried couples – even in separate rooms. There was too much sneaking around that went on, and too much to spike the interest of his adolescent daughter. "I'm sorry," he said. "You're going to have to find another inn."

"Your Honor," Felix said. "It's nearly midnight." Curfew had come and gone hours before.

The mayor stood up and turned his back to them, staring at his wife's tribute wall. He snickered as if he'd just remembered a joke.

"You," he cried, turning and pointing his finger at Felix's nose. "You will be married tonight – right here."

Felix shook his head. "We don't have a license."

"I'm the law here," the mayor boasted. "Who do you think issues the licenses and performs the ceremonies?"

The cook peeked out at them from the kitchen, his belly wedged between the frame and the door, making him look like an over-stuffed sandwich.

"Don't just stand there, you red-faced buffoon," the mayor told him. "Get my wife's camera."

"I don't feel married," Magdalena whispered.

She knew she should be grateful that at the very least she'd procured another document for her new identity's paper trail. It had been what Marek Andel wanted and had perhaps been what he'd died for, but their so-called wedding still felt hollow to her. It was rescued only by the sweet and familiar reality of their wedding night and the extravagant comfort of a well-appointed bed. While their room at the mayor's inn was sparsely decorated – only a bed, a night table, and a small dresser topped with a washbasin and a pitcher of boiled water – it radiated warmth and charm. It was embellished with a turn-of-the-century photograph of the Prague castle steps after the first snow, and a stack of French postcards that lay in the drawer of their nightstand, next to a pocket book of the New Testament. Theirs was the honeymoon suite.

Magdalena collected a postcard of a curvy brunette who was naked from the waist down; bent over with her face between her knees. She ran its dog-eared corner from Felix's Adam's apple down to his groin, sweeping her hair across his chest.

"And you don't look like my husband," she said, pattering her fingertips over his stomach muscles.

"Really?"

"I mean you don't look like Maria Ciccia's husband. He should be a Spaniard, I think. Or a Greek." Magdalena leaned in to kiss him and wove her fingers into his hair.

"Maria Ciccia's a fabrication," he said. "You and I are real."

"But we're not really married," she said. "You're married, but to a forgery. A Maria Ciccia who happens to look exactly like me."

Magdalena jingled her bracelet, holding up a cameo charm her mother always claimed resembled her as a little girl. "What are we going to do?" she asked him.

Felix rolled onto her, crunching the sheets beneath them. He nestled his face into her hair and neck, inhaling her skin cream. It mixed with the strong, briny smells of his mouth. Her shoulder tasted of a fig. It was the same sweetness he'd detected when they were still children and Magdalena dipped her finger into a gravy boat and let Felix lick the sauce of giblets and onions from its tip.

The memory seemed far away now, when only a week ago he would've said it was like yesterday. Everything before the moment he watched young Mr. Krev garrote his father floated in the background like a distant dream. His father had once told him that a boy becomes a man when his father dies, even if he's long been the master of his own life. He becomes the true man of the house – not just of his own house, but the house of his ancestors. He becomes the sole guardian of his family name.

"What was he like?" Magdalena asked. "The man who killed your father?"

He brushed her hair from her face and settled next to her. "He was nothing," he told her. "Barely a man, with a face like a baby's."

Chapter Seven
The Czech-Polish Border:
December 24

Magdalena was saying something. So quietly. Her arms were wound tightly around Felix's neck; her forehead was pressed to his collarbone.

"Chilliest land," then "strangest sea," she said, and Felix realized that she was reciting *"Hope" is the thing with feathers* by Emily Dickinson. It was Magdalena's version of a prayer.

Felix kissed the top of her head.

A man with a fur collar squirmed, while his wife, or perhaps sister, admonished him for making it difficult for her to breathe. She wiggled her elbows and kicked the shins of a young boy – maybe fourteen – and then his mother.

"Watch it, bitch," the mother said, kicking back.

The commotion crushed Felix and Magdalena closer. He clinched his arms around her and their bellies rubbed together. Magdalena's stomach growled ferociously. She hadn't eaten since the prune tart a day and a half earlier. Neither had Felix, but she could hear nothing coming from his empty belly.

"I smell oranges. Don't you smell oranges?" The man in the fur collar sniffed the air like a hound.

"Somebody has oranges and coffee," the woman with him said.

"Shut up," Felix whispered, and Magdalena nuzzed closer to him.

But she smelled it, too. Coffee and oranges. They were close to the back of the train, so it must've been coming from the caboose. An afternoon snack for the engineer.

The aroma taunted her hunger and stirred a part of her memory that she'd long since locked away. A time before war and hiding and love; when a German on the street was merely a tourist and a train was nothing more than a mode of transportation.

It was when she was twelve years old and her parents took her to Palestine; a place she would always remember by its perfume of coffee, oranges, and jasmine. The desert there had seemed to her a beautiful, sleeping woman. If the mountains were her body, the desert was the palm of her hand, cracked with the lines of her destiny. The hot air was her breath.

The memory of that naked land comforted her now. It was a part of the earth that had always existed and always would exist exactly as it was – Germans or no Germans. Moses had walked those lands in the same fashion as a modern-day desert tribesman, with animal skin water pouches, camels, and swaddled clothing to protect against the heat of the day, and warm the bones through the chill of night.

It was on that trip Magdalena first identified herself as a Jew. Although her mother had never converted, her family celebrated the Christian holidays of her father's faith and paid only lip service to the Jewish holy days. These were customarily days that her mother observed alone – or not at all.

Bless her father, she thought. It had been his idea to come to Palestine and properly introduce her to her half heritage. He was a scholarly man who had little patience for Jewish rituals practiced in the home, but a journey to the Holy Land was something he could sink his teeth into. Her father had known obscure details about even minor happenings that occurred more than a thousand years past, and he pontificated with a lusty joy that made Magdalena and her mother look at each other and giggle.

"They schemed and Allah schemed, but Allah is the greater schemer!" He quoted the Qur'an as if it were *Macbeth*.

One night, when it was too hot to sleep, Magdalena recalled getting up to open the wooden shutters in her room. The air outside was dead still, suffocating, but the full moon had gushed a friendly blue light that illuminated the street below.

As she looked out her window, she became aware of two men standing in the shadows across the street from her hotel. They looked like they were conducting business, but it was odd for them to be out on the street at that hour. Jerusalem was a holy city, and not one for late nights. The shorter man with big feet embraced his companion and danced slowly with him for a few moments. The two men went down to the ground together, in an embrace, until the shorter man lay on top. This man raised himself and knelt over his companion, while his hands explored his outer and inner clothing. Once satisfied, the short man got up, leaving the other man unmoving on the floor.

It was the first act of violence Magdalena had ever glimpsed; yet it was performed so gracefully that she didn't realize she'd witnessed a murder until many years later – when her father was already dead of fever and she and her mother were ensconced in the Andel's cellar.

Murder, it occurred to her, had lost any sense of ambiguity since then.

Magdalena tilted her head up at Felix and endeavored to smile at him. She wanted to tell him her story about Palastine, but he was deep in thought and bore a grave expression. He bent down and spoke into her ear. Magdalena couldn't hear what he said over the trundling of the wheels, and he just shook his head. She watched him for a long time, but he was lost to her.

"I'm sorry," was what he'd said.

The mayor of Ceský Krumlov had plied them with prune tarts and an overly sweetened pot of coffee before hurrying them out of his pension. Their train had been delayed till mid-morning, but the mayor had wanted to make sure his newlyweds were able to make a stop at Pringel's Jewelry Store before their departure.

A cousin of the mayor, Pringel had promised to attach Benito-the-pig's gold-plated heart to Magdalena's charm bracelet for no cost, provided Felix look at wedding rings he could sell him at cost.

"Wouldn't you rather something with a little more *gravitas?*" the jeweler pressed. "This piece of tin will only chip."

Max Bruch's *Violin Concerto No. 1 in E Minor* wailed incessantly from a gramophone, while Pringel tapped his pen to the music and appraised the little trinket.

"I don't care if it chips,'" Felix had told him. "She wants her initial in the center." Somehow it had seemed important to him.

Felix now hated himself for having taken Benito the piglet's gold heart to Pringel the jeweler. An attachment to anything – let alone something as frivolous as a lucky charm – only created trouble.

Look what it had done to his father, he thought.

"Yes, of course I told him it'll chip," Felix heard Pringel say. He was talking to an apprentice – a tall man with a mop of dirty blonde hair. Thin as an insect, but strong, with legs built for long strides. He looked right at Felix.

Recognition burst onto the man's face and Felix felt a sudden inclination to run.

"My friend!" The man leapt through the curtains and gasped. "I hope I'm not being too familiar." Removing the magnifier loupe from his right eye, he pocketed it and then brushed his fingers through his hair. It would not be tamed.

"Not at all." Felix took his outstretched hand and combed his memory for the man's name. All he could remember was that he'd never liked him.

"You look so well! But my best days are behind me," the apprentice sighed.

A Grepo – in civilian clothes except for his death's head button and SS lapel pin – turned at the sound of him.

"I'm sure that's not true," Felix said. "You seem to look fit."

"I shouldn't complain," the apprentice whispered. "But I hate this damned job. Tell me, do your parents still come down here? Or are you the man of the manor now?"

"Well," Felix started.

"You remember that dining table I fashioned from a felled tree?" he asked. "Good work I did, didn't I? Is it still there?"

"In the dining room."

"Good, good," the apprentice refrained, wiping smudges off a long glass case.

"I'd heard you went to Germany," Felix said. What he'd heard was that the apprentice – his father's former handy-man – had taken his grandparent's German citizenship.

Cheap opportunist was what his father had called him, *but the joke will be on him when he gets drafted for the army.*

"Germany!" the apprentice exclaimed. He fiddled with an earring tree, and looked up just as the Grepo pushed Pringel aside and lurched towards him.

"You," the Grepo sputtered. "I knew it was you."

"Now, now," the apprentice said.

"We've been looking for you."

"Me? But I've never seen you before in my li—"

"Coward – deserter!"

The apprentice spun on his heel and stabbed the sharp tip of the earring tree into the Grepo's eye, twisting it as he pushed the man down. He snatched a handful of jewelry before jumping out of the ground level window and disappearing into the crowds of the Christmas rush.

While the other shoppers gasped at the dying Grepo, Felix pushed through the exit doors and grabbed Magdalena's hand, dragging her away from a tea vendor.

"That man!" One of the shoppers called, pointing at Felix. "He knew the murderer!"

Felix and Magdalena had been arrested for a charm bracelet, while the apprentice, an army deserter, was free. The apprentice had refused an attachment to anyone or anything and that's why he was alive somewhere, while everyone who happened to be in Pringel's jewelry store that morning was arrested and loaded onto a transport to Poland – even the obliging customer who'd fingered Felix.

These were the inverted rules of war time, Felix told himself.

And now, hardly a day later, they were standing in a cold, noxious train car. One filled with disease and despair, and soon, probably, death. Felix couldn't help but think he deserved such an end. Magdalena, however, did not.

"Can you see anything?" Magdalena asked. Felix had become pinched between the wall of the train car and a Jewish man smelling of sour breath and menthol. He squinted to see if he could get another look through the wooden slats and tripped over an old woman who had died during the night and lay curled up on a bed of feces and hay. Felix swallowed hard.

"Just more ice," he said. "But it looks like we're slowing down."

The charms of Magdalena's bracelet – Benito's heart, a single rose, her cameo and a tennis racket – dug into Felix's skin as the train rumbled to a halt. They were only a few kilometers from the Polish border, in an isolated stretch of countryside, but would have to wait in the freezing boxcars, squeezed together bone to bone. Kicking and grumbling and pushing.

Felix heard the engineer curse, "Damnation!" as the man shambled out of the engine car and disappeared under the train. The rhythmic clanging of his wrench as he moved along the train's underbelly sounded vaguely like church bells.

About two cars over, a compartment door opened. Hurried footsteps chomped through the snow, running from car to car, opening door after door. Shouts were heard, and questions – it was too difficult to hear exactly what was being said – until their door cranked open allowing the air to waft in like a spirit. It smelled of burnt cashews.

"Speak with the tongue of Jan Hus!" shouted a village girl who stood at the door.

Her face was pink and ruddy and bore a look of surprise that somehow made her appearance seem ordinary – as if she just happened to be coming by and was merely startled to see so many people at once.

The girl wore the brown robes of a cult that worshiped the martyred Czech saint, and held in her hand a leather lump that looked like a kidney, but was meant to symbolize Jan Hus's actual tongue. It had been lanced from the saint's mouth only minutes before he was burned at the stake for heresy.

As the Hussite girl secured the lever, she reached into her pouch, flinging a few withered apples and a handful of garlic into the boxcar. Some of the prisoners dove for the apples while others just stood there, unmoving.

"*Achtung! Halt!*" a German officer howled.

The young girl froze for a moment, then took off across the open field. Her violet babushka fluttered at the back of her head as she dashed through the icy countryside. Felix wanted to call to her and tell her to take it off, but it was too late. Magdalena buried her head into his shoulder as the girl's skull exploded.

"Shoot them! Shoot them all," the officer screamed.

Magdalena's knees buckled and Felix held her up, hooking his arms under hers.

The elderly prisoners crouched under the train, while the able-bodied jumped off the platforms and scattered like bugs. Felix pushed Magdalena out of the car and dove down next to her. He seized her by the scruff of her coat collar, yanking her to her feet. As the shots fired, people began to fall – a boy of about twelve, an old man, and a mother whose infant was smothered when her body collapsed into the snow.

Felix held Magdalena's hand, dodging around the others. At the edge of the field, they broke off from the pack and sprinted towards the forest. Magdalena struggled to keep up – clutching Felix's hand, panting. They were in one of the densest forests in Europe; one the Germans had considered clearing in order to cut down on escapes from their transports. In the end, it was cheaper to chase the runaways down. During the summer, the dogs could easily pick up the scent of their ripe flesh and in the winter, they tended to freeze to death anyway.

"We're going to die out here," Magdalena said.

It was nearing nightfall when a seductive peace settled in the forest around them. No twigs crunching, no wails or heavy breathing. No more shots. Their clothes were drenched in sweat. It was possible they'd been running for hours.

Magdalena's lungs ached and she couldn't bear to move anymore. She crouched to the ground and curled up into a ball to keep the frigid wind at bay.

"Stay here," Felix told her.

Magdalena nodded, trying to focus her mind on anything that could trick her body into feeling warmer – boiling milk, sunbaked aluminum, the dry, blistering days in Palastine. Felix seemed to have been gone a long time when she startled at the sound of his voice. It had awakened her from a wild, desperate dream that she could remember only in terms of its color – red.

"There's a house over there."

For a moment, Magdalena stared at his face, not recognizing him.

"They have a statue of the Blessed Mother at their gate," he said. All blue robes and ivory skin, the statue of Mary had been freshly painted and positioned prominently at the entrance to the property, as if she alone decided who entered.

"She spoke to me."

Her lips had looked fleshy as they moved, beckoning him into the house. Spittle had flown from her mouth.

"The woman of the house? She spoke to you?" Magdalena asked.

Felix had a reckless look in his eyes, like a man who hadn't slept in days. It occurred to Magdalena that neither of them had really slept since Marek Andel's death and that Felix might have been delirious.

"God help us," she said. It was the last prayer she would utter until she was well into mid-life.

Although it was easy enough to make the decision on the snow-crusted ground, under a bare chestnut tree, their nerve wavered once they saw the lights and chimney smoke of the lone cottage Felix had stumbled upon. A small barn sat behind it near the opening of a wheat field.

"I want something to eat. I want some tea," Magdalena said suddenly. "I want to go home. Mama. I want Mama." She wished she was back in her old room – not the room in Marek Andel's cellar – but *her* room with her lavender bedspread and clotted cream walls.

"We can hide in there." Felix pointed at the peeling, wooden structure. "They won't even know."

Felix kissed her hot, furrowed brow, wiping her tears with his fingertips. He lit a match – his third to last – as they entered the barn. There weren't many animals, only a few caged rabbits. The far right corner had been fashioned into a chicken coop, where two chickens stared them down. In the center of the structure lay a large pile of manure with flaxen streaks of hay in it.

"Get under there," he said. If they came looking for them during the night, he hoped the dung's stink might cover enough of their scent to fool the dogs.

Magdalena dug herself into the mound, packing the dung around her body as Felix blew out their match. He slipped in next to her, tunneling his arms around her torso, and hummed a few bars of "They Can't Take That Away From Me" into her ear. He thought he heard something – a soft murmuring, like a prayer being whispered into the dark – and stopped singing. Magdalena was already asleep and Felix pulled her closer.

He heard the prayer again, but sleep was overtaking him now and he was too tired to fight it. It was the Kaddish Vera had requested of him before she died. He listened to the prayer, its Aramaic words guiding him into his dreams.

Outside by the gate, in the scant moonlight, Mary finished the Kaddish. She could see a half dozen flashlights beaming haphazardly into the forest and hear the incessant barking of German Shepherds. She could see the shadowy outlines of the men who were controlling the animals – pulling their leashes, giving one word orders, *"Gehen! Ruhe!"*

One of the dogs sniffed into the air and looked Mary's way, catching her gaze. He growled at Mary, but she clapped her hands – pale as milk, her blue robe shimmying – and shooed him away like she used to with the goats in Nazareth when they made trouble in her garden. The dog heeded Mary's warning and took off deep into the forest, followed closely by the other dogs and their masters. She watched the flashlights bounce until they looked as faint as distant stars.

"Wake up."

"Mmm," Felix grunted.

"Get up and stand up."

A man stood over them, holding a lantern and poking Felix with the scoop of a shovel. He was about forty and wore a neat, cotton shirt of powder blue. His hair was black, and no longer than his eyelashes.

"We planned to go before dawn," Felix said.

The man expelled a deep breath and scratched his fingernails across the stubble on his cheek. It sounded like the stroke of a soft brush on a washboard.

"It's already before dawn."

He lowered the lantern close to their faces, and bent over to get a good look. He studied their eyes and leaned back on the handle of his shovel. Felix remembered the statue of Mary at his gate and took the Infant of Prague figurine out of his pocket, holding it up in the light. The man straightened his back.

"The dogs usually come by now," he said.

He motioned for them to get up and held the shovel close to his hip, like a weapon. Felix and Magdalena tried to brush the dung off their clothes, but it was no use.

"Wait here," he told them.

He left the lantern in the barn and disappeared into the murky, morning air. When he returned, he carried a bundle of field workers' clothes in his arms, and two thick coats patched with burlap.

"My wife is warming water for a bath," he said.

Felix stripped his clothes off quickly, and helped Magdalena undress – wrapping one of the bulky field coats around her goose-pimpled skin.

"Where are we?" Felix asked.

"Svělto on the Czech side." The man extinguished his lantern. "Next big town is Bielsko-Biala, then Krakow."

He led them to his cottage in the pitch darkness, the brittle snow collapsing beneath their feet.

His wife, an older woman with gray and strawberry hair, was sitting by the kitchen fire, roasting bits of bread with cheese. The fire's gentle fever washed over them and Magdalena shivered.

"There might be others," Felix said.

The man looked over to his wife and she nodded, rolling her apple-green eyes. She lifted a tiny Infant figurine – even smaller than Marek Andel's – out of a wooden trinket bowl and hung it around her neck.

"They've come before," the man said. The last time had been near the harvest, when a fellow with sores on his back wandered into their house. He'd eaten himself sick and vomited blood and potato dumplings all over their kitchen tiles.

The man wound up an old gramophone and played ragtime music, nervously tapping his slipper to the tune of Scott Joplin's "Maple Leaf Rag."

"I can play this on the accordion," Felix said. The man seemed offended at Felix's mention of it. His wife placed steaming borscht on the unvarnished kitchen table, flanking the sides of the bowl with two tin spoons.

"You're too kind," Magdalena said.

"My wife's birthday."

"Too kind," she repeated, but the man wouldn't look at her.

Felix and Magdalena bathed quickly after the meal, drying themselves with kitchen rags before stepping into the field workers' clothes – starched and clean, smelling of soap and minerals. The wife had boiled two eggs along with the bath water and gave them a hunk of rye bread.

Felix thanked her and she finally endeavored to smile. She thought him handsome and it was her birthday, after all, she reasoned.

"Take the small Brimmel road," the man directed. "It's longer, but less traveled and links with roads leading to Prague."

Their passports were gone – collecting dust in a south Bohemian police station – so it wasn't as if they had many choices.

Magdalena looked down at her charm bracelet and was struck in that moment by how meaningless it was; as meaningless as Felix's watch, with a black market value that hovered somewhere between butter and chocolate. If they'd traded it for some wine and liverwurst the way Felix had wanted they would've never gone to Pringel's jewelry store. They would be in Bratislava – perhaps in a hotel having honeyed tea and cured salami – their passports and marriage certificate folded into their undergarments.

Magdalena pinched Benito the pig's heart off her bracelet and threaded it through the buttonhole on her peasant's blouse.

"Please," Magdalena said. She unfastened the bracelet and dangled it from her fingertip. "I'm glad to see it go."

The man turned away, but his wife accepted the bracelet and tucked it into her stiff, white brassiere.

CHAPTER EIGHT
PRAGUE: DECEMBER 25

The back of the munitions truck was filled mostly with rifles that had seen better days. Having jammed on the battlefield, they were to be melted down, as the Germans had neither the time nor inclination to fix them. The rifles, Felix thought, made it a pitiful ride. They were jagged and uncomfortable to crouch on, but the driver had been eager to take their bread and boiled eggs for his inconvenience. He poured over the German menu Felix had stolen from an upscale restaurant and accepted its pages as travel documents. Felix had taken a chance that the driver was illiterate.

"And it was on the River Pegnitz on a day just like today that da da doo anticipation of whether you would to agree dee dee dee," the driver sang, forgetting the words to "On the River Pegnitz." He knew none of the songs he liked to sing and inevitably had to drop off after a couple of verses. Undeterred, he was crooning short blocks of "Hello, Again, My Long At Last Love" as they entered the Prague city limits three and a half hours later.

It was mid-afternoon, and the sky was white with the gloomy comfort of a coming snow. The coal-tinged air, still heavy from a run of cold nights, gave the yellow gaslights a luminous glow.

Despite their circumstances, Felix felt pleased to be home.

The driver parked and Felix lowered Magdalena onto the pavement before bidding him farewell. Felix watched the man, bow-legged and arthritic, enter the pub at the corner of Karlova and Liliova streets.

"I hate this part of town," Magdalena said.

It dressed in a false gayety that she found disingenuous in the best of times and grotesque under their present circumstances.

"There's always Jaro's."

"Jaro," Magdalena said.

Felix knew she'd never liked his Uncle Jaro either. Too handsome, too rich, two times divorced, and he was always leering at her. Not to mention the fact that Jaro used to procure women for Felix when he first started playing for the national team. Not girls – women – and they had indulged all of the carnal fantasies of his fifteen-year-old self. Although it was long before he and Magdalena had fallen in love, she couldn't forgive Jaro for it, and he could hardly blame her.

But Jaro spent the winter at his country house in Český Raj, a hundred kilometers north of Prague. He left his penthouse empty, giving his maid the time off with pay.

"It's worth a chance," he said.

Magdalena nodded. Felix saw she hardly meant it, but there was no where else to go and they couldn't very well stay on the streets.

They avoided Old Town Square by taking a longer way around the back of St. Michael's Church, where marble angels leapt from the stained glass windows like doves frightened by a noise. Guarding the church's rear entryway was a statue of Christ. New. It hadn't been there last month. He was depicted in his agony, and already black with coal dust except for a gilded crown of thorns.

Magdalena peered up at Him and His eyes – so cleverly sculpted – appeared to return her gaze.

For Magdalena, His look had always been one of apathy: the same one He'd been giving her since she was a child suffering through the Lutheran masses her grandparents made her attend. He looked bored on that cross, staring towards the heavens the way an assembly line worker stares at a clock during the last twenty minutes of his shift. Perhaps for Christ, she thought, this was a full time occupation. With all of the civilizations that must exist in the cosmos, Magdalena imagined He must have a great many people to save and die for, and had lived out this melodrama a million times in a million different solar systems.

In an alleyway hardly a block from Jaro's penthouse, a German officer was shaking down a man who'd bought cheese from a black market vendor. He pushed him up against a wall and pocketed his purchase.

"Prosím Vás. Bitte!" The man begged after a kick to the belly and chin. A thin stream of blood trickled from under his loose tooth.

"What are you looking at?" The German spat at Magdalena. She didn't realize she was staring.

The cheese man took advantage of the distraction and tore away down the street, but not before the German ripped his gun from his belt and fired into a gaslight, an apartment window, and past the head of an elderly man carrying a sack of baked goods. The man fell on his bad knee and his daughter's still warm strudel tumbled out of his sack and into the sewer by the street side. The German ran by him, kicking his fallen bag out of the way and shouting threats into the dark.

Felix hurried to the struedel, wiping it off on his coat flap and slipping it back into the sack. He gave it to the old man, who tucked it into his cape and limped away down the alley corridor.

"Is there a back way?" Magdalena wrung her hands on the ebony door handles of Jaro's building. There were iron and baroque carvings of Old Testament parables etched into the wood of the front doors, and no modern fixtures like doorbells. The doors hardly looked like something that belonged with Jaro and his velvet smoking jackets.

Felix heard keys jingling, a muffled cough, and quiet footsteps. He pushed Magdalena into the shadows as a man appeared from around the corner.

"Hello, sir," Felix said.

The man's hands were shaking and he dropped his keys. Felix bent down to pick them up. He smiled, appealing to the man's eyes – red and swollen from wiping them with the cuff of his coat.

"I didn't mean to startle you," Felix said. "I'm not a policeman or anything."

"I can see that," the man said, appraising Felix's rumpled appearance. His voice was nasal and rough.

"I'm Jaro Andel's nephew." Felix held out his hand and the man shook it. "He lives on the top floor. My wife and I are in a bit of a bind and find ourselves locked out." Felix unclasped his hands. "We were visiting my uncle at his country house, in Český Raj. We'd hoped to return much earlier, but our train was late, and then this. I left the keys in Raj. It's embarrassing, really."

The man said nothing, but moved closer to study Felix's face. Felix offered an eye for the man's inspection, and then thought better of it, tilting his head back into the shadows.

"I thought that was you," the man said, breaking the spittle bars connecting his lips. He stepped back, revealing a tailored coat that had to be twenty years old, and bared his mother of pearl teeth.

"By golly, you whooped the Russians last year. I thought we'd lost for sure, but you were as fast as a kitchen mouse and scored right under their noses." The man scratched his eye and sniffled.

"One of my favorite games," Felix told him. "You should've seen their faces."

"I did. I was there." The man relaxed some, and began fumbling with his keys again.

"So your uncle lives here?" he said. "So do I, but I don't know him. Well, maybe if I saw his face, but not by name, no." He coughed and cleared his throat. "Damn this winter," he chuckled. "My sister's house was too drafty for me. Miserable. I should've never gone out – but it is Christmas." The neighbor unlocked the door and held it for Felix.

"Yes, of course, Christmas," Felix said. He'd completely forgotten.

"My wife, Maria."

Magdalena stepped out of the shadows and took the neighbor's hand. He nodded at her, thrusting his fists into his coat pockets and leading them to the elevator.

"My brother thinks you're the best left wing in Europe. Even better than that Norwegian – the albino." The neighbor rocked from foot to foot as if he were about to tip over.

"Is he as big a bastard as he looks?" he ribbed. "You must think so. He put a stick through your leg." The neighbor closed the elevator doors, pulling the up lever.

"That was a Swede and I still have the scar," Felix chuckled. "It's a doozy."

The neighbor rambled on about hockey until he got off on the fifth floor. There, he stood outside the elevator gate, pressing his thumbs together and wiping his nose.

"I'd like to offer you a drink, but I'm so damned sick." He said it as if he was passing painful gas. "Are you going to be able to get in up there?"

Felix smiled and told what felt like his first bit of truth in a long time. "My uncle has a spare key hidden."

"Yeah," the neighbor said. His key ring slipped off his index finger and dropped onto the tile floor with a clang that echoed throughout the foyer.

"That you, Pepík?" A tenant called up the elevator shaft.

The neighbor pulled his collar up over his neck and exhaled. He waved Felix along, waiting for him to close the elevator gate and start ascending to the penthouse before he turned to his door. Felix and Magdalena heard him fiddle with his door handle as the elevator rose and listened for the sound of the man's apartment door opening and closing, but it never came.

Uncle Jaro's apartment looked down on the chic shops of Pařížska Street from half-moon windows. They arched from the floorboards – a series of exquisite planks in wood the color of caramel – and scaled the twelve foot ceiling.

The fireplace was filled with dry logs and Felix endeavored to light it. He crumpled newspaper pages and crushed them into the ruts between the kindling wood. He rolled one of the pages into a tight tube and lit it on the kitchen stove – then ignited the rest of the news pages with it and stoked the fire with his breath.

Next, Felix went to Jaro's liquor cabinet and uncorked a Moravian red. He poured it into a highball glass and tasted it, swirling it around the crystal engravings. It had been open for a while and was tart, but could still be drunk.

He pressed the glass into Magdalena's hands.

It had begun to snow and Felix looked out the windows and watched the light, feathery dust collect on the stone ledge. He followed each, tiny snowflake from its creation in the gray-lined clouds to its tumble through the atmosphere and final rest on the ledge.

When he was only a boy, he'd once glimpsed what he thought was eternity through a window. He'd seen the view – his backyard – thousands of times, but in one singular, astonishing moment he saw the sky and what lay beyond it. He saw the tiny bugs on the surface of the grass, the microbes deep in the earth, the flowers and vegetables as they grew, the dew drops on the leaves and the cells that made up the leaves – all simultaneously – the way God would see them.

As he gazed out Jaro's window, his vision again blurred and sharpened to a vivid intensity, the way it had when he was a youngster. He saw the snowflakes now with the same omnipotence, getting drawn into the swirling wind. He heard Vera Ruza's shallow breath, as if it alone was propelling the snowflakes from the clouds, and he shuddered. His father's voice came to him in a hum – the same hum Felix was used to hearing around the house before his mother died. He realized how much his mother's presence had made a family of them, and how he and his father had drifted apart after her death.

"Do you think we should answer it?" Magdalena whispered.

The dirty lavender sky, the snowflakes, the swirling and dotted-line patterns of the air, and Vera's breath all disappeared from him, the way a dream evaporates as the mind rouses itself from sleep. But thoughts of his father remained.

"I'm sorry?" he asked.

"The door."

There was a noise – like the creaking of a house during a windstorm. Felix was about to dismiss it, but then he heard a tentative rap. Felix moved to the door and cracked it open. The sick neighbor was standing in the door hutch looking blotched and half frozen.

"Hello, again."

"Hello," the neighbor said. "May I come in?"

Felix gestured inside and the man slipped into Jaro's apartment in his stocking feet.

"Can I take your coat?" Felix asked. The neighbor held his shoes in his hands. They were soaked, as if he'd been walking through puddles.

"No, thank you. I'm still cold. The hallway – it's cold. I've been there for some time."

"I see."

The neighbor was rubbing his feet on the woolen, Oriental rug.

"May I offer you some slippers?"

"Please."

Felix went to Jaro's bedroom and sifted through his uncle's closet, retrieving a pair of soft moccasins. He stopped to warm them briefly by the fire.

"I wanted to call on you downstairs, on the fifth floor, but thought I should wait until later."

The man pressed his feet into the warm slippers and wheezed with pleasure. "I don't live on the fifth floor."

"My mistake."

"I don't live here at all. I lied to you." The man raked his fingers through his thick, black hair.

"I don't understand."

"You wouldn't. You see, I'm taking the same chance you did – when you asked me to let you in. Did you really think anyone would believe that story you told?"

The man took a monogrammed handkerchief – *HP* – out of his pocket and blew his nose hard. His eyes were watering again, and he wiped them with his sleeve. They were puffy and rough, making it difficult to tell his age. He could've been twenty-five or forty.

"My name's Jura Srut. I don't live here, but I do come here now and then."

Felix took a closer look at the man's top coat. It was a fine coat, but at least twenty years old and the sleeve edges were frayed and unmended. "Is my uncle a friend of yours?" he asked.

"I don't know him." Srut stifled what would have been an enormous sneeze and swallowed hard.

"Look, my uncle should be back by the end of the month…" Felix started.

"I know you don't belong here. And I know if you stay any longer it'll bring nothing but suspicion on this place. You understand now?" Srut took out his handkerchief again and wiped his nose. "Do you think I could sit down? Eat something?"

Felix and Magdalena followed him to the dining table. Jaro had never been one to clean out his cabinets and Magdalena discovered several dusty cans of beans and vegetables in his kitchenette. She set the table and offered up the small bounty, watching Srut devour cold sauerkraut and kidney beans with his fingers. When he was done, he wiped his face with his soiled handkerchief.

Felix poured Srut some wine, and then divided the last few sips between himself and Magdalena.

"This is really what I needed." Srut cupped his hands around the glass and took a large swallow. "Do you mind if we sit by the fire?"

Srut stretched out in Jaro's chair and hung his feet over the blaze. The firelight turned his inky eyes saffron.

"Look," Felix said. "We have nowhere to go."

Srut huffed and rolled his eyes.

"Come on, a famous guy like you should have plenty of friends."

"A famous guy like me attracts a lot of attention."

Felix went through the possibilities in his head, each a dead-end for one reason or another. Admittedly, he disqualified some of his friends for the most remote character flaw. His friend, Brana, for example, would never pitch in enough money when a bill came. With a friend, the stakes were higher and there was too much common information. They were safer in the hands of strangers, who couldn't know where they were most likely to hide, or describe them down to their birthmarks.

"We have each other. And you, if you can help us find a place to go."

Srut rubbed his toes, stealing glances at Magdalena. Felix moved closer to her.

"You're a Jew," Srut appraised. "You don't look so Jewish though. What are you, a half-breed?"

Magdalena looked to Felix, then nodded. Srut shrugged and scooted next to the fire.

"Look, I'll see what I can do. These people here in this building... they're not my *friends*. It's a men's building, with a lot of bachelors or divorced patriots. I work for them from time to time. I carry messages or packages, and they give me some food. Sometimes money. They know I know how to get in and out of places without being seen, and that I can pass." Srut started to wipe his nose with his wet handkerchief, but Magdalena handed him a linen dinner napkin. He stuffed it into his pocket, throwing the old one into the fire.

"I've got a dirty race, too. The dirtiest one, but only half like you. I'm a gypsy. See? You're surprised. I can pass, I told you. Almost everyone I know is gone - been rounded up - but not me." Srut looked into the fire again, warming his cheeks and neck.

"I'll get you a place and we can talk about payment later," he continued. "First thing I want is somewhere to sleep. You got a pillow?"

Felix went back into Jaro's bedroom and returned with a pillow. Srut grabbed it out of his hands and stretched, bunching the pillow under his neck.

"Did you know I love nothing as much as I love the smell of coffee?" The gypsy sighed. "It smells so much better than it tastes."

"We don't have any, I'm afraid." Felix didn't know if Srut was challenging him to find some, or simply reminiscing about his favorite pleasures.

"No, you have no coffee, but you have a fire, and that's the smell I like second best." Srut leaned over and poked at the smoking embers. "People like to say that gypsies will start a fire in the middle of a living room with whatever they have available, as if they were outdoors, like primates."

73

"People like to say a lot of things," Felix told him. "They like to say the Jews are responsible for all of our hardships."

Srut shrugged and continued poking into the hearth, smiling at the crackling wood. "Maybe it's true. If it is, I don't care. When we ran out of kindling, we would steal a neighbor's door and build a fire in the middle of our flat. A lot of people don't like that. It's their prerogative. They don't like it, and I don't want to die for it. It's as simple as that."

CHAPTER NINE
NEXT DAY

It was the gypsy who'd taken all of the big chances and Pepík knew it. He'd known him for most of his life; a boy with black, hooded eyes even then, fleeting by on his stolen bicycle. Pepík's mother had told him to stay away from that kind of trash, and he could remember one time when he and his friends threw pieces of bread from their lunch at Srut when they saw him begging for food outside of a delicatessen. Pepík wondered if Srut remembered that incident. He often searched the gypsy's eyes for a hint of bitterness, but the man's eyes, like his voice, betrayed nothing.

Even without that past episode to pollute their current rapport, it was uneasy business dealing with the man. Jura Srut looked so normal, but he had his gypsy ways and required a constant stream of crumbs, no matter how small, thrown at him to do even the most menial errand. The irony was not lost on Pepík.

"Well, at least something to drink, Srut. I'll make us some coffee."

Pepík had always been a follower, and probably always would be; he'd accepted this fact about himself. Only now he followed a better sort, a more upright crowd than that of his social-climbing mother and former wife. His life as a divorced man and his uncanny skill for matters of business were the only things that had ever been all his own and he loved them the way some men love their children. Even the terror that had gripped him when he moved into his apartment two years before and began to discover the goings-on in the building was for Pepík something to be savored. It was *his* terror, not his mother's or his wife's, and it gave him a silent strength that he carried with him now when he walked down the street. Women even liked him better, and much of it was due to Srut.

He'd stumbled upon Srut again accidentally, as he had most of the good fortune in his life. Srut had been standing in front of him in line at the Commercial Bank on Wenceslas Square. Pepík didn't recognize him right away. At first he was only a dark-haired man with a large mole on the right side of his neck. It was when Srut tried to pass himself off as one of his neighbors, a man Pepík knew had moved to Austria, that he took notice. The woman at the window was suspicious right from the start, but Pepík was amazed at how unruffled Srut's answers were; easy lies humming and whistling from his mouth like songs from a chain gang. Before he was able to give it any thought, Pepík stepped into the exchange and vouched for Srut's sincerity.

"I'm new to my apartment house," he told the clerk. "But I've seen this man in it many a time and I'm sure he must be who he claims to be. Yes, Ehrenreit. That's the name on the bell."

Srut never did thank him and Pepík had to chase after the gypsy for nearly a block before the man would engage

76

him at all. This was how their lives had become intertwined and how Pepík was able to prove himself to the other men in his building. Srut was fearless and established himself as quite an asset to their group of pampered bachelors who'd become an extension of the Prague Underground. Despite an immutable open hand, Srut had always come through.

And what a puzzle he was. For such a clever man, he had no mind at all for business and often took an inferior payment, say of bread instead of meat, for a more dangerous assignment. Then, as if he'd thought better of it, the gypsy would demand payment of clothes or butter for merely delivering a message. Pepík had dealt with Srut for over a year now and was no closer to understanding him.

"You need what? An apartment? Look, I can't just sneak a bunch of gypsies into a place – you know that. Nobody cares about those arrests - it's the one thing people like about the bloody Germans. Sorry." Pepík lit his cigarette, and stepped back to avoid Srut's sneeze. A pearl of spittle landed on his round, metal-framed glasses, and he wiped them with his shirt.

"They're not gypsies, I told you; they ran from the country. Got arrested last week in Krumlov and they tried to take them into one of those camps. It can't be good to have them staying up there. What if the owner comes home?"

The kettle started squealing, so Pepík picked up his cane and hobbled over to his kitchen, pouring two Turkish coffees into his ex-wife's Italian cups. He arranged the cups and their matching saucers on his mother's old kitchen table, and motioned for Srut to sit down. The gypsy did, moving his cup towards Pepík and leaning in too close.

"You're not looking any better," Pepík told him. "You should take care of yourself."

Srut nodded and took a cigarette out of his coat pocket, lighting it off the candle next to his elbow.

"So you got a place or what?"

Pepík stared at Srut's hand, unable to look up from the dry skin, cracked and peeling at the knuckles. "How many did you say?"

"Just two. A couple. One is a Jew."

"That's hardly a surprise." Pepík cradled his head in his hands, curling his fingers around what hair follicles he had left. He didn't look up when Srut spoke again.

"I thought maybe that Henrik could take them."

"Yes, alright, yes, Henrik. He could probably take them. Provided they're really not gypsies."

Srut nodded his head and Pepík gripped his cane, rubbing his fingers over the intricate iron work on the handle. "Jesus, Maria, and Joseph, I think you'll be the death of me after all."

Srut patted Pepík's nervous hand and offered him another cigarette.

CHAPTER TEN
DECEMBER 30

Felix fell back next to Magdalena. They followed Srut's crisp pace past the Church of St. Barbora, its Gothic façade scowling at them, and continued on to the Vltava River until they reached the Charles Bridge.

The old bridge was swaddled in mist and deserted except for a couple of maintenance men who were cleaning the statue of Jan Hus. They polished and scoured the unlucky saint, whose lot was to spend eternity encased in stone, covered in hundreds of years' worth of soot; watching, yet unable to speak his mind about his ravaged homeland. Felix wondered if perhaps the Hussite girl with the violet babushka had been united with her beloved saint upon her death. He hoped so.

They passed the ancient clock tower in Old Town Square, and climbed uphill, high into Letna. There, although it was only a fifteen-minute walk from the city center, it had the look and feel of a quiet suburb. It could've been another town.

"The fatso," Srut said. "That's his house."

The outside was simple and boxy, with two inlaid pillars – also squared –flanking the doors. It was a two-story place, with another small half-story attic that pointed into the sky like a dancing shoe.

"We've got to go round the back," Srut told them.

They entered the house through the cellar, shaded by several large trees that even in the wintertime, with their limbs bare, were able to provide cover for the back yard. Their bark was thick and knotted, and every branch looped like a part of a puzzle, knitting a protective layer against neighboring houses sitting beyond the small creek that passed behind the property.

Once inside the cellar, Srut sat them by a row of wine cabinets, turned on the single light fixture that dangled from the ceiling like a spider, and went up the stairs leading into the house. He listened at the door, scratching and making snorting noises.

"Come on, Henrik," he rasped, but fifteen minutes went by before he heard the familiar hard-stepping that characterized Henrik's entrance into any room.

"Is that you, Schmoodla?"

Srut barked.

Henrik unlocked the door. "Poor girl," he said, holding out fresh bread and currant jam thinned with soft gelatin. He rumbled down the steps setting off countless creaks as each plank of wood brayed under his weight.

It was the way Henrik maintained himself that gave him the look of a man of indulgence rather than gluttony. He wore tailored suits without a hint of the dandy, and a neatly waxed mustache. Even his thinning hair had dignity, as he made no more effort to camouflage it than he did his massive girth.

"Mm. Hello," he said, putting the tray of bread and jam on a crate next to the young couple.

Felix began to introduce himself, but Henrik motioned to the food.

"Eat, no? All this other nonsense I can find out later, or from our friend here. Srut, there's enough for you, too, but not here. You come upstairs with me."

Srut followed him, disappearing into the yellow light of the kitchen.

It was in the quiet darkness of the cool, stone cellar that Felix and Magdalena ate, whispering to each other. They already missed Jaro's apartment. It had been their last respite of normal life.

But the fat man's cellar was not completely without its charms. While it offered no luxuries, it did look a bit like Marek Andel's cellar and reminded Felix of a night when he was spying on Magdalena through a crack in that cellar wall. It was before she'd kissed him while he read Mary Shelley's *Frankenstein* to her under the light of a lantern, and before they'd made love for the first time, while Vera and his father drank a midnight tea in the kitchen above them.

Magdalena had braided her mother's hair, separating it into three equal parts with her silver hairbrush before her fingers went to work, as fast as a typist's, braiding down to her mother's waist. Vera did the same for her, kissing the top of Magdalena's head and smoothing her wayward curls with licked fingers. When the ritual was done, Magdalena and her mother looked remarkably alike and much closer in age.

Felix tried to imagine Magdalena with salt and pepper hair and crooked lines framing her eyes and mouth. He ran his fingers over Magdalena's shoulders, envisioning what her skin would feel like after it had turned to crepe paper.

Henrik and Srut were gone for less than an hour. They re-entered the cellar the same way they left it; Srut like a cat and Henrik like a buffalo.

"We don't want to be any trouble," Felix said.

"Your very existence is trouble," Henrik quipped, leaning into the wall for support. "Now you, lady, are the Jew, and you, of course, are the hockey player. It would do no good to have you recognized." Henrik dangled an unlit cigarette between his pinky and ring fingers.

"Welcome to your new home. At least until we can find you a more permanent residence. Ha! Pepík was sure you were gypsies dressed up to look normal like Srut over here." Henrik had a robust, dirty laugh, as if he were always among men.

"Where do you stay, Mr. Srut?" Magdalena asked.

"Different places." Srut took a cigarette from Henrik's pocket and lit it.

"Nobody stays here on a continuous basis," Henrik explained. "It's isolated enough, and I live alone here, so it makes for a good stop along the road."

He plodded over to a large wooden bin that sat at the far end of the wine shelves and opened it, patting the cushions inside.

"You can make a comfortable bed with what's in here," he said. "A hot pipe runs along the bottom of the wall opposite the wine shelves. It'll keep you warmer at night. You can make your bed right up next to the wall, it's clean."

Indeed, everything in Henrik's cellar was as scrupulous as his fingernails. There wasn't a cobweb in sight, and even the characteristic layer of dust that covered most bottles in a proper wine cellar was absent.

"If you need anything, please don't call up to me or knock on the door. I'll be checking in on you often enough.

And if you have an emergency, some sort of catastrophe or I don't know what, then bark like a dog, or cluck like a chicken, or something. Just make it sound authentic."

That was the end of their instruction.

"Okay, then." Henrik motioned for Srut.

As Srut passed by, he blew a cloud of smoke their way, and with it came the smells of strong cheese and blood sausage.

If there was ever a moment when Jura Srut allowed himself an instant of reflection, he never showed it. Not in the weeks they'd seen him coming and going at Henrik's house – often stumbling downstairs drunk and falling asleep sprawled over their bedding.

Srut's belly was always stuffed and he bragged about eating smoked ham and chocolate with *the fatso* as he called him. Henrik was good to them. Of course, he was better to Srut, but they couldn't complain. He fed them simply, but well, and was always full of some sort of talk from the market that day or about a book he was reading. Henrik seemed as isolated as they were and in as much need of human contact. He even brought them books to read. Sitting under their lone light fixture, Felix and Magdalena could revel in the *Arabian Nights* and *The Count of Monte Cristo*. It gave them things to talk about other than their troubles, and the characters took on the familiarity of people from a nearby village.

There'd been no talk of going to another safe house since their first day at Henrik's, and life had taken on a curious sense of routine. Henrik gave them drinking and washing water, and let them up into his house twice a week, late in the evening, to have a bath. A night owl who suffered from bouts of insomnia, he let them take as long as they liked, while he read and snacked in his kitchen.

It wasn't long into their stay when Felix and Magdalena got some insight into Henrik's life beyond wine, food, and books. He had a lady friend who came over for a regular appointment. Their dangling light fixture would tremble and flicker as cries of "My darling, toss your hair! Your blonde hair!" would escalate.

"Do you think she's as fat as he is?" Magdalena whispered, as she and Felix lay awake.

"Maybe we should ask Srut. He's probably met her."

Srut introduced them when he came barreling into the cellar one afternoon, shushing them with a sharp motion of his hand. He did so with authority and absolute conviction, despite his wearing a long, blonde wig and coral lipstick. Srut swept their blankets up in his arms in one motion and stuffed them behind some crates. He then led them to the back of the pantry, where they crouched at the rear behind vats of dry goods.

Above them, Henrik strode towards the front door with contrived confidence. Orders were barked at him, but the dense cellar walls muffled his protests. Two sets of boots, each heel digging into Henrik's parquet floors, started marching towards the cellar.

As the door opened, Felix could hear Henrik.

"Would you like some wine? I have excellent wine. Please, let me select a bottle. This could all be very civilized."

But the men in the boots ordered him to shut up. One put his Luger to Henrik's temple as the other stomped down the stairs. The German officer didn't rush, but looked around as if strolling, lifting the tops off barrels and opening crates.

The officer was so close that Magdalena could smell him – damp wool imbued with the tang of citrus. His hands reeked of moldy lemons – the kind her father had used to clean his leather upholstery, mixing their juice with mild nut oil and applying the mixture with a rag. Her father's Skoda, his reading chair, and his belts all had smelled that way, and it reminded her of when she was a little girl, only waist high, who would wrap her arms around her father's legs to breathe in his aroma. She hated that the German smelled like him.

"Mm-humph," the man snorted, holding a match up to the dried herbs that hung from two rows of shelves. The shelves were filled with various jars of pickled goods and the German officer examined each one as if he were expecting to find severed fingers.

When his inspection was over, he trudged out of the pantry, dropping his lit match onto a fallen branch of dried marjoram. Srut extinguished the small fire with his hand, the way a vigil light is put out in one smooth, watchful motion.

The German officer had left both the pantry and cellar doors open. He stood at the top of the stairs reporting his findings to an uninterested commandant.

"Get this degenerate out of my sight," the commandant sneered.

Henrik said nothing as he was escorted out of his house. The only trace of his presence was his wearied stepping, which was at rhythmic odds with the one-two, one-two of the boots that hauled him away.

They were gone in a matter of minutes, leaving the house lonely for its master.

Srut stood up first, testing a cramped pair of legs with a creep to the pantry door.

"This is a trick," Magdalena said. "They'll be waiting for us outside." Magdalena tore her hand away from Felix's and huddled close to her barrel.

"We have to keep moving. They'll come back."

"I don't think they've left," she said.

"It don't matter." Srut peeled off his wig and stuffed it into a crate next to the wine shelves. He lit a cigarette and crossed his long arms. "If they're still outside, like you say, and know we're here, why would they wait? They'd just douse the place with gasoline and let us burn."

Srut puffed at his cigarette. With his thumb and index finger, he wiped the lipstick off his lips, smearing its traces on the hip of his gray trousers. "I don't think they're looking for us."

"Of course they're looking for us," Magdalena said. "Someone must've seen us come in. Or thought it was suspicious that Henrik was always looking for so much food. Those black marketers have no scruples. They would turn anyone in for a favor."

"Lady, I don't think anyone would look twice at how much food fat Henrik was bringing home, and no black marketer would turn in one of his best customers."

"Oh, and people always do what's expected of them don't they?" Magdalena pulled her blanket and sheet from behind the crates and folded them into small squares. She stuffed the left-over jars of canned fruits and vegetables into an empty potato sack.

"They didn't look very hard for us, did they?" Felix crept to the cellar doors leading outside, and tried to get a view of the yard through the crack between them. "I don't see anyone, but I don't have much in range of vision."

"Probably back at Gestapo headquarters with poor Henrik. They don't treat men like him well down there. If they don't beat him to death during his interrogation, he'll be on the next train to nowhere tomorrow."

"You know why he was arrested?" Felix went over to Srut, searching his eyes. The gypsy, true to his fortune-telling ancestry, offered glimpses into possible truths, but always left plenty of room for interpretation.

"No, but if it was political, there wouldn't be anything left of this house and we'd be riding right along with him. Poor fag, one of his *friends* must have turned him in."

"One of his friends?" Magdalena pressed towards him. "Like you, maybe?"

"M, stop," Felix said.

"All they'd have to do is offer him food or money," she spat. "A little trade in information and he doesn't even have to brush his wig out."

Srut flicked his cigarette butt to the floor. "We've all got to get out of here," he said. "And you're going to leave that bag of food and the blanket here. We can't walk through the streets like we're going camping."

Magdalena clutched her stores harder, and turned towards Felix. "So he can stab us in the back the way he did Henrik?"

"I can stab you in the back whether you leave with me or not," Srut told her. "Henrik's dead," he said, softer now. "At least he will be. Let's pray he doesn't decide to tell his life's story during his interrogation."

CHAPTER ELEVEN
FEBRUARY 20, 1944

It was past midnight when they left through Henrik's backyard, taking refuge behind the knotted branches of his trees, and walking along the creek, their shoes chawing deep into mud-encrusted leaves. Magdalena wore their blanket slung over her shoulders, and Felix carried the potato sack filled with canned goods.

The creek ended, disappearing into a sewer, and the three of them sat at the edge, eating canned plums and pickled eggs. Morning would be breaking soon, and a light fog had descended onto the hilly regions of Prague, providing them with some cover.

"Can't we go back to Jaro's?" Magdalena asked. "Things were good there."

Srut wiped his nose with his coat sleeve. "Henrik has friends in that building. The whole place might be filled with SS – if not right now, then soon – questioning, arresting, tearing apart all of those beautiful homes."

"We can't just walk the streets," Felix said.

"There's a place to go. Not a good place. Too many people already."

Srut rolled up the blanket and tossed it to Felix. He climbed up the embankment onto the street and made sure to walk a full twenty paces ahead – never looking back. It only took thirty minutes to make it to the Palace Lucerna in the city center. There, Srut stopped and waited for them to catch up.

The Lucerna was a gilded structure of iron trellises, domes and archways leading to a theatre, a nightclub, a restaurant and several shops. Before the war, it had been the vortex of the town center. Now, a chain-link curtain descended over each door and entryway, giving it a sorry look of good times past.

"Wait here for a few minutes," Srut said, stopping them at the door of a luxury goods shop. A salami, rutted like a dried turd, made a pitiful window display.

After a quarter of an hour, Felix spotted Srut's face in the small portal window of an office building across the street. He was motioning and mouthing for them to hurry up.

"We thought you'd forgotten about us," Felix said.

"Be quiet," Srut whispered. Already he'd had a run-in with a doughy clerk who'd been coming in earlier and earlier as the weeks wore on. He was a weak and nervous type, no doubt escaping some manner of tyranny at home. A mother, a wife, a disappointed daddy. Exactly the type who could reclaim a small portion of his manhood with a call about a suspicious character with dark features.

Srut nodded towards a door. There were chains and chunky padlocks covering its corroded metal façade and he brushed them aside as if they were cobwebs, easing the door open with his shoulder.

A strange sort of darkness greeted them inside. While there were no windows or perceptible light sources, there were several white plastic tarps that glowed in the way snow glows in the night, even without a moon. Srut led them to one of the tarps - one that folded down like a bedspread, exposing a workman's table.

"It's this way," he said. Srut crouched under the table and disappeared into a hole.

Felix helped Magdalena into the tight pathway. A fiddle played and a woman hummed in the distance, getting louder as they came towards the end of the tunnel, where a black velvet curtain descended over the mouth of the hole as if it were the entrance to a theater. They could hear voices in conversation. Some were animated and jovial, while others hushed as though they were trying not to wake a baby.

"We're here," Srut muttered. He pulled Magdalena inside. She lost her footing and skinned her knees on the hand-crafted nails that stuck out of the entrance hole like a cat's claw.

"Oh, cunt. She's bleeding," a trill woman's voice called out. The woman came closer and pulled up Magdalena's woolen skirt, wiping her knees with a damp cloth.

"It's all right. It's nothing really, girlie." The woman flashed a rotted smile. Her tongue curled between a missing front tooth and a small, yellowing fang each time she spoke, giving her a pronounced lisp. Soon other faces gathered around her to get a look at her scraped knees and offer a diagnosis.

"A lot of blood is good. It'll clean out the cuts," a gaunt man of an indeterminable age told her. He had no gray hair, but his skin hung on his face like heavy drapery and his lips coiled inward as if he'd neglected to put in his dentures.

They were the faces of trolls, contorted not by time, but by exposure and erosion. Only Srut and a young girl no older than fifteen were untouched by the hard-earned ugliness of the group of eight or so gypsies that surrounded Magdalena. The young girl's skin was smooth, like butter caramel, and her long, dark hair was thick and glossy. Her face looked like an apple with a small bite in it for a mouth.

"We're under the Palace Lucerna, aren't we?" Felix's eyes circled the room, if it could be called that. Parts of the walls were made of rock and mortar like some of the oldest base structures of the castle, and the floors were brushed dirt. It was, as Srut had described it, "a hole."

Velvet curtains, hats, and stained silk dresses littered the place like discarded theater props, pilfered from the Lucerna nightclub above. There was no ventilation to help dilute the oppressive pong. In fact, the only way in and out seemed to be the ramshackle tunnel that started in the office building across the street.

"How about that?" Srut said. "We're living in a palace. Or at least in the palace dungeon." Srut sat down on a mottled mattress, partly covered by chiffon show gowns and stretched his legs out, pointing his toes and bending his ankles.

The lisping gypsy took Magdalena's hand and led her to a pile of torn materials and lacy petticoats. As soon as she'd sat down, the gypsy picked up one of the white petticoats strewn about, spit on it several times, and used it to blot Magdalena's knee.

Srut nudged Felix aside and held his hand out to the beautiful young girl that had stood silent and watchful since their arrival. The girl burrowed into Srut, wrapping herself around him, and kissing his neck.

"This is my wife, Milada," the gypsy said. Felix offered his hand, but it went ignored.

He went to sit under the hole they'd come in from, and surveyed the different characters – figures in a Goya painting – that mingled before him. It was mid-morning when he started to doze. The last image Felix glimpsed before entering a deep sleep was Srut, naked and bobbing on top of his wife, who lay splayed on a purple velvet curtain.

Morning and night passed in the hole. Music, conversation, and sleep were conducted in varying shifts. He watched Frida, a sleepy-eyed imp with short, skinny legs and an enormous bosom and belly, read a deck of playing cards for Vit, her cousin by marriage. He wanted to know if his wife was still among the living.

"Her spirit is strong," Frida promised.

She pointed to the tunnel and told Vit to be alone. He should sit in the dark and try to touch his wife's spirit. Only his own heart could tell him if she lived; Frida couldn't make such predictions. When he left, Frida sighed with weighty breath. She looked down at her cards and drummed her fingers over the two of hearts and two of clubs before erasing the collage of images and burying her face into a stained, blue baby's blanket.

The smell was something Felix would never get used to. In the corner, there was a bin large enough to fit a crouching man. The bin served as a toilet and was emptied into one of the many crevasses that pockmarked the tunnel. Two brothers, Tagur and Multa, were in charge of the bin, keeping it covered, and wiping splatter from the crooked wall behind it. They often argued about whose turn it was to empty the contents and then inevitably did the chore together.

Marital relationships were conducted in full view, and often during the middle of conversation, eliciting an occasional acknowledgement from the entwined partners. No thought was left unspoken, as diplomacy had been left behind above ground, if it had ever existed. Felix couldn't help feeling that he and Magdalena had become members of a tribe.

Srut was the only one who left the hole, returning with bread and mayonnaise, sometimes cheese and apples. Food was shared equally among the clan, leaving bellies far less than half full. Conviviality and game playing - fiddle sticks, jacks, and shells - distracted from the lack of milk and eggs.

Milada, Srut's wife, appeared to garner no status from being the partner of their provider, but Srut was treated as a king. His was the only ass allowed to sit on an actual cushion, and his back the only one granted a mattress to stretch on. Even Milada would lie on the floor next to him, so that he was able to sleep without straining his neck. Srut was also, without question, the cleanest of them all. Where he washed was a mystery, but it was a necessary element to his looking like a normal person when he went above ground. Of the others, only Felix and Magdalena used some of their drinking water every day to wipe themselves down.

"I want to go with you," Felix told Srut on their fourth day.

"You smell too bad." Srut grinned and pretended to clean his fingernails.

"I know where we can get food. A lot of it. But we need to do it at night."

Srut said nothing else about it, until Felix awoke to his gentle kicking some hours later.

"Up, up."

The hole was quiet while the fiddler slept coiled on a piece of burlap, and the lisping gypsy woman squatted in a corner talking to Tagur and Multa, the brothers. It had the tempo of a nightclub at three in the morning.

Srut led Felix up a short flight of stairs and pointed towards a door with a frosted glass window panel. It was a small room, which held two large sinks with deep basins. The porcelain one was used primarily for washing paintbrushes and splashed with a multitude of colors. Felix took off every scrap of his clothing and stepped into the larger sink to do his washing. He scrubbed his body, using his underwear as a washcloth and lathering with the harsh, black workman's soap.

"You forgot perfume," Srut teased, as Felix emerged looking clean.

Felix took the lead away from him, pushing open the front door and taking a deep breath of fresh night air. There was a glossy sheen on the cobblestones, and he wobbled on his first step outside.

"Which way?" Srut asked him.

"To Vinohrady."

"Vinohrady?"

"I used to make it in ten minutes skating on the Vltava."

Felix pushed past Srut, and jumped up onto the sidewalk. He took a running start and slid across the veneer of ice, spinning gracefully before angling his feet in a hockey stop at the curb's edge. Srut followed him, his arms flailing. He managed to stay on his feet, but dropped off the curb, tripping forward with three heavy steps that almost sent him into a parked Skoda.

The gypsy laughed and it occurred to Felix how innocent the laughter was. How something so natural on any given Friday or Saturday night during peacetime was now punishable by death. It was only the barest thread of reason that kept them from putting their arms around each other's shoulders and singing bawdy lyrics, loud and off tune, as they wound their way through the streets.

Instead, Felix and Srut left the quarter like they would the bedroom window of a secret lover. They crouched from doorway to doorway and walked in the shadows formed by a bright full moon.

"How long have you known Milada?" Felix's voice blended into the night current like the hiss of a whisper by a riverbank.

"I don't know. I remember when Frida was pregnant with her."

"I've known Magdalena since we were five, but she's still a mystery to me in so many ways. Is Milada?"

"What?"

"A mystery."

"No."

"You know her so well?"

"No."

Felix and Srut prowled behind the National Museum, crossing into the residential streets of Vinohrady. There, more than anything, it was the gardens that conveyed the pleasures and burdens of commitment. The fruit trees and rose bushes that studded the lawns took considerably more care than the ferns and ficus trees that were popular in places like Uncle Jaro's apartment building. Each home displayed the unmistakable touch of a woman.

"This was my father's house," Felix murmured.

Srut ogled the three-story house with copper gutters and French chateau windows. Like most city properties, it had a small front yard embraced by short arms of stone and concrete that met at the center, joined by a black iron gate with bars interlocking like fingers.

"Rich bastard," he groaned.

The gypsy pulled two cigarettes from the inside pocket of his coat and lit them with one of Henrik's monogrammed butane lighters. He handed one to Felix.

"We can go in from the back," Felix said.

The shrubbery looked the same, but his father's hammock – normally rolled into a hanging sack resembling a beehive – had been removed. Roughly in its place was a wooden bench carved with hearts. Troll figures and costumed animal statues now cluttered the garden. His mother's mermaid had been hoisted up from between the rosemary bushes and hung on the door of the garden shed like a warning to them all.

"The cellar door to the pantry is rotten," Felix said. "If we give it a good kick, it'll crumble."

Srut sat down on the head of a stone raccoon, and chewed nervously on his cigarette butt, biting off bits of paper and spitting them onto the ground.

"No one can hear what goes on in the pantry, unless they have their ear to the kitchen door. We can be out of here in ten minutes with enough food to feed us all for a week."

Srut shrugged his shoulders, taking a deep drag before stubbing his cigarette out on the raccoon's nose and pocketing the butt. The cellar doors were tilted slightly above ground the way they'd been at Henrik's house, and Felix lifted his right leg, bearing down twice and separating the two doors. The wood crumbled as he'd predicted, leaving a hole the size of a ripe melon and allowing Srut to reach inside to lift the metal pole barring their entrance.

Srut had to feel his way in the dark, but Felix knew exactly where he was going. He went to the foot of the stairs leading into the house, then lit a lantern his father had kept hung on the railing.

In contrast to the garden, which had been remodeled, the clean, ordered pantry remained exactly the same, with the exception of a couple of bare shelves where his father had stored marmalades. Those were evidently a popular treat in this household.

To the right of some pickling jars, one large nail was staked into the mortar of the stone wall. From it hung a pair of Felix's old skates, black and worn in, patched a half dozen times on the instep. He took his skates off the nail and slung them around his neck. Felix had worn them for luck at every home game and his mother had spent countless hours mending their insides. He'd even worn them in Bavaria, for the Olympic Games.

"Start loading," Felix whispered. "There should be sausages and hard salami hanging inside the cupboards."

They worked swiftly, filling their pockets and the small burlap sacks that Srut brought with him. They tied the sacks onto their belts like medieval merchants. Famished from a perpetually under-filled belly, Felix pried open a jar of pickled pig's feet and began to gnaw.

When the door from the kitchen opened, Felix half expected it to be his father - but the man who stood there held a PO8 Luger and a queer sort of anxious smile on his face. His pajamas were childlike yellow and he wore a black, pencil-thin mustache, no doubt the suggestion of a fashionable wife. His hair was parted to the side and straight, like his Fuhrer's, and his posture was unmistakable; he was a former military man turned bureaucrat, fatter with every successive year of war and the spoils it had brought him.

"You've come to the wrong house," he hissed, before raising his Luger and pulling the trigger.

CHAPTER TWELVE
SAME NIGHT

Felix heard the whistle of a bullet as it passed his ear. With part of the hoof bone still in his mouth, he hurled the lantern at the German, shattering his jaw and throwing flames onto the staircase. He launched the pig's foot at the man, hitting him hard in the neck and compelling him to drop his gun over the railing.

Leaping up the stairs, Felix gripped the German's throat, while Srut beat at the fire with a doormat, trying to stop its immediate spread to every piece of wood – barrels, crates, shelves, furniture – that stood in its path.

The gypsy looked up at the German's face, his blackening tongue and distended eyes transforming from panic into death. Felix continued squeezing, staring into the man's gaping eyeballs, while Srut hollered at him to move on. Felix could've dug his fingers all the way into the muscle if it wasn't for the Luger firing off beneath the stairs. Only then was Felix able to loosen his grip and let the German tumble into the flames.

The gun was popping off like a firecracker as Srut and Felix scrambled to get out of the house. Felix's shoulder burned and he held it close to his body, maneuvering the prickly bushes of his neighbor's garden. As they jumped a stone boundary wall, Felix felt his shoulder tear at the joint and he slumped into the grass.

"We can't stop now," Srut panted. He lifted Felix to his feet, feeling a warm stream of blood flow over his fingers.

"You're shot."

Only a few feet to their left, a man in white pajamas and rubber boots stood watching them. The man switched on his hand light and put his palm over it as Srut jerked his head in his direction. He could see a squall of police lights coming in the distance.

"Mr. Svoboda?" Felix whispered. "Mr. Svoboda, it's me – Marek Andel's son." Svoboda moved a step closer, shining his hand light onto Felix's face.

"Come inside, quickly," Svoboda whispered, motioning to his back door. "Go in the studio and be quiet."

Srut shuttled Felix into the open door, seating him at a wooden workbench. This room was where Justus Svoboda sculpted his stone angels. Many of them were variations on his late wife, Barbora, and her miniatures looked down on them from several ledges – smiling, beck-oning, pleading, beguiling – posed covering her breasts with her arms or standing naked without inhibition as if she were clothed and waiting in line at the post office. Svoboda always carved a miniature with his tiny hands before embarking on a larger sculpture for a mausoleum or a public building.

"What did you do to yourself, boy?" Svoboda shined the light on Felix's shoulder and helped Srut remove his bloody coat and shirt.

"There was a gun in the fire," Srut explained. "It went off from the heat."

"From the heat, eh?" Svoboda examined Felix's shoulder. "It looks worse than it is. It's a graze with a lot of blood that's all. The dislocated shoulder - that's the real problem."

Srut looked down at Felix's sagging limb and was reminded of the grisly pictures he'd enjoyed as a boy. They were of men who'd gotten the rack, and if they survived spent their lives grossly disfigured with their arms and legs crooked and distended like knotted noodles.

"Hold him, will you?" Svoboda went to a metal cabinet, and pulled out a bottle of Russian vodka, new, but already half empty. He took a handkerchief from his pocket and wet it thoroughly with the liquor before stuffing it into Felix's mouth. Holding his arm like a trombone, Svoboda bent and lowered it. Felix clenched his fists. He writhed, kicking Svoboda close to the groin, and the sculptor fell to the floor. Srut gripped Felix's shoulders and sat on him, biting his nose. Felix couldn't move. He began breathing hard and Srut held him this way, biting down enough to keep him still, but not draw any blood. Svoboda was finally able to get up and do what needed to be done. He came to Felix, taking him at his elbow and shoulder, then jerking his limb twice until it snapped back into its proper place.

Felix grunted, his teeth grinding on the vodka-soaked linen, and then collapsed onto the bench. Svoboda took a swallow from the vodka bottle and passed it to Srut, while he tugged the handkerchief out of Felix's mouth. They polished off the rest of the liquor, Svoboda taking the last few drops before lifting the bottle in salute and placing it with a thump on the workbench.

"Can you walk or what?" Srut asked as Felix sat straddling the bench – hunched over with his head between his legs. There was a small puddle of vomit next to his boots.

"He can't walk," Svoboda told him. He draped a blanket over Felix's shoulders.

"I can walk."

Svoboda spun the blanket around Felix's neck and brought his face close. He wrinkled his pug nose at the smell of Felix's clothing.

"There's a fire next door, surrounded by police and onlookers. You don't think you'd arouse any suspicion do you? Or how about tomorrow morning with your filthy clothes and no papers? You don't have any papers, do you? I didn't think so. No papers, no clothes, and an injury. We should give you a clown's nose and a cowboy hat to complete your costume."

Svoboda sat down and took Felix's face in his small hands.

"Are you sure they'll be looking for you? Did anyone see you do it?"

"They might've heard us."

"The only one who saw us is dead," Srut said. "He died in the fire."

"Are you sure?"

"He died before the fire," Felix said.

Svoboda looked Felix in the eyes. "I hope you did the job right."

Heals chopped above them, scattering across the second floor before clip-clopping down a flight of stairs between the studio and the kitchen. They sounded like a pair of high-heeled bedroom slippers making their way across Spanish tiles. And they were.

A slender woman in wide curlers and a shimmering champagne robe entered the studio. She wore feathery spike-heeled sandals that showcased her fine arches and red toenails. Nodding once at her new houseguests, she crossed her arms over her breasts.

"This is my wife, Dasa," Svoboda said. "She can finish helping you. I'm going out there like a good nosy neighbor."

Svoboda lifted a brown topcoat from a hook on the kitchen door. He tucked his pajamas into his galoshes and donned a captain's hat, a relic from the Great War, and left through the same door they'd entered. Dasa continued to stand there, hands on her hips, as if she were about to chastise a naughty nephew.

"You're still bleeding," she said. Dasa disappeared into the kitchen and came back, this time holding a damp cloth, white tape, and bandages. She lifted off Felix's blanket with two long-nailed fingers and dropped it onto the vomit, stepping down and swirling the blanket around with a pointed toe. She tended to Felix's shoulder like a practiced nurse.

"We owe you congratulations," Felix said. "On your marriage."

"Oh that." She smiled and smoothed the front of her robe, retying the square knot at her waist into a bow. "Justus and I have been married over six months now. Knew him a long time before that."

She took a cigarette from a tapered metal drawer, lit it, and then tossed the pack and lighter to Srut. "Why don't you clean the rest of that up on the floor there and any blood you might see dripped around."

Dasa picked up Felix's coat and shirt with a sharp poker that hung on the wall along with Svoboda's other tools and placed the bloody items into a bag. The statuettes of Barbora, Dasa's predecessor, lay pasted behind her like wallpaper.

"I'll be right back."

Srut smoked his cigarette down to the butt, while Felix let his burn.

"This is some mess," Felix whispered.

Srut wasn't listening to him. He was busy rifling through the sacks still clipped onto Felix's belt. Svoboda had tossed the belt onto his concrete floor as he removed Felix's coat and the skates around his neck.

"Nothing's broken," Srut said. "Sausage?"

"I can't eat."

"Suit yourself." Srut sliced a thick chunk of sausage with his penknife, folding it into his mouth. A syrupy drop of saliva dripped from Srut's bottom lip. Srut slurped, wiping the juice away with the back of his hand before cutting another piece.

"Magdalena will be worried if I'm gone much longer."

Srut chewed and nodded.

"Don't you worry, Srut?" Felix lay down on the workbench, carefully positioned on his good side. He spoke like a man with a fever.

Srut waited the few seconds it took for him to drift off into sleep. "I worry," he said.

Felix didn't stir when Dasa clicked back into her husband's studio carrying an armful of clothes. There were janitor's jumpsuits, security uniforms – nothing military – only the kind a night clerk might wear to guard an office building, along with a few heavy sweaters and woolen jackets. She laid them on the long, steel table next to her husband's workbench and separated them into outfits.

"These should fit, more or less."

Dasa bent down to take in Felix's face. In her first display of tenderness, she reached onto a shelf above

Barbora's naked likenesses and unfolded a large cotton sheet. She puffed it up like a parachute and let it float gently on top of him, leaving only his nose, eyes, and hair exposed. She then cocked her head, signaling for Srut to follow.

"He's out cold," she muttered.

Srut walked behind Dasa, letting her lead him through the dark kitchen and into a living room lit by the moon. Like Svoboda's studio, the house was decorated in the fashion of magazine articles featuring "Homes of the Future." Steel and chrome, concrete and wheat-colored wood framed the soft leather and suede upholstery. The light fixtures jutted like robotic arms and legs from the floor, ceiling, and various tables, ending in swollen joints that held bulbs in sizes Srut had never seen before. Some were the size of a half-melon, while others were barely larger than a thumbprint. He wondered what the place would look like if all of these lights were turned on and he could see the hues and textures of the geometric patterned rugs and indecipherable art works.

"Cig?" Dasa asked.

She sat down on a sofa that looked like two planks of wood nailed together into an L-shape, and held up by four tin cans. Srut took the pack from her and lit up, choosing an uncomfortable chair made of a few leather straps and some metal rods.

"I understand you killed a man tonight."

Srut lifted an eyebrow. "I need a drink."

Dasa swung over to a table littered with crystal glasses and decanters. The light reflected off them, looking like the Manhattan skyline in *King Kong*. She poured two glasses of good rum, neat, and handed one to Srut as she passed him on the way to her seat.

"Once those jackals are done putting out that fire, they'll knock on every house in the quarter." Dasa talked about the Germans as if they were door-to-door salesmen.

"What if they come before we've left?"

"Oh, we'll do what we always do. Shoot you, I guess." Dasa tossed her head back and laughed like a woman who'd been smoking for forty years, though she was thirty-one. Her shoulders stiffened and she sat at attention when the back door opened and Justus Svoboda's rubber galoshes sloshed into the kitchen.

"In here," Dasa rasped, as a shivering Svoboda entered the living room, rubbing his arms. He walked straight over to the bar and poured a glass of rum, taking it in one swallow, before pouring himself another.

"Fire's still burning. It's spread to half the house and could take the whole thing down." Svoboda took his drink and sat next to his wife. "Only the daughter got out, and she was unconscious." He drank the rest of his rum and took Dasa's from her hand. "So far, they think it's an accident."

"That German tried to kill us. He's the one who started the fire."

Srut gulped his rum and lifted his glass. Svoboda nudged Dasa, and she got up, took their glasses, and went to the bar.

"That's not how the SS would look at it. Fleischmann was a prick, but he was their prick. And you were in his house."

"Not his house."

"That depends on your point of view."

"Do you want us to leave now?"

Svoboda took off his galoshes and massaged his cold, sockless feet. "Come on. Let's go check in on our young friend."

Felix hadn't moved at all, and Svoboda touched his foot, shaking it like a hand, until he groaned and fluttered his eyelids.

"Come on. I've got a better place for you to sleep."

Felix got up, disoriented, and swayed for a moment before finding his balance. His shoulder stung every time he moved, but he'd felt worse.

"This is good," Svoboda said, looking over the clothes Dasa had brought down. "You might as well get in these now. It's cold upstairs and your own clothes are, how can I say this, *offensive*."

He selected janitor's jumpsuits, a couple of wool cardigan sweaters, and two jackets – one gray and one blue. "These are comfortable and will look just as they're supposed to after you've slept in them."

Srut removed his grimy clothes and folded them. He buttoned each button on his clay-red Italian shirt and charcoal jacket. They were his only good clothes, and he was hopeful Dasa might launder them before they left.

Svoboda helped Felix change into his jumpsuit and sweater, fashioning a tightly knitted moss green scarf around Felix's neck and elbow as a sling.

"You look like out-of-work-plumbers." Svoboda laughed, and Srut saw into his nature. The sculptor's shrewd eyes, no bigger than hazelnuts, made their judgments quickly and absolutely, as they had about Felix while they stood in his backyard under the beam of his hand light.

"And don't forget this." Svoboda put the Infant of Prague into Felix's hand. "I found it in your pocket – snooping, I'll admit."

"Quiet!" Dasa's voice hissed from the living room and brought the house to a standstill. There were footsteps outside and the doorbell rang in chorus with a thumping on the front door. Dasa hurried to the door, keeping her cigarette wedged between her lacquered fingers.

"You need something?" she asked the two uniformed men. They answered in German, which Dasa spoke fluently, but refused to practice. "Yeah, I'm up. The whole neighborhood's up."

Svoboda crept into the kitchen and crouched, his hand inching towards the vent where he kept his gun.

"Look, there hasn't been any coffee for three weeks. All I can do is boil up some water with a little rum." Dasa exhaled and Svoboda could almost hear her eyes roll. He listened to the familiar snap of German-made boots as the young men came in, following Dasa towards the kitchen.

"Why don't you sit down?"

The men remained standing and one of them yapped at Dasa.

"Here, take this. I know you got a lot more important things to do out there than wait for a woman to boil water." She handed him a glass of rum and poured a second glass for the other one.

The yapper made it clear to Dasa that he disapproved of liquor, especially on the job, to which she replied, "Me, too."

"Well, I hope everyone's all right over there ... oh... oh," Dasa lamented as the younger one, a Sudeten German, informed her of the tragedy that had befallen the Fleischmann house. All of them dead but a daughter, he explained. And she was in critical condition.

"My God. It makes me grateful for the good life I have," she said without enthusiasm.

The men told her to stay inside – that the neighborhood gapers had been a nuisance to the firefighters – and then one mumbled something Svoboda couldn't quite make out.

"I gave you my last bottle, friend. You're welcome to look around. Believe me, I won't miss it. My husband tips the bottle whenever he gets the chance."

The men gave Dasa a cool greeting as they left, leaving her to contemplate the mess they'd made of her floors with their wet and sooty boots. The air in the room was thicker from the smoke in their jackets then the cigarette Dasa stubbed out into a kidney-shaped ashtray. She was lighting another cigarette as Svoboda returned to the living room.

"I didn't give them any of the good stuff." Dasa's hands went up to check on her hair, loosening some of the tight curlers, then giving up and starting to unravel them altogether. Her fingers were expert at keeping the cherry of her cigarette from fouling her coif. "They weren't looking for trouble. They were just looking."

Svoboda's laugh came upon him like a bucket of cold water and infected Dasa, who tried to suck on her cigarette in between guffaws. They walked arm in arm through the kitchen and back into the studio, where they were met by a quiet, abandoned space.

Felix's father's house was illuminating its corner of the neighborhood. Gone were the secret room where Magdalena and her mother had lived, and the bed Felix had slept in since he was a boy. Gone was his Olympic uniform – cleaned and boxed for posterity – although his victory skates hung from the fingers of his good hand.

Felix and Srut looked out of place outside the burning house, even in their clean janitors' clothes. No janitors lived in Vinohrady and it was too early for them to be going to work anyway. The neighbors had been sent back to their homes, so there wasn't even a crowd to hide in. Only policemen, firefighters, and SS officers dispatched to the scene. The streets had been blocked off and were being guarded, so there was no leaving on foot.

"We should've stayed back there," Srut said.

"And wait for the Germans to search the place?"

"They were willing to hide us, you idiot."

"Then go back," Felix said.

"Us, not me. The man had no interest in me."

Two more fire trucks pulled up to the scene. The firemen jumped out of them, rushing to battle the flames that were now licking even the roof. They left the second truck unattended, and Felix snatched two fireman's hats from the ground, donning one and tossing the other to Srut. He grabbed Srut's arm and broke into a run. When they reached the vehicle, he pushed the gypsy into the driver's seat.

"I don't drive," Srut told him.

They crawled over each other – switching places – careful to avoid the petals. Though Felix had downed the rest of Srut's rum as they left Svoboda's house, his mind was, under the circumstances, remarkably lucid. Even the large wheel seemed manageable with his good right arm as he edged the truck away from the burning house.

Felix nodded at a fireman, signaling him to move aside and the man did, letting the fire truck rumble past him as he continued fighting the fire.

"We might just get away with this."

A few meters past the convoy of emergency vehicles, Felix looked to his left and caught the eyes of another fireman. The young man stood there, a cup in his hands, mouthing a confused expletive, until his eyes finally swelled in outrage.

"Help me hold the wheel." Felix shifted gears, and smashed the foot pedal to the floor. The truck drew a low, gurgling breath before expelling a roar and then a bellow as its tires squealed down the cobblestone street, eager to catch up to the motor. They screeched past the two officers who'd visited the Svoboda home.

"Nein! Halt!" the Sudeten German yelped. He reached into his pocket and pulled out a whistle. Fumbling, he placed the whistle to his lips and blew, turning his cheeks blood purple. A pair of SS officers, friends of the ill-fated Fleischmann, instantly seized control of the situation. The taller officer, sporting a prominent gold canine tooth, ordered the policemen to their wagon, while he and his cohort got into their Mercedes sedan and pulled out onto the street in pursuit of the stolen fire truck.

Felix's one-armed driving wasn't so much of a problem as the truck bounced down Vinohradská Street, but when he had to turn, the fire truck was sent into an unsteady weave. His right and left side wheels lifted up off the pavement, setting down one after another - *Fee Fi Fo Fum.*

The gypsy had no feel for the vehicle, and pulled down too hard, forcing Felix into a tug of war until Srut relaxed his grip and let Felix take over the helm again. Felix lowered his speed. Most of the roads were far too narrow to allow either of the cars behind him to come up alongside. He could crush them easily against a building if they tried, and part of him welcomed the opportunity. In his rear view mirror, he glimpsed the driver of the Mercedes pounding his fist on the steering wheel.

"Fucking Czechs," the driver ranted to his gold-toothed partner. "What kind of crazy swine steals a fire truck?"

"He's stinking drunk – look at his driving," the partner told him.

"Does he think we won't shoot him because he's drunk?" The driver fired a couple of shots out the sedan's window, but they bounced off the back of the fire truck.

"Up yours," Srut shouted, flicking his fingers off his chin.

Felix was growing tired. His shoulder stiffened with every passing minute, and the pain had spread to the muscles of his neck and back. He was starting to see double, causing the fire truck to careen through the street, riding up onto the pedestrian pathways, and taking the turn onto Spálená Street too quickly. The truck fishtailed into a crystal shop, shattering shelves of vases, champagne flutes, punch bowls, and candlestick holders.

"We're dead, you know," Srut said. He banged his fist against the side window. "Can't you get on an open road? One leading *out* of Prague?"

Felix ignored him. Gershwin's "Rhapsody in Blue" was thumping through his head, focusing his attention.

"Stop humming!" Srut hated humming.

Gershwin always played in Felix's head during a game, swelling with drama during poignant parts and ebbing in the interim. He'd known he was destined for the National Team when he played a game in concert with his inner orchestra, never missing the ching of a symbol or snort of a horn.

As Felix turned down Narodní Street, he passed the National Theatre, its winged statues hanging from the façade and posed like naughty hostesses. The ladies wore gowns that exposed a little too much breast or thigh under the ruse of oversight.

The Goddess of Soliloquy, a tall, slender schoolgirl of a muse, batted her stony eyes at Felix, and parted her lips as if she had something important to say, but decided to keep it to herself. She and her sisters giggled and flew towards the fire truck, hitching on to the ladders that flanked its sides.

In his mirror, Felix could see the flapping of the goddess' wings, but he tried to ignore them, concentrating on the sound of Gershwin's trumpet and his grip on the steering wheel. As he turned onto the embankment, he felt the vehicle lighten under his grip. The truck glided along now, lifted up by the marble wings of the goddesses. The women winked at him and moved as if they were treading water.

Srut was saying something, or at least his lips were moving. He looked confused and angry. The Goddess of Soliloquy poked her head into Felix's window and began whispering to him. Srut rattled off a stream of curses.

"Do what she says," Felix demanded.

Srut stopped cursing and glared at him. "She? Says what?"

"Get out there," Felix said. "When we enter the tunnel, start throwing whatever you can off the back of the truck."

"They have guns, you ass! You fucking go out there."

"Can you spray the water at them?" Felix asked.

The goddess's lips were still perched at his ear. Her voice was familiar, but Felix couldn't place it. In the distance, he could see the mouth of a tunnel they would be entering in a few moments – the road laid out like its tongue.

Srut looked at Felix, letting his friend's unnatural calm infect him. They had, after all, no plan other than the one

Felix was offering and Srut preferred the offensive to the defensive any day.

Srut reached down behind his seat into a chest of tools wedged there. He grabbed a wrench and flung it through the rear window glass of the cab, shattering it and leaving only a few jagged shards sticking out of the back window frame like shark's teeth. Icy air flooded the cabin and Srut held his breath on instinct. He was still holding his breath when he snatched a hammer from the chest of firemen's tools and knocked out the remaining pieces of glass. Srut then hoisted himself up off his seat and climbed out onto the perch that sat between the driver's cab and the real business of the vehicle. He rounded the corner and gripped the handles on the side of the truck, moving along to a short ladder that would take him to the roof.

He heard the first shots come ricocheting off the horn of the rear siren. The second shot took the horn clean off, sending it crashing into a stop sign and nearly taking Srut's head off as it rebounded. Srut pulled himself up to the roof like a snake onto a tree branch. Once there, he lay flat, catching his breath and allowing the bullets to whiz over his head and pummel the sides of the fire truck.

He had no more than a few seconds to get a good lay of things before they entered the tunnel, but Srut was used to working in the dark. It was doing these things on a moving vehicle that terrified him. Srut didn't trust planes, trains, or automobiles.

He bellowed as the tunnel approached; it was a battle cry that hadn't come from any of his known ancestors. His people had never been soldiers. When the dark tunnel enveloped them, Srut pushed up with his shoulder into a coil of cable. He rolled it onto its side and sent the cable off the back of the truck and into the trailing cars like a big snowball. The cars behind them swerved, barely avoiding it.

Crouching on the roof of the fire truck, he was barely visible to the police car and indiscernible to the Mercedes Sedan now. The only light came from the single dome light of the police car. He didn't know the goddess had told Felix to cut their emergency lights as soon as they entered the tunnel. She was looking out for Srut, even if he couldn't see her.

One by one, he dangled his legs over the side of the roof and lowered himself until his toes found the silver perches flanking the sides of the truck. With his one free hand, he grabbed and fumbled at anything he could, unhooking latches and rattling the extension ladders until one came loose. The ladder scraped against the road, still hanging on by a solitary latch Srut was unable to reach. Stretching his leg out, he kicked at the thing's ribs, loosening it. His free hand gripped a lever for balance and he heaved back, ready to swing. Raising both of his legs, he gave the stubborn ladder one final kick.

Srut's wail rose in pitch as he watched the ladder unfold to a cacophony of squeaks and crunches. For a moment Srut forgot about the fact that he was hanging from the side of a stolen fire truck, and swung back and forth howling in victory. The ladder slid partly under the carriage of the police car and curled up like a scorpion's tale, smashing the windshield.

The lever Srut had been hanging on gave way, leaving him suspended with the passing concrete chipping away at the thick soles of his boots. He didn't notice at first that the drop of the lever coincided with a rush of water that blasted from the rear of the truck, drenching the cars behind them in a punishing charge.

While the water sprayed, the ladder extended to its full length and crunched under the wheels of the police car, forcing it to come to an abrupt stop. The sedan slew from side to side, trying to get around the vehicle before grazing the tunnel wall and spinning out of control. It finally smashed into the police car, wedging it between its bumper and the wall.

"Stop! Stop!" Srut cried.

Felix had seen the cars behind them crash, but it wasn't until the goddesses unhanded the vehicle and flew back and away towards their home on the National Theatre's facade that he was able to see Srut and hear his howling. The last few bars of "Rhapsody in Blue" beat in Felix's eardrums as Srut scrambled back up the rear of the firetruck.

"Let's get out of here." Srut crawled into the cabin from the back window and rummaged through the tool pack, picking out whatever he could hide in his clothes. He took a screwdriver, a rope, and a small, rubber coated mallet that made the pocket of his jumper sag like a stocking filled with oranges.

"Where the hell are you going?" Srut said.

Felix took his foot off the brake and began rolling the vehicle down the embankment road. It led two ways: one slid down a ramp to a small island on the Vltava and the other dead-ended at the Charles Bridge.

"Time we got rid of this thing." Felix shifted the gears and the truck lurched forward suddenly, whooping as it careened off the road past trees and picnic benches. An iron railing couldn't slow it down and the truck leapt off the cobblestone beach of the island, belly-flopping into the water through a layer of ice. After the initial splash, the truck sank into the river like a fat lady lowering herself into her bath, easing in until only her head bobbed above the water.

Felix and Srut climbed from their windows to the roof and jumped off the end of the truck onto the cobblestones. Police lights flashed along the embankment road, and a shot shrilled from above, clipping a tree branch at the riverside.

"So much for trying to convince them we drowned." Felix grabbed Srut's hand and dragged him onto the frozen river and under the Charles Bridge, where they were hidden from view.

"Come out with your hands up," a voice boomed through a bullhorn. A squadron of SS officers positioned themselves on the bridge.

"Give yourselves up peacefully and your families will be spared. Your families will be spared." The officer repeated each sentence twice, like a bad chorus in a German folk song.

"They want to kill us."

"Of course they want to fucking kill us," Srut said.

The gypsy kicked the side of the bridge and a loop of coiled roped peeked out from his pocket. Felix snatched it up.

"Hah!" he grunted, unraveling the rope, and wrapping it crisscrossed around his torso. He measured a long train of it before tying it around Srut.

"What are you doing?"

"They might fucking kill us, you know, but they're going to have to catch us first."

Felix had Srut lace up his skates and wrap an extra coil of the rope around his injured shoulder to keep it steady. He told the gypsy to sit down on the ice and hold his knees together, making himself into a ball. Felix then started skating in a wide circle under the bridge, gaining speed, and dragging Srut behind him.

Srut held onto the rope and slid in ovals behind the left wing of the Czechoslovak National Hockey Team. They made several passes under the bridge before Felix broke out, crouched low to the ice.

Shots rang out from a dozen officers on top of the bridge, chipping the ice around them as Felix wove from side to side with Srut's frozen ass in tow. Half the squadron ran down the stairs in pursuit, but only one of them could balance well enough to aim and fire while sliding across the ice in his boots. As his fellow officers fell and misfired, the graceful German picked up a good speed and was able to get Felix and Srut back in his sites. He fired off several rounds, but was ultimately foiled by one of his own men, who blew a hole in the ice and sent him flying through the air.

With the Germans scrambling behind them, Felix and Srut skated well past Old Town, and climbed up the embankment stairs where the river curved and hid them from sight. Felix's shoulder hurt like hell, and Srut retied Svoboda's green scarf around it. The gypsy then removed Felix's skates and hung them around his own neck; he helped Felix slip back into his shoes. Srut tied his jacket around his waist to cover his wet, numb ass and coiled the rope again, stuffing it into his loose trousers and giving himself an ample crotch. Dog-tired, they rejoined the city at dawn.

Chapter Thirteen
Dawn

"I need to eat," Felix said. His legs were shaking. With the adrenaline draining away, pain, rum and fatigue were retaking his body.

Srut knew a place. It was a place he used to go to when he was hungry and didn't feel like earning a meal from Henrik.

The coffee house and patisserie, called simply Café, was a bare, ugly place that had changed little over time. The only smidgens of charm that Café possessed were small, crystal chandeliers which hung over each booth like diamond powder puffs, clashing with the dull, russet upholstery and uncovered tables. It was also the easiest place in Prague to dine and dash, as the staff was chronically lazy and indifferent. Germans, for this reason, were conspicuously absent, further attracting a clientele Café could've never hoped to host during better times.

Srut and Felix sat at a big table, as if they were waiting for friends, and ordered coffees and sweets they had no means to pay for. Srut chose an assortment of crème pastries, signaling the waitress to keep the check, as they would be ordering more. She walked away without writing their order and came back some ten minutes later with one coffee and several minutes after that with the other. The pastries came following her cigarette break, which was taken in full view of her hungry customers. She stood inside, to the left of the front door, looking out of the picture window and smiling whenever she saw a woman wearing a hat that she fancied.

The pastries were heavy, Viennese-style towers and tubes, filled with jams, candied nuts, crèmes, and custards tasting less of sugar and cream than powdered milk and shortening. Felix ignored them in favor of coffee and bread, while Srut spooned the crèmes out of every shell, leaving several carcasses of crust strewn about the chipped porcelain dish. He ordered more coffee and pastries, while Felix took a newspaper from a neighboring table.

"Fire didn't make the paper," he said, snapping the newspaper page, and skimming stories of alleged German victories. Felix's eyes stopped at the bottom right of the front page.

"Someone tried to steal the Infant of Prague last week," he said. Running his hand over his vest pocket, Felix tapped his father's figurine. He sighed deeply; it hadn't been lost in the chase. "A special envoy from the Vatican thwarted the robbery." The article went on to describe another foiled theft that had happened a few weeks before Christmas.

Srut had no patience for the news, except the sports pages, and found his eyes wandering from woman to woman, scanning Café for a beauty. A redhead with fingers like ivory piano keys peered over a coffee-stained menu. Her lime-colored eyes strained to allow a better look at Srut. He rubbed his hands over his unshaven face before blowing her a kiss.

"It says here they suspect rebel involvement in the first robbery, which seems utterly ridiculous," Felix said.

"Hmm." Srut licked his lips slowly. He looked up, expecting to lock eyes with the redhead once again, but was instead met with a glare from a pair of small, brown irises.

Svoboda, Srut mouthed.

Svoboda noticed him, too, letting his eyes sweep their table, but betraying little other than casual recognition. He buttoned up his bulky topcoat and turned to pass Felix and Srut. Bumping up against Felix's outstretched leg, he excused himself, glancing back at the two of them once more before leaving to the right, towards the top of the square.

As their waitress redressed a false eyelash, Felix slipped past the front door and headed in the same direction as Svoboda. Srut ignored his friend's absence, flipping through the newspaper once more before getting up to ask about a toilet. He never returned to his table, and their waitress cursed like a whore when she realized she'd been stiffed.

Though ice still hung like snot from the noses of gargoyles, it was the first pleasant day in a month. Felix was comfortable without gloves and didn't bother buttoning his jacket all the way to the neck.

"Excuse me, sir, I think you dropped this," Svoboda said from behind him.

Felix turned and forced a curt, polite smile, taking the crescent change purse from Svoboda's hand. The yellow daisy threaded through Svoboda's buttonhole greeted Felix like a big, happy face. Svoboda nodded, tipping his fedora, and then walked on without a glance back in Felix's direction.

The little leather pouch was dyed the blush of a painful sunburn and contained five things: a one hundred-crown note, several food vouchers, a calling card for a furrier by the name of Dvořák – the address circled, an appointment card from a Dr. Novotný reminding him of a 4:30 checkup, and a key.

"Did he give you that?" Srut had come up beside Felix. He seized the hundred-crown note and kissed it.

"We eat. Tonight we eat!" He put his hand on Felix's good shoulder. "Magdalena eats, too. Everybody eats."

"Everybody eats," Felix repeated. He squeezed the cards and the key in his palm.

At Dvořák the furrier's, a gilded sign the size of a fish salver hung from two iron hooks above the arched, wooden door. The sign rocked back and forth like a playground swing, its fancy cursive poised on the gentle breeze.

The key Svoboda had given Felix didn't fit the outside lock, but the door was open, and led into a foyer furnished with a circular couch made of satin and royal blue velvet. A headless mannequin stood in the far right corner with one knee bent against the other and its hands floating like fresh flower petals at its side. It was draped in a large brown sable coat and looked like it was waiting to be asked to dance. Heavily framed drawings of glamorous Parisian women in a range of furs lined the walls like ancestors.

The door behind the mannequin was locked and the key from the change purse opened it, spilling into a modest ballroom, complete with mirrors, buffed yellow wooden floors, and an enormous overhead light studded with crystals and sporting electric bulbs that craned their metal necks like swan heads. Only two of the bulbs were working, and cast a dense, amber light into the room.

"Hello?" Felix called.

"I'm glad you came." Svoboda was leaning out from behind a mirror – one that opened like a door into another room. "We were worried about you last night."

He stepped out from behind the glass and met Felix and Srut in the center of the ballroom. A mustached man followed him, as well as a short gentleman with more salt than pepper hair and a face that was creased with dozens of tiny wrinkles. The short man, clad in a black overcoat buttoned to his neck, stood back by the mirrored door, his hands folded in front of him as if he were merely an observer.

Srut knew the mustached man. His name was Pokorný and he lived in the bachelors' apartment building. He'd met him once or twice and remembered him as being a friend of Henrik's.

"This is Kamil," Svoboda said.

Kamil Pokorný, with good teeth and a bad complexion, nodded and held out his hand. He avoided Srut's eyes and turned only to greet Felix.

"And who's that?" Srut demanded, pointing to the short man by the mirror.

"That, Mr. Srut, is Monsignor Merillini."

Felix looked over at the Italian, studying the man's quiet demeanor. He radiated a pensive nature and a deeply personal form of power. Srut circled around them.

"I didn't think you church types liked to get your hands dirty in this sort of thing," Srut said. "Except for shaking hands with Hitler and Mussolini whenever it suits you, of course."

Srut always enjoyed exposing hypocrisy and double talk. He made no effort to disguise his self-satisfied posture, and crossed his arms as he waited for Merillini's retort.

"Mr. Srut," Svoboda said. "Monsignor Merillini is here at great personal risk to himself. Perhaps if we understood one another better, there would be less suspicion between us."

"Perhaps," Srut aped.

"Let's begin then, shall we?"

Svoboda sat first, cross-legged on the floor. Pokorný, Felix, and Srut followed, while the Monsignor remained standing.

"Your fire is being called an accident." Svoboda lit up a cigarette, using it as a pointer to punctuate his sentences. "More important, it's been reported that the two drunkards who drove the fire truck into the water have probably drowned. They may still drag the river for show, but it's not in the best interest of the men who chased you to make any big deal out of it. You made asses of them."

"Did any of them get a good look at us?"

"No."

"Then we're invisible again."

"You, dear boy, are hardly invisible." Svoboda aimed the cherry of his cigarette at Felix's nose.

"What is this?" Srut swept his arm around the ballroom. "We don't even know these men and you bring them to meet us like this is some sort of cocktail party?"

"You know me," Kamil Pokorný said. "You know my full name and you know where I live. I don't even know you have a home."

"That's right. Where would a dirty gypsy like me go to lay my head?" Srut had never spoken to Pokorný before now, but he'd always been annoyed by his aristocratic cheek-bones and scanty lips.

"And you knew Henrik," Pokorný said.

"Too bad he couldn't come to the party."

"Stop." Felix put his hand on Srut's back. "Please."

Svoboda took a tiny pillbox out of his breast pocket, opening the top with his thumb. "You look like you could use one of these," he told Felix. "It's for pain."

Srut grabbed the box as Felix reached for it. He tossed it to the side. Justus Svoboda's eyes didn't follow the flight of the pillbox and paid even less attention to the scattering of white pills. Pokorný leaned forward, but Svoboda remained as relaxed as he had the night before after two full glasses of fine rum. Monsignor Merillini clasped his hands in front of his waist, blinking his eyes as if it took considerable effort.

"Mr. Srut, we're all men on equal footing," the Monsignor said after a brief, silent interlude. "Each one of us could expose the other, and set off a desperate chain of events. Would it be worth it for anyone here to add more gravestones to an already full plot?"

"Maybe for you. I don't see any priests getting rounded up."

"Not yet," the Monsignor acknowledged. "But if Herr Hitler has his way with the world, it shouldn't be long."

Srut snickered and looked the Monsignor straight in the eye. "I would think not."

Srut smoothed down his jacket and kicked the empty bottle of painkillers. He pointed his shoe and started crushing the white pills under his toe one by one.

"Why don't I tell you about myself," Svoboda said gently. "And then you can decide whether or not you want my pain killers."

Felix leaned forward and put his hand on Srut's elbow. He could feel the Monsignor staring at him, but didn't meet his eyes. Instead, he looked to Svoboda.

"Do you know why my father was killed?" he asked.

Svoboda nodded.

"Your father was my friend, although I only got to know him well in the year before his death. We were neighbors prior to that. Fellow widowers. We would wave to one another in the garden and give each other a babka cake on Christmas."

Svoboda's cigarette had burned half-way to his fingers and was clipped of ash like a good haircut. He hadn't smoked it yet, and his breath still smelled of cinnamon.

"He knew what was coming, and I was powerless to help him at the time. I had other involvements." Svoboda inhaled deeply.

"What involvements?" Srut's eyes had changed since the night before, when he'd drank rum in Svoboda's living room as a guest. Now they looked skeptical and haughty.

"Mr. Srut, you of all people know. Wasn't it you who carried guns to a villa in Barrandov and found sanctuary for your friends in poor Henrik's wine pantry?"

Srut sat up taller, crossing his arms over his chest.

"Ah, the Chief. And I thought you were just a scribble of handwriting. To what do we owe this honor – you showing yourself like this to us? Aren't you afraid I'll trade you in for a few marks and a good piece of meat?"

Svoboda laughed as if his wife had whispered a joke into his ear.

"I'm not Zeus, Mr. Srut. And not apt to turn you into a swan because you've looked into my face – even if I could. One has to take chances sometimes and venture into trust.

After what I saw last night, I happen to think the two of you are a pretty good bet."

Kamil Pokorný chuckled.

"What are you?" Felix asked. "And who were you to my father?"

Svoboda wove his fingers together and opened his palms. "I'm a patriot, first and foremost. And I'm an artist. I can sculpt a monument for a city square, or perhaps a replica of a precious artifact."

"Like an Infant of Prague," Felix said. The words his father had spoken to him on the night he was killed came back to him now. *Take this,* he'd said, crushing Felix's fingers around his little Infant. *It's all that we have left to win this war.*

"I didn't know the Prague Underground was interested in religion," Srut said.

"The Prague Underground is faith personified. We are, after all, David to their Goliath." Svoboda smiled and leaned in towards Felix. "And your father was one of our disciples."

Felix catalogued his father's known offenses: hiding Jews, enjoying degenerate art, and believing in Christ and not Hitler. They were deeply personal offenses – ones that expressed private values and loyalty to long, meaningful friendships – like to Vera, Magdalena's mother. But nowhere among them could he see how Marek Andel II, a regional banker and son of a hops farmer, could've gotten involved with the Prague Underground, the Infant of Prague, and the likes of Krev, the young killer, and his Nazi bosses.

"Your father wasn't the richest banker in Prague," Svoboda said. "What he had was will; the will to move large sums of money for dubious assets. I'm an artist, as I said. The Germans think me frivolous, but your father – he could become involved in things. His valuable council and tireless work on their behalf helped them lose more money than they gained – and money is the most essential element of a war. Money and propaganda, of course."

Felix's temple began to throb, overwhelming the dull pain in his shoulder.

"He helped the Germans procure treasures from the Catholic Church," Svoboda continued. "And I helped him cheat them by producing glorious fakes. Unfortunately, one of my fakes was unmasked."

"The Infant?"

Svoboda nodded.

"But the Infant is back at the Church of Our Lady the Victorious," Felix said. "At least that's what I read this morning."

Svoboda raised his palms and looked to the Monsignor.

"Is it? I don't think so," he said. "Not the original, at any rate. I don't know where the original is and neither do the Germans or the Catholics, for that matter. But your father did. I'm afraid he hid it somewhere and its location died along with him."

Srut flicked his cigarette, letting it bounce off the toe of Svoboda's shoe. "So you let him die to protect a statue? Is that how the Chief of the Prague Underground operates?"

To the gypsy this made no sense at all. A nationless people, gypsies stuck to their clans and had no more than a passing interest in the state that provided them infrastructure. It was why Srut could pass, but he would never pretend.

"Mr. Srut, nobody does anything for me or me for them."

Kamil Pokorný nodded in silent agreement and played with his mustache, its gray hairs yellowed from heavy smoking. "You wouldn't even be alive if it weren't for his hand," he muttered.

"It's all right, Kamil. I'm sure Mr. Srut is quite clever enough to have survived without any of our help," Svoboda said. The Monsignor affected a closed-lip smile.

"Are we being conscripted?" Felix asked.

Svoboda nodded.

"Of course, you're free to go right now and never look back. Or we can try to take care of each other's immediate needs. You could help us, as we, in turn, could provide better for you and those in your care." Svoboda removed a mirror from his breast pocket and put his cigarette out on it, blowing the ashes off his reflection. "You are aware, I'm sure, that nightclub basements in the middle of town are no place to hide. Do you honestly think that your comings and goings have gone unnoticed? In those crowded buildings with all those nosey cleaning women?"

"Could you find a place for our wives and Srut's family?"

"Is that what you want?" Svoboda directed his question to Srut and the gypsy gave no answer. "How many of you are there?"

"Eleven, including ourselves," Felix told him.

"Ah. Then that makes nine. The two of you will need other arrangements." Svoboda cleared his throat. "Mr. Srut, does your wife look like you?"

"She looks like a gypsy."

"She's pretty," Felix added.

"We're not putting on a beauty pageant. We need her to look Czech, not pretty. I'll get some clothes together and see what we can do. Dasa's good at these things."

Chapter Fourteen
March 18

When they met under the Manesův Bridge on the Old Town side of the river, Svoboda produced two envelopes. It was late, close to curfew, and a frenzy of hurried feet clattered above them on the footpath.

"Boleslav Miška." Srut opened his envelope first. His new name suited him no better than if he were a dogcatcher called Socrates. Felix looked over his papers and back at Svoboda.

"These are copies of my papers. My name."

Svoboda nodded. "All things considered, I thought it would be more dangerous to give you a different identity. You're rather recognizable to the young men in uniform."

"And if they connect my name with my father's?"

"That's not so likely on a routine check. There are hundreds of Andels in Prague."

Svoboda put his arm around Felix and kissed his forehead. "I'll need to see you again two days from now. Let's meet in the café of Obecní Dům. Of course, you'll need to bathe – will that be a problem? I have some clothes for you here." Svoboda held out a shopping bag and Srut took it from him, riffling through its contents and holding up only one dark suit jacket.

"What about Srut?" Felix asked.

"It's less suspicious for all of us to meet separately, in twos, if we're not to hide under bridges. People get nervous when they see a larger group together."

"Then let's meet in private." Srut smelled the suit jacket and stroked the silk lining against his cheek.

"I have to insist, Mr. Srut. After all, I'll need to meet with you as well when I move your wife into her new hiding place. I'm making her arrangements."

"And the others?"

"And the others, yes."

"How soon?" Srut bit off the end of Svoboda's answer.

"Mr. Srut, it isn't easy to find people who are willing…"

"How soon?"

"Who are willing to take in a gypsy family."

"How soon? You think the stench from our shit hasn't raised any suspicions yet?" Srut scrunched up the suit jacket into a ball and threw it at Svoboda's feet.

"I don't know, Mr. Srut," Svoboda said. "Your wife, a few days. The others…perhaps two, three weeks."

"Ha!"

Felix glared at Srut.

"I was just asking a question." Srut's tone was normal again. He was forever assessing people – testing their boundaries.

"Two weeks." Svoboda held his fingers up in the form of V for victory. He'd abandoned his pleasant tone and took in a deep breath to cleanse himself of Srut's bad manners. "We should get out of here, gentlemen. We're not the only ones who meet under bridges."

Srut rolled up the bag full of fine clothes and put it under his arm, turning his back to Svoboda and waiting for his friend to join him. Felix was stopped by the sculptor's hand.

"Two days."

Svoboda watched the men walk away with Srut in a defiant lead. Kamil Pokorný emerged from the back of a pillar, where he'd been crouched with his ready gun. Monsignor Merillini stepped out of the shadows and placed his hand on Svoboda's shoulder.

"Perhaps we shouldn't have let them go again," the Monsignor said.

"Or we should let them go and never come back." Pokorný tucked the pistol inside the waist of his trousers and sauntered over to Svoboda, shaking his head and pushing the wayward hairs of his mustache away from the corners of his mouth.

"You don't like them, I know. But my friend, you've always had appalling judgment." Svoboda patted Pokorný on the back and cast his eyes back to the Monsignor.

"Kamil, will you follow them and bring young Felix and his wife back with you to my house tonight? Upon further reflection, I'd rather he leave the gypsy den right away."

Svoboda and the Monsignor watched Kamil Pokorný disappear up the stairs to the street level. The Italian narrowed his eyes and looked out into the fog as if he could still catch a glimpse of Felix Andel as he made his way back to the Palace Lucerna.

"You're quite right about him," the Monsignor said. "It appears he's an idealist, like his father."

"And like you?" Svoboda asked.

"No, I'm afraid." Monsignor Merillini slid his hands in the pockets of his coat. "I'm a realist."

CHAPTER FIFTEEN
MARCH 21

Justus Svoboda twirled his walking stick like a hobo. He'd carved it on a summer day, when he and his wife, Barbora – it was her thirty-ninth birthday – stripped naked to swim in a shallow pond at the back corner of his country property. It was before the war, when he had not a care in the world except for his late wife's cough.

Today, the stick was part of him, like a pair of worn-in leather slippers. He took it with him whenever he left his house and it gave him the appearance of a happy man.

"Such a rare day shouldn't be wasted on a tram," Svoboda said, shaking his head at the passengers – *zoo animals*, as he called them. He and Felix were walking to Svoboda's favorite café in Obecní Dům for their meeting, already once postponed.

Finished in 1912, Obecní Dům was an Art Nouveau masterpiece and also the newest building in Old Town. It was painted in creams and golds, underscoring its youth. Svoboda strode through its gilded entrance doors like a count, offering his arm to the pretty hostess as she led them into the hall. An oval-shaped ceiling of red, gold, and eggshell hovered over them, supporting a second floor balcony bar that belonged in an opera house.

"Your usual table, Mr. Svoboda," the hostess said, gesturing to a round, intimate table for four. It was perfectly positioned, looking out onto the street from an arched, leaded window, and into the café with the front door and upper balcony in full view.

"You might recognize Andrea," Svoboda said, indicating the young woman. "She's one of my models."

Andrea smiled through crooked teeth and full, ruby lips.

"She's in the living room on the consul," Svoboda continued. "The girl with the beautiful spine who sits holding her knee with one arm and playing with her toes with the other." Svoboda mimed the upper part of the pose, including the closed-mouthed look of disappointment that Andrea wore as surely as a hairstyle.

Felix remembered the sculpture, particularly the one enormous breast that hung from under the girl's arm like a fresh roast. It had repulsed him.

"Very beautiful," he said.

Andrea smiled again, and Svoboda whispered into her ear. She scratched a short series of symbols on her notepad, and tucked it back into her skirt as she walked away from their table. If she had worn her hair up, she could've looked in vogue with the dozen or so chandeliers made of thin, upright tubes of frosted glass. Instead, she wore her hair as long and straight as a Chinese girl with a full set of bangs cut a little bit too short, like her skirt.

"Is she one of your people?" Felix whispered.

"One of *my* people?" Svoboda said. "I gave her our order, son, she's bringing it to the bar." Svoboda waved to a cigarette girl and tapped Felix's elbow, but Felix shook his head and the girl turned away.

Felix watched her go, his eyes darting from table to table, fixing on rings, fur collars, and calf's leather gloves peeking out of cashmere pockets. Finally, they focused on the shine of a gold canine tooth that glimmered from the side of a German officer's mouth. A square bandage lay in the middle of the man's forehead. Felix stared until the gold-toothed officer, perhaps sensing him, turned his face – the bandage staring back at Felix like a third eye.

"That man with the bandage," he whispered. "He was one of the Germans chasing us the night of the fire."

"You're staring at him," Svoboda said. "Now smile and wave. That's right."

Felix waved like a German, with closed fingers and a flat palm. Svoboda nodded at the man as well, like he'd shared a drink with him at a party somewhere. The gold-toothed man didn't acknowledge their greetings, but let his eyes linger on Felix before fixing his gaze back on his skinny girlfriend.

"I have to go to the toilet," Felix said.

In the men's room, Felix leaned against the gold-flecked tiles. Splashing cold water on his face, he drank some of it and wiped himself down with a white linen cloth. He dampened the linen and swabbed the back of his neck, folding the cloth and placing it in his pocket when he was done. Exiting the toilet, he walked past the now empty table where the gold-toothed German had sat. Felix went straight to the bar at the front of the café, ordering vodka.

Upon hearing Felix's Czech, the bartender insisted on immediate payment, wiggling the drink between his fingers and holding it out of Felix's reach the way a housewife clutches her pocket book in front of a gypsy vendor.

"I'm with him." Felix gestured to Svoboda's table. The bartender stepped backwards, his lip quivering, and spilled a good quarter of the vodka out of the glass.

"It's on the house," he said. "On me."

Felix took the glass and sipped it, watching the boy polish the bar with fast, round strokes, his eyes cast down as if
he were averting them from his naked mother. Felix turned
his head back to their table, not registering the man who'd
joined Svoboda at first. It was as if he were peering over into
a dream.

Next to Svoboda sat Josef Goebbels, the German Minister
of Public Enlightenment and Propaganda; Hitler's good
friend and trusted right hand. Lída Baarová, Goebbels's
Czech mistress, was with them, smiling and smoking her
cigarette. To Felix's knowledge, Goebbels had no interest
in hockey, but Lída was a different story. She was a movie
actress, and they'd traveled in the same social circles. They'd
shared drinks on many occasions and a bed on one. Felix
downed his vodka and started for the door, but ran straight
into a man about his size.

"Excuse me," he said, before recognition set in. Krev
shoved by him, ignoring his beg of pardon, and proceeded
to Goebbels's chair. He was wearing an old, clay-brown suit –
barely above cheap – that didn't fit well in the shoulders
and had probably been a hand-me-down. Marek Andel's
murderer bent down and whispered into the Minister's ear,
enduring a sharp reprimand, before marching back to the
street side doors where he stood on guard. His castigation
had discomfited him and his cheeks burned red. Felix's stare
caught his attention and Krev narrowed his tiny, blue eyes.

"Felix! There you are!" Lída Baarová's voice fluttered
like her eyelashes. "Justus was about to send someone in
after you." Lída floated over to him, holding her cigarette
over the heads of the seated diners she passed. As she
moved closer, Felix could hear her thighs caressing each
other beneath the silk lining of her deep-water blue suit,

trimmed with Chinchilla. She held her arms out to him in a joyous, girlish manner, displaying every gift her lover had ever given her. Her neck, wrists, fingers, and ears glittered almost as much as the crystal glasses that sat atop the tables.

"What's wrong, darling, are you ill? You look so pale. But gosh, it's good to see you – it's been ages." She kissed both his cheeks and looped her arm around his, leading him to the table. "Now, I didn't know you knew Justus."

"Well, I…"

"We were neighbors once," Svoboda said, standing upon Lída's return. Goebbels remained in his seat. "Minister Goebbels, I don't think you know our young star here. He represented Czechoslo – forgive me – the former Czechoslovakia at the winter Olympic Games in 1936."

"He didn't win." Goebbels spoke in a flat, nasal tone. He mocked Felix with a smile.

"We didn't win."

"But you will next time, when the Games resume in Germany on a permanent basis."

"Yes, next time."

Goebbels signaled the waitress, who leapt to their table.

"Please, sit down," he offered. Lída was already seated, cozying up to her lover and tucking her lovely, dark head in the crook of his neck.

"We're discussing a Christmas present for Minister Goebbels's, uh, mother," Svoboda said. "He'd like me to make a bust of her favorite of his six children."

"It's a little early for Christmas, isn't it?" The question sprang unthinking off Felix's tongue, and he wished he could take it back.

"Of course, but these things take time. There need to be sittings, photographs taken from every angle."

"Hilde's a very special child," Goebbels said, his gaunt face and neck displaying scribbles of veins. "Her essence can't be captured just like that." He snapped his fingers.

Felix took the damp, linen towel out of his pocket, blotting his forehead and upper lip. "Hot," he said.

"I don't want to talk about Christmas," Lída whined. "Let's talk about my birthday, can't we, darling?"

"Birthday, birthday. All I hear is birthday."

"It's going to be a masked ball. Isn't that clever?" Lída cooed.

"There are other things going on in the world." Goebbels smiled, patting his mistress's nose with his short, slender index finger.

"Not for me," Lída sing-songed. She kissed his cheek. "I wish we could have my party in Prague and not in Kutna Hora. Or how about Rome? Couldn't we do it in Rome?"

"All the arrangements have been made, pet. You know how I love Kutna Hora."

Lída sat up, down but not out, and stretched her long fingers across the table. "Kutna Hora it is." She waved her hand, playing her smile for all it was worth.

"I'll have my secretary call you," Goebbels said, pulling Lída up with him. Svoboda nodded, standing to shake the Minister's hand, and Felix followed in suit. His hand trembled as he held it out to Goebbels, who ignored it and made way to the door, drawing Lída behind him. The Minister's limp, the result of a clubbed foot, was almost undetectable except for a slight stiffness in his gate.

"Oh, Felix," Lída sang, as they walked out into the brilliant sunlight. "You'll come to my party, won't you?"

Krev held the door for them like a proper valet and followed his master outside. He turned around once more, his upper body swimming in his ill-fitting suit jacket and his fingers tugging on his feathery mustache. He glanced back into the café as if he was amazed, though not quite impressed, that such a place could exist.

Chapter Sixteen
Same Day

Svoboda lowered himself into his chair, looking deadly serious, and having lost all the gaiety he'd demonstrated on their stroll to the café. His walking stick leaned against the leaded glass of the picture window, as if abandoned by a tourist. Svoboda ordered another round of whiskeys and paid for them.

"What in God's name just happened here?" Felix gulped his liquor.

"It's remarkably straightforward, son," Svoboda said. "Minister Goebbels is giving a party for his mistress, Miss Baarová. He wants me to sculpt a bust for her birthday gift, as a surprise. The child's portrait was a ruse."

"I don't care about the portrait," Felix told him. "Who was that man? Krev, the blonde boy."

Svoboda leaned back, scratching his cheek.

"Ivo Krev? Ruffian, that's all. Errand boy for Herr Doktor."

"What did you call him?"

"A ruffian." Svoboda shrugged. "Unfortunately, there's little shortage of Czech youth who think nothing of betraying their country for a fleeting opportunity."

Herr Doktor, Felix repeated to himself. "Did my father know him?"

"Who?"

"Goebbels, *Herr Doktor* as you called him."

Svoboda tipped his chin up and shook his head. "Not directly."

Felix looked into the empty chair where Goebbels had sat. It was an inanimate object that held no residue of the man, just as the Art Nouveau Café tinkered along as if the Minister had never been there. Even the bartender, who'd trembled at the sight of him, was back to pouring double vodkas and playing a game of Aces with himself behind the bar.

"How about indirectly?" he asked. "Was Goebbels – *Herr Doktor* – the collector who was duped into buying the fake Infant?"

Svoboda folded his hands. "Of course."

Felix's head didn't spin. Nor did his blood drain and his head pound the way it had when he bumped into Ivo Krev. But he felt a sense of finality in this revelation.

"Of course," he repeated. "And now he wants a sculpture from you? How ironic."

"Ironic it is." Svoboda appraised Felix's expression. "But it's only one piece of the puzzle."

Svoboda took his walking stick from the window and held it firmly in his hand, balancing the bottom point on the ruby carpeting.

"This is going to be the last birthday party Minister Goebbels throws for Lída, and the bust is a parting gift."

"Is he…are you planning to kill her?" Felix asked.

"No, she's a little fool. Not a harmless fool, mind you – never lifted a finger to help anybody. Minister Goebbels, to his great regret, is being forced to dump her like yesterday's garbage."

Svoboda slid his hand down from the knotted handle of his staff.

"Minister Goebbels would like to marry his little consort, but the Fuhrer will have none of it. A Nazi Minister could never leave his German wife and Aryan children for a Slav. An actress, no less."

Svoboda put his stick on his lap and folded his hands in front of him on the table, drawing his shoulders in, and making himself look small. "There's a mole in Goebbels's office," Svoboda whispered. "I placed him there. He's helped us dangle the Infant of Prague under the Minister's nose."

Svoboda chuckled and drew his knuckle to his lips.

"Is the Infant of Prague that important to him?" Felix asked.

"Not from a religious point of view or even from the point of view of a collector. You see, over the past year, the Infant has become a painful thorn in the Minister's side."

Felix shook his head and leaned forward.

"You haven't been to church much in recent times have you, son?" Justus Svoboda smirked and gave Felix a wink.

"What does Josef Goebbels have to do with the Church?"

"He'd like to say, 'nothing,'" Svoboda said. "But unfortunately for him, that's not the case."

Svoboda took a mighty swig of his whiskey.

"The Catholic Church's propaganda machine has been using the Infant of Prague as a mobilizing figure in helping to turn the tide in the war. Largely thanks to Monsignor

Merillini, the Infant has slowly become fetishized by the disgruntled Catholic masses. This makes the Minister... uncomfortable."

Svoboda narrowed his eyes and breathed, savoring the moment. "The Church has stepped up its manufacture of the little replicas of the Infant and has been selling them or giving them away anywhere they can, while we – or what is left of us in the Prague Underground – have stepped up production of our own. We've been printing pamphlets, leaflets and spreading rumors about the Infant's role in certain elements of the war."

"What elements?" Felix asked.

"Heydrich's assassination for one. Did you know that the Czech soldiers who killed him parachuted into the country wearing their little Infants on chains around their necks? They even visited the Infant of Prague – to pray to Him for the success of their mission – on the very night before they threw the fatal bomb that ripped apart our esteemed Reich Governor."

"I didn't know," Felix said.

"Because it didn't happen. Not quite that way, at least. I should know. I helped plan the killing and I can assure you no effigy of the Infant Jesus was involved."

Felix sat back in his chair. His cousin had been one of the many shot in retaliation for Heydrich's murder. He'd been an ill-fated citizen of Lidice – a town that was literally wiped off the map as Hitler's wrath spread throughout the country. The men of Lidice had been shot in front of their families, and the women and children sent to concentration camps. The town was then bulldozed into nonexistence.

"Thousands of Czechs died for that assassination," Felix whispered.

Svoboda closed his eyes, as if saying a silent prayer. "But not in vain. No other Resistance movement has been able to pull off something of that scale – not France, not Poland. Heydrich may have only been one man, but his bloody end showed the Germans and the whole world that their big-wigs can be taken down by little more than a ragtag group of inferiors."

Svoboda gripped Felix's wrists and lowered his soft voice even further – until Felix could scarcely hear what he was saying.

"The Infant – like the fish during Roman times – has become a secret symbol of like minds and has begun emboldening our population. They may not be ready to form an uprising on their own, but if we started the grum-blings of one – fired the first shot as it were – the populace will be confident enough to support it."

Felix scratched his fingers through his hair and rubbed his hands over the light stubble on his chin. He looked out the window at his fellow Czechs, who marched across the pavement heading home from work to the comfort of a light supper. They didn't look emboldened to him. Task-focused, they went about their business day by day with only the hope that there was still a future for their homeland.

"The Resistance now lives in the symbol," Svoboda told him. "And that symbol is now in the hands of any believer who is given an Infant of Prague figurine from his pastor – or buys one for a couple of crowns at a trinket shop."

"Goebbels can't be taking this very well."

"Your father is proof of that," Svoboda said. "Only a man as trusted by the Church as your father could've gotten the Infant out from under the watchful eyes of the Diocese. Goebbels paid your father a considerable sum to get him to steal the Infant. He wanted to replace the Infant with a fake and wait for its obsessive minders to discover the fraud. Goebbels could then publicize the fact that the Czechs had been praying to a false god and present the real Infant as proof of the Reich's invincibility."

Felix marveled that Goebbels, the brilliant propagandist, had been bested by his humble, Infant of Prague-worshipping father and suddenly felt a tremendous swell of pride. It was followed almost immediately by the shame Felix felt over the last words he'd spoken to his father – boasting about his own understanding of the real world.

"My copies of the Infant were too good, you see – all of them: The one we gave Goebbels, the one at the Church of Our Lady the Victorious, and even a spare that your father kept hidden," Svoboda continued. "But that was our idea all along – mine and your father's. Of course, as the weeks turned into months and no hysterical claims of dupery emerged from the Infant's minders, Goebbels became agitated. He had the Infant your father sold him inspected by an expert other than the one we arranged. When Goebbels discovered the fraud, he couldn't very well march into the Church of our Lady the Victorious anymore and demand that the Infant be authenticated. Not without the real Infant in his hands. It would've been obvious to anyone that he'd orchestrated a stunt and once again, the missing Infant's power would only be reinforced – as if the Infant of Prague had mystically vanished from a bumbling German propaganda minister."

Bumbling indeed, Felix thought. A short passage from Hebrews came to his mind. It had been a favorite of his father's – one Marek Andel had repeated often in company and uttered as a meditation when he believed he was alone: *Faith is being sure of what we hope for and certain of what we do not see.* Felix was certain his father had been reciting this verse to himself as he tangled with Josef Goebbels in the months before his death. Even as Ivo Krev attempted to garrote him. Somehow, this thought gave him comfort.

"What now?" Felix asked.

Svoboda fingered the card for Goebbels's private secretary. He tapped his nail over the Reich eagle which lay embossed into its center. "He thinks the holder of the Infant is someone close to him. In reality, our mole has been his blackmailer." Svoboda sat back, further contemplating the Minister. "Goebbels hasn't the slightest idea someone like me has been pulling the strings. Oversight can be a consistent point of failure for men of extreme hubris. I'm too unimportant to consider, yet if he would only connect the lines – he'd know it could be nobody but me."

Felix remembered the brand new Infant figurine his father had given Krev, and the way Krev had shaken it next to his ear, as if it could tell him something.

"How did you get the Infant? Did my father tell you where he'd hidden Him?"

Svoboda took a deep breath and folded his hands. "The Infant of Prague is lost – gone. And it's of no concern to the Prague Underground anymore. Its loss is of great concern to the Monsignor, of course, but even he's given up any hope of finding Him. The copy – one of my copies – remains at The Church of Our Lady the Victorious where the Infant has been for centuries. It's housed in the same case the Infant was housed in and wears the original vestments the Infant wore. No one is the wiser. No one but you, me, the Monsignor, the Pope, and naturally, Minister Goebbels and his young thug."

To Felix, it was inconceivable folly for someone like Goebbels – a man who felt the weight of a world war and the fate of an entire nation on his shoulders – to be distracting himself with holy icons from a religion he disdained. To be killing and pilfering and plotting over what was essentially a bad purchase.

"He's gone mad," he said.

"Not mad, obsessed."

Svoboda pulled his drink to his chest.

"Felix, thanks to our mole, Goebbels is under the impression that he's devised a trap for the thief and blackmailer that will come into play at Lída's party – a party we now have a reason to attend thanks to your celebrity and acquaintanceship with the pretty Miss B."

Felix started to protest, but Svoboda went on with his story.

"But the only one caught in a trap will be him. Dear Minister Goebbels will be posturing before all of his powerful friends – his every word and movement documented for posterity by his own league of propagandists. He plans on exposing the Infant that night and broadcasting his triumph over God."

"Goebbels is no fool," Felix said. "He's not going to be doing any broadcasting until he gets his hands on the real statue."

"But that's where you come in." Svoboda raised his empty glass and chinked it to Felix's. "Goebbels will have every reason to believe that he's going to get the Infant because you're going to slip him a little note that tells him as much. You, the son of Marek Andel, will reveal yourself as the real blackmailer."

Faith is being sure of what we hope for and certain of what we do not see. Reciting his father's verse was an invocation for strength. The strength to do what was right for Magdalena, who could do little for herself given her status as a Jew – who would find all this talk abhorrent.

The strength to finish what father had begun.

Felix shook his head, inhaling deeply through his nose. He stopped, sniffing, catching a whiff of something very sweet. He knew it from his mother's garden – the scent of lilies of the valley. Vera Ruza's hands had smelled of the flower, and Magdalena's hair often smelled of it, too. Vera was always running her fingers through Magdalena's hair. His father's shirt collars had smelled of it. Vera could tie a perfect Windsor knot.

Felix felt his father's presence all of a sudden. It was the first time he'd felt any remnant of his father since his death. And it was a close feeling – almost as if his father was sitting at the table and their feelings for one another were as warm as they had been while his mother was still alive. Barely touched by the war and the stress it had brought into their household.

"How will I get him to unveil the Infant and make a fool of himself if I don't have the actual statue?"

Svoboda smiled.

"You won't. You see, I couldn't care less about his lofty plans for his silly party. I do care very much, however, about who is there and how many cameras will be recording the big event."

The leader of the Prague Underground leaned forward, squeezing his next words into Felix's ear.

"That club-footed devil is going to die. And we, along with every high-ranking Nazi and flashing camera in the whole place, are going to watch him gurgle his last breath."

Die, Felix thought. Yes, of course. Herr Doktor must die. Ivo Krev must die. It was the only thing since Marek Andel's death that made any sense.

CHAPTER SEVENTEEN
PRAGUE: MARCH 21, 1956

The Vltava River ran in a straight line between the Castle Sverak and Prague's city center, offering Felix a passing glimpse of Obecní Dům and its once famous Art Nouveau Café. He watched as a woman lounged behind the leaded glass of one of the arched windows and raised a dainty cup to her lips. Dressed in a fine, old coat with a fox fur collar, she stared with palpable longing over the glassy surface of her tea, as if she were waiting for something extraordinary to happen. Felix craned his neck to take her in before the train veered to the left, shuffling into the main station.

Though it had been cold until recently, the faintest scent of corn poppy had begun to seep into the air, mixing with the fading winter smells of burning coal and left-over piles of soiled, melting snow on the roadsides. Felix dipped his head out the window, letting the air slap his face until their train squealed up to the platform.

It was only a little after six, but the station was already beginning to empty as people settled into their homes for supper. Felix and Liebermann caught a tram that rattled and dinged its way to the industrial outskirts of Vršovice, dumping a handful of long-faced bureaucrats and factory workers at a new housing complex that had been built next to one of the city's largest breweries. The aroma of yeast hung in the air, obscuring even the sulfur-rich smoke that belched from nearby factories.

"Pardon," grunted a plump woman in a peasant's skirt. She rolled her 'r' for emphasis and elbowed Liebermann in the ribs as she cut them off to exit the tram.

She turned back, making sure to catalogue them; the lumpy man in a dull suit the color of mud and the thin one, a little too fashionable in a teal suit that matched his eyes. She'd never seen these men before, but relished taking an instant dislike to them.

Felix smiled at her and tipped his hat, but she looked away, curling her lip. Liebermann followed her into her apartment building and hurried to hold the elevator door for her. His chivalry was met with a glower. Once she entered the tinny elevator box, he slammed her head into the door, jammed the door shut and sent the woman to the storage cellar, where she would wake up some hours later. There was a woman like her on every floor, watching the comings and goings of neighbors, reporting anything the slightest bit outside of routine, and her absence would be like a small holiday to the people who lived in her building.

Liebermann slipped out the back way of the apartment complex and met Felix at the brewery's garage. There, everything was exactly as it should be. The garage had been unlocked, the keys to the beer wagon had been hidden behind the front driver's side tire, and ten beer barrels filled with Prague's finest pilsner squatted in the back under a heavy tarp. One of those barrels – close to the rear, but not obviously so – was empty, padded on the inside and complete with a breathing tube.

"I hope your agent is as thorough and reliable as your brewmaster," Felix said.

"He's a bit oily, I think." Liebermann reached across the ample front seat of the beer wagon as he started to drive. He lit yet another cigarette for Felix, who'd been chain-smoking since they left the train station. "He calls himself 'a friend.' I don't think that's funny at all, do you?"

Felix ran his hand over his breast pocket. It held the only thing that didn't belong to Conrad Horst – his and Magdalena's wedding photo. He tucked his finger past the seam and stroked the water-stained corner of the image.

"I always prefer dealing with the low-levelers," Liebermann reflected. "Doctors, clerks and their like – not the movers and shakers like this *friend*. Of course, he is able to smuggle the woman out of prison, after all. What clerk could do that?"

Felix took a deep drag off his cigarette. The padding under his business suit was beginning to chafe his thighs and he was tired of being Conrad Horst.

"I've been there before," Felix said. "It's for the politicals, not the ordinary criminals. The guards are vicious – purposefully so." He'd spent over a year in the prison, and remembered scratching Magdalena's birthday into the floor where he slept.

Liebermann chuckled. "Always full of surprises, aren't you, Father?"

"Security isn't much lighter at night, I can tell you that."

Liebermann didn't appreciate the ongoing commentary. He liked the Jesuit, but wished he had stayed where he belonged – on the outside, giving the orders, greasing the wheels.

"Come on – it can't be so bad," Liebermann said. "Everyone loves a good beer – we should be welcomed with open arms."

The shrieking inquisitor came into the room again and began his routine. *We know someone from Vienna tried phoning you at your flat! And that you made several calls to Rome. What are you plotting?*

The room was bare except for a chair and table, and had a permanent sallow yellowness that covered the walls, ceiling, and floor. The enduring tang of nervous perspiration infused the air and cheap furniture. Magdalena sat in the yellow chair with her stomach growling ferociously. She had become an artist at appearing to be listening, while letting her mind wander into its many secret compartments.

There were always two of them, but never at the same time: one who spoke in a calm, rational voice and another who was like the frayed, free end of a live electrical wire. Hands waving, spittle flying, eyes trembling, the ratty voice becoming hoarse, until he'd finally have to take a strong drink. The foul breath was the hardest to endure, and the most difficult to ignore. It usually became worse once the voice started to fail. The throat would be irritated and the alcohol would create a stale, fetid smell when it attacked the raw membrane.

It was funny that she hadn't seen him – her *friend*, as he called himself – in almost a day. He'd promised to get her and her Ales out of there, but promises were what people like Friend traded in. Still, he was the only one of them with any intelligence and he'd let her glimpse her son, just as he'd said, when they first arrived at the prison. She'd gotten to see Ales's left hand, his slender fingers coiled around one of the bars on his cell door. She'd even called his name and he had called back to her.

Magdalena wondered if Friend was with Ales. She wanted him to be. She hated the thought of her son with these men. Eleven was an impressionable age and she didn't want her son to learn just yet that stupidity and violence were rewarded with power in their country.

Seven weeks ago you scratched your nose at your grocer's stall. Who were you signaling?

Magdalena's stomach was starting to adjust to the hunger. They probably wouldn't feed her for a few days. She took her focus away from her empty belly and trekked into her memory, piecing together a vignette. Magdalena remembered pouring over an American comic book with Felix as they lay on her bed in her secret room at his father's house. Late into the night, they huddled close, holding a small lantern over Superman and Lois Lane. The flimsy book was worn and curled at the edges, silly and childish in its simplicity, but gave her hope that the Americans could swoop down at any moment, save her and her mother, and free Czechoslovakia.

"They seem so invincible, don't they? The Americans?"

Felix agreed.

"Then why is it taking so long?" Magdalena buried her face into his lap and stroked his thigh with the tips of her nails.

It was their intimate moments she remembered most often. Felix's soft, seductive murmurings at night when their heads hit the pillow, and his naked body – the way it took on the look of smooth salt hills under the light of the moon. He would grip her fragile wrists, and she would wrap her limbs around his body as they lay in bed whispering their dreams into the dark. It was when making love with him was as natural a part of her life as bathing. It was what brought Ales into her arms, and allowed her to savor the salt and pepper taste of his skin after a hard day out at play. That taste – as wired into her as the desire for sleep, the need for water – was the flavor of love in its essence and her last tether to her former self.

How sweet and distant that memory seemed — as if she'd made it up to comfort herself, the way an orphaned child might invent a famous father. It stiffened, losing its animation, and turned brown and bone, like a century-old photograph. She could've tried to revive the image, but she was too tired and was further pulled into the present by a sugary string of drool that slopped over her inquisitor's engorged bottom lip and landed on her knee.

"It's a beer delivery," Liebermann explained in butchered Czech. Felix sat next to him and smiled at the prison guard, nodding his head and playing the idiot.

"At this time of night?" the guard demanded. He grabbed the stack of paperwork from Liebermann's fist and combed over the names, dates and specifications.

"Big man wants good beer," Liebermann told the guard. "It's good, no? For you, too. For everyone. Good job, well done. Have one on me, he says."

The guard gestured for Liebermann and Felix to get out, aiming his gun at their chests. He opened up the back of the wagon and leaned in over the beer barrels, hitting random kegs with his night stick. He demanded that Liebermann tap one of the kegs.

"Mmm, good, no?" Liebermann urged, as the guard tested the brew. The guard blinked in the affirmative. He stomped back to his station and dialed his telephone, cupping his hand over the receiver as he spoke.

"He wants to see you," the guard grunted, waving them along with his pistol, and making Felix and Liebermann march – hands raised – down a flight of unlit stairs into the basement. There, they were led through a long series of corridors and a maze of disjointed hallways lined with padded cells, and ushered into a pea-green room lit by florescent light tubes. The guard left, locking the door behind him.

Felix looked over at a simple, metal folding table that hosted an audio recorder, a pen, notepad, and a small, brown bottle. A large Gladstone bag sat under it. There was nothing else in the room – not even a chair. Only the table, what lay on it, and the bag. The brown bottle, Felix realized, was a vial of Thionyl Chloride. A powerful battery acid, it was often showcased during interrogations, though it was rarely used. They'd never used it on him, at least, though they'd threatened countless times to pour it into his eyes and on his genitals. He'd often wondered why they didn't just do it.

"The beer was too cold." The voice came from behind them. Neither Felix nor Liebermann had heard the lock being tripped and the door opening.

"It's a cool night," Felix said. He started to turn around.

"No, no, no. No need for that," the man instructed, and Felix pivoted back.

"Did you bring my money?"

"Do you have the woman and the boy?" Felix asked.

"They're being loaded onto your truck, of course."

"By whom, Herr–?"

"Friend."

"So nice to finally meet you in person," Liebermann said.

Friend took out a small, light gray handkerchief, blowing his nose in three quick snuffs. An interrogation light clicked on and his head spun like a startled bird. Liebermann watched a man with second-rate clothes – new, but poorly made, copying styles from two years past – push open the door. His hair was thick and dirty blonde, with a greasy center part, and his mustache was unruly. Errant hairs poked out of it, tickling his lips and nostrils.

"Gitanes?" he crooned, offering the French cigarette by name.

"Sir," Friend allowed.

"What's with your hair?" Friend's superior asked.

Friend had dyed it that afternoon. He brushed his index finger along his newly black goatee, smoothing it as if it had been a terrible mess.

"My wife's idea."

The superior lifted an eyebrow. "The night clerk was very excited about the arrival of a beer shipment. Strange time of night for such a thing."

Felix felt a peculiar overlap of time and experience much stronger than *déjà vu*. Even stronger than his sensory memories of the prison – its dank smell, the way the walls had a look of pock-marked skin. He turned to peer at the men, trying to block the beam of light with his hand, but it was so bright that he could only see them in silhouette.

"What would we want with beer at Pankrac this late?" the superior inquired.

VICTORIA DOUGHERTY

"It's not about beer," Friend told him. The Czech agent's arms hung at his sides as if he had no need for them. "It's about the kinds of informants we cultivate." He nodded towards Felix and Liebermann.

"These Germans are your *informants?*" the superior said.

Friend took a deep breath. "Our networks are different here than in Paris."

"This certainly isn't Paris, is it?" the superior chuckled.

It was in Paris that Friend's new superior had a string of espionage successes – all due to finding, or rather being found by – the right informant.

"The French make excellent goods," the superior mused, taking a wet-lipped drag off his Gitanes. "We'll make them even better once France falls to us. It's only a matter of time. I estimate by 1959 the question of Western Europe should be resolved."

He put one hand in his pant pocket and the other on the audio recorder, patting it as if it were a housecat. "Maybe we should all make our way upstairs," the superior said. "To check out this beer party."

"I'm following a lead," Friend explained.

The superior cocked his head. "With German beer wagon drivers?" He clicked his tongue at Friend.

"They may know something about that physicist from last fall; the one who disappeared from his house arrest."

The superior snorted. "He turned up in America, of all places." His career hadn't gone as well since he'd been transferred out of Paris.

"Of course I, personally, don't give a damn about any physicist," Friend told his boss.

The superior chortled. "I suppose if you did, he'd still be in Gdansk." His hand was trembling ever so slightly and he slipped it into his jacket pocket.

Friend smiled. "You shouldn't, either. Not tonight anyway. Water under the bridge."

Friend knelt down and retrieved a bottle of Calvados from behind the Gladstone bag. He opened it up and sniffed it before offering it to his chief.

"I don't like it," the superior said, pushing the bottle away. "A beer every once in a while, or a Becherovka – for health – nothing else."

Friend took a generous sip of the Calvados. "You work as hard as anyone here," Friend told him. "I have a couple of glasses in the observatory. Nice ones. We need some civility – even in this place."

The superior took a deep breath, letting his eyes wander over the bottle as if it were a woman. He dug his hand further into his pocket and leaned on his hip. "Alright, one sip," the superior grunted. "But only because it's Calvados." He took the bottle by the neck and let the warm apple brandy flow down his throat. "This is enough party for me tonight," he said. He took another gulp of the brandy and wiped his lips with his sleeve. His hand was steady now.

"Don't forget this," Friend cautioned. He tossed him a palm-sized tube decorated with silver trim and painted foliage. It was breath cologne labeled *Fenouil.* "From France."

The superior smiled, displaying a horsy grin that made his lips all but disappear.

He took another swig of Calvados and corked the bottle, holding it under his arm.

"It can't hurt to be careful," Friend continued. "A word or two, overheard, could send the wrong message again."

"A wrong message, you say?" the superior sneered. "Like an unscheduled beer delivery? Son of a bitch."

Liebermann watched Friend perk up as the superior opened his mouth wide, preparing to receive a spray of the breath cologne. Friend took his handkerchief out again, as if he were about to sneeze, and covered his mouth with it. He lifted the Thionyl Chloride from the table, flipped the cap off the brown bottle and sprayed a stream of the acid into his superior's mouth. The man shrieked and fell to his knees, spitting and wheezing through his burning lungs, scraping at his blistering tongue with the pads of his fingertips.

Friend drew a coiled wire from his belt and whipped it around his superior's throat. A thin stream of blood budded from under the wire and trickled down onto the man's collar, the cotton absorbing it like linen stationary drinking ink from a fountain pen. Friend pulled his superior close to his chest and held him tight, waiting until the man's body went limp before dropping him to the floor.

Felix closed his eyes and listened to Friend's breath – slow and steady with only the slightest huff – and the squeak of the wire as Friend rolled it into a tight loop and refastened it at his waist.

"Krev," Felix whispered.

The Czech agent cut the interrogation light and ran his fingers through his hair. Felix could see him now. His features, still plain and boyish, had hardly changed at all.

"Ivo Krev."

Krev looked up from the dead man at the sound of his name.

"Do I know you?" He studied Felix for a brief moment before reaching under the folding table and taking the Gladstone bag. He slung it over his shoulder.

Felix shook his head. "What are you doing?"

"Plans have changed," Krev said.

"You have no idea." Felix was speaking his native Czech now.

Krev opened the door and looked out into the hallway making sure it was clear. He motioned for Felix and
Liebermann to hurry along.

"Close the door," Felix said.

Krev cocked his head.

"I said close it." Felix pulled a Walther P.38 pistol from
under the rubbery padding in his business suit. It was one
he'd taken from a German guard years before, during the
war, and had hesitated to bring along with him.

"Are you mad?"

Krev's face registered no recognition of him.

"Herr Horst?" Liebermann demanded.

"Your pistol, Mr. Krev," Felix said.

Krev retrieved his pistol from its holder and threw it to
the floor. Felix picked it up and handed it to Liebermann.

"Go to the wagon and get our cargo out of here," Felix
instructed the German. "Assuming Mrs. Melan and her boy
have been loaded into our beer keg?"

Krev nodded.

"If you're lying you'll regret it."

"I did it myself," Krev told him.

Felix motioned for Liebermann to go, but the German
shook his head.

"I wanted to do it," Krev muttered. "I've risked everything to do this, don't you see?"

Liebermann put his hand on Felix's shoulder. "We have
to get out of here, or else no one is going anywhere. Not us
and not our precious cargo."

Felix cocked his pistol.

"Look what I've done," Krev rasped, glancing down at
his superior. "He was dull-witted and weak, but he would've
taken pleasure in killing you."

Felix swallowed hard. Sweat beads budded across his forehead and began rolling down into his eyes, like tears.

"I don't know what this is about." Liebermann spoke softly into Felix's ear. "But this room isn't padded to muffle the sound of a gunshot, my friend. It would, however, stifle his screams if we lock him in here."

Ivo Krev's shoulders slumped into a posture Felix thought uncharacteristic of him.

"Oh, no," Felix said. "Mr. Krev will be coming with us. But I think that was his intention all along."

"Simpletons," Krev narrated as they pulled away from Pankrac prison, light by three kegs of strong beer. The prison glowed behind them, partly shrouded in a creeping fog—barbed wire wrapped around every gutter, railing, and fence like Christmas lights. "And not all simpletons are gentle, the way they're portrayed in novels."

Felix stared ahead as Liebermann pulled onto the road. They were a good ninety minutes from the border at Domažlice, but would still be well short of dawn by the time they arrived. If they were lucky, no discoveries would happen till the morning, when a new, more sober assemblage of guards would come for the shift change.

"Everyone has to believe in something," Krev murmured.

"What are you talking about?" Liebermann had had just about enough of the Czech agent.

"What's there to believe in here anymore?" Krev lamented. "I used to believe in Germany. My mother was German, you know." The Czech agent was sitting on his Gladstone bag – his hands tied behind him.

Liebermann eyed him in the rearview mirror. "She must've left quite an impression," the German quipped. "You told me you hated Germans."

"I like German music." Krev's mouth turned up into a grin. "I haven't always been a good man, Herr Liebermann – I'll grant you that – but I do keep my word. In that regard, you and I are quite alike, wouldn't you say?"

"Shut up," Felix said.

They spent the rest of the ride in silence, pulling onto a grassy trail about three kilometers from the border. From there, it was a quick drive through a patch of forest and into a large clearing bordering several unused hectares of farmland. The once-rich soil had been left to dry out and become infested by weeds, the apparent victim of a Five-Year Plan.

"What are we doing?" Krev inquired.

A gentle wind blew, swaying the thinnest branches and causing their stiff new leaves to rustle.

"Emptying a beer barrel, Mr. Krev," Felix told him. "You're going across the border – just like you were planning."

Krev thrust his chin forward. "I don't like confined spaces."

Felix fixed his eyes on the Czech agent and asked him with all seriousness, "What do you like, Mr. Krev?"

There was a soft whistle in the air. Felix slipped out of the wagon onto the new, spring grass. The crescent moon provided little light.

"I've always wanted to go," Krev detailed, as Felix gestured for him to follow. "I've been abroad many times, but I never had the courage to stay. They don't make it easy for men like me to defect, you know. I know too much and I'd be hunted down, disappearing into a grave or a gulag one day."

They walked around to the back of the wagon and Felix untied Krev's hands. He made the Czech agent pull down the ramp.

"Would you mind if I had a rest?" Krev entreated. "My arms are stiff from—you know, my boss back there." Krev shook his head. "I know his wife. We went together for a while after the war." He looked up at Felix. "You think I'm an animal, don't you? And you're right. I am an animal." Krev put his head into his hands and knelt down.

"Roll one of those barrels onto the grass and empty its contents into the ground," Felix said.

"How will I breathe when I get in that thing?"

Felix stepped closer to him.

"I'll make sure you're delivered safe and sound to the West German authorities, Mr. Krev."

Krev closed his eyes briefly and took a breath. He looked as if he was going to cry. He hung his head and lifted his elbow slightly. "Why are you doing this?" Krev implored.

"I'm helping you."

Felix strode up onto the ramp. There hadn't been time at the prison to open the barrel that hid Magdalena and her son. He'd only been able to tap on it – three times twice – and get the same pattern in response.

Krev sprang to his feet. From his sleeve dropped a small billy club that fit easily into his hand. He reached up and bore down on the back of Felix's skull, knocking him to the ground.

Felix came eye to toe with Krev's left shoe and followed the man's trouser seams and shirt buttons all the way up to the Czech agent's face. Krev's features shifted shape, his nose elongating and eyes becoming deep-set and black, before they morphed back into the blandest of Slavic characteristics.

"Srut?"

"I wasn't sure at first it was you," Krev whispered.

"Srut? Are you there?" Felix mouthed. He lost consciousness, his mind roaming through a dream that mingled the past and present. The dream ended and Felix found himself floating; watching his body lie in the grass as if he were sky gazing.

Chapter Eighteen
March 21, 1944

"Just a few weeks," Felix mumbled to himself, sitting in the Woodrow Wilson train station at twenty minutes until two, and sporting the smart travel clothes that Svoboda had given him. He felt older in the brown fedora from Pilak, the best men's hatter in Prague, and wore his authority like a new father.

Svoboda had given him his instructions that morning, surprising him with a train ticket, and the address of an apartment he'd secured for their next rendezvous in Prague. Felix would be staying with a man named Pepík in a south Moravian province, keeping low until a few days before Lída Baarová's birthday party. This way, to anyone in Prague, it would seem as if he were in Bratislava, training with the rest of his team.

Already twice since their meeting with Goebbels, Felix had been recognized on the street. Once by a fan, a youth of about fifteen, who'd catalogued every goal Felix had ever scored and recited the list in a fast, fervent way – as if he was saying a Hail Mary. The second was more worrisome. It was an old neighbor, curious about why Felix was in Prague at this time of year. "Aren't you playing anymore?" he'd

asked. Felix had mumbled something about family business and assured the man he was going back to Slovakia
promptly.

Svoboda would make arrangements for Magdalena.
Felix had hated leaving her so suddenly – especially when
Magdalena hadn't been feeling well, her stomach sour
from nervous tension. But Svoboda had insisted Felix leave
quickly and without ceremony. It avoided unwanted hyster-
ics, he claimed.

"Why can't I come with you?" Magdalena had asked
early that morning, after Svoboda left their attic room.

She knew why – that she had no papers yet, that she
couldn't possibly get on a train – but she asked anyway. Felix
smoothed her hair and let his hand wander down over her
shoulder and her collarbone, then lower. He kissed her as
tenderly as he knew how.

"You'll love London in the spring," he said. "The parks
are wonderful. We can take long walks."

"I hear it rains all the time."

"Not all the time." He kissed her just under her jaw bone.

"Who says you'll be there by the spring anyway – and
don't say Svoboda."

"I say," he said.

Making love did not change her disposition, but it
did settle her stomach a little. She sipped the coffee Dasa
had made for them as she watched Felix get dressed. She
counted his scars – most of them sustained in practice and
not during an actual game. *Animals*, she'd said under her
breath.

"I want to leave together. I think we should tell him
that."

Felix exhaled.

"I mean when it's time to actually leave the country."

Felix sat back down on their bed and took her hand.

"M, that's the surest way of getting arrested."

She sniffed. "At least we'd be together."

"Yes, together on a cold train. We've been there before."

Magdalena shunned the memory. She pulled her knees up to her chest and wrapped her arms around them.

"I'm scared," she said.

"Number forty-nine bound for Vienna," the voice over the loudspeaker called, and Felix got up to buy some sweet buns and hot grog for the road.

"Mister, you dropped something. Your wallet, I think," a man said to him as he was finishing his transaction at the concession stand.

"No, it's right here, I'm about to pay –" but he stopped as he fumbled through his coat, digging his fingers into every pocket. Felix whipped around towards the man and found himself looking at Srut, the gypsy waving his pocket book – the contents of which: money, papers, a piece of ribbon from Magdalena's hair – held Felix's entire life. Srut's eyes were different than he'd ever seen them, open like a frightened corpse that had seen his death coming and registered in that split second that there wasn't a damn thing he could do about it.

"Yes, you must mean my... thank you," Felix said, reclaiming the pocket book and tucking it into his vest. He walked with Srut in the direction of the station offices, the gypsy digging his lean fingers into the underside of Felix's wrist.

"They're all gone," Srut whispered. "The hole was raided by the police."

"When?"

"Last night." Srut bit into his cracked bottom lip. "The fiddler was shot. So was Milada. The others were dragged away."

"Did you see it?"

Srut shook his head. "I was out."

"Multa. He's alive. The only one. He was in the storage room when they came and he hid under a tarp." Srut's lips pursed together, baring his teeth. "They didn't even search that room. They knew where they were going."

"Could they have followed someone in and out? Multa, maybe?"

"Don't be stupid. You know it was him."

"Who?"

"Svoboda."

Felix shushed Srut, squeezing his friend's shoulder. "This is horrible," he said. "But we have to keep our heads. We knew that hole could be raided at any time."

Felix led Srut behind a newspaper kiosk and pulled the fedora over his eyes. He angled in front of the gypsy as a young woman, blonde with creamy skin and jade-colored eyes, walked by them. She was wearing a Mother's Cross – a swastika at the center of a crucifix, dangling from a simple blue and white ribbon tied around her neck. They were given to women who had born children for the Reich.

"He did it. I know he did it like I know my own blood," Srut told him. His breath was both stale and overripe – a spoiled ham on a bed of wilted grass and blackened apples. "We have to get out of here. I know a place. It's not good for long, but we'll figure something out. We have papers."

"Srut, I'm going to Roznov."

Srut pulled back, still holding on to Felix's coat.

"You're not thinking. He'll kill you. Or get you killed for his stupid tricks."

Felix straightened his trench coat and stretched his palms and fingers. "They're not tricks to me."

"Do you think your father would be proud to see you like this? He wanted you away from it and you come back like a pigeon to take his place."

Felix checked a clock on the wall behind Srut's shoulder and shook his head. "I'm sorry about Milada and all of it. I'm sorry about everything. He'll help you. Go to him – I know he will. Not everyone is out to get you."

Felix turned from Srut, breaking his grip, and started in the direction of the platform, feeling the gypsy's eyes on him until he stepped up onto the train. When he looked around his compartment, he was comforted for a moment by the banality of the travelers around him.

"Srut," he said out loud, startling himself, and causing a round-bottomed grandmother to look up from her old movie magazine as if the word was meant for her.

"Joan Crawford," she said, pronouncing it Yown Krovard, and pointing to a picture of the actress in a white feather boa and satin slip dress. Felix nodded and pushed the fedora over his eyes, keeping them wide open, but pretending to sleep for the one hundred and eighty minutes it took to reach Roznov.

Chapter Nineteen
Same Day

Even as Magdalena stood without the protection of valid papers or Felix's arm draped over her shoulders, she was able to relish what the new season had to offer. It was one of those beautiful days in a series that had coaxed the last, remaining spring buds out of their tight, emerald gift-wrap. The air – full of rainwater and fresh river fish – had a smoky perfume in it, carried over from a night of coal heating. Magdalena watched the streets dry in a slow creep, as the early morning sun gained strength.

She and Dasa Svoboda were costumed in plain spinster's clothes, so as not to draw any attention. They wore comfortable shoes, since their day would be spent walking or standing, staying off trams that could be boarded by security detail.

"It's only till noon – when we get your papers and we're home free."

Dasa picked one of Magdalena's long, dark, hairs off the lapel of her beige jacket and secured Magdalena's light brown wig with two more bobby pins pulled from her own hair.

She intertwined her fingers with Magdalena's and turned to lead her into the marketplace, but was stopped by a splat that sounded like milk and potato salad being flung onto a concrete floor. Magdalena stood behind her, hunched over, her shoes and stockings flecked with tawny drops of bile. She was letting another stream of stomach juices, coffee, bread chunks, and yellow beets from last night's dinner crash onto the sidewalk.

"We have a sick girl here, could you move along?" Dasa snarled. An older woman stared with disapproving fascination.

"I'm fine. Let's get this over with," Magdalena said. She wiped her mouth and straightened her posture, looking much better. "It's just nerves."

Taking one deep breath, she took Dasa's hand again and they rounded the corner to face the crowded outdoor market.

"This looks like a slave auction," Magdalena whispered. She'd never actually seen such a thing, but had read about them in a book of Arabian folk tales her father had given her as a child.

The bales of bread, sacks of potatoes, buckets of withering carrots, jars of milk, and crates of dirty turnips at the stalls looked as lonely as any of the slaves in Magdalena's imagination.

"It's not so bad today," Dasa said. "There are usually more people and all of the good vegetables are gone by now."

The women walked together, stepping into the bread line first as Dasa turned to her friend and mouthed "not so bad" once more. This first line wasn't slow, like the others, as all the bread was thrown together into a large tub and there was no illusion of choice. A loaf was meted out in exchange for a coupon, while a serious-looking youth directed shoppers away and into the next line.

"Over there," Dasa said in a hush. "Don't look. That's Tadeas. Your papers will be inside the sack of flour he gives us."

Magdalena looked over at the midget who sat Indian style on top of his podium, taking coupons and distributing flour sacks. His Errol Flynn mustache twitched every time he made a calculation, and his meaty hands, no longer in length than a teaspoon, handled the coupons with expert dexterity, as if he were shuffling cards.

"Stop staring!" Dasa scolded, as Magdalena inspected Tadeas's slicked-back hairstyle.

Magdalena looked away, but held her head up with a bit more confidence. Tadeas was less than an hour away by time and ten meters to her left by distance. She watched his silhouette from the corner of her eye, bending and turning as if he were practicing calisthenics.

She thought of Felix – his touch had been so gentle that morning, when she'd wanted something else. Passion, perhaps. Maybe aggression. His careful handling of her somehow felt like a goodbye, and she supposed it was. At least goodbye for now. The thought made her feel nauseous again.

Magdalena turned to her right, half expecting Felix to be there. Instead, her nose hit the brim of a man's hat, and her eyes caught the profile of a pimple-faced German officer readying his whistle. The whistle blew and the officer began waving his arms in stiff, rousing motions like a bad conductor.

"Dasa, what's going on?"

The pimply guard positioned his rifle, aimed, and let off two good shots into the air before the howl of sirens scattered the rest of his comrades as they ran for cover. The boy lowered his rifle and accidentally discharged it into the crowd, causing panic.

In the Northern corner of the sky, what appeared to be geese flying in a V formation glided towards the city, as if coming back to enjoy a Prague spring after a long winter's exile.

"Get to a bunker!" A woman yelled, running to an open cellar door, where the owner of a nearby hardware store was directing people to shelter.

"Better to die by the Americans than by the Germans!" The man cheered as he leapt up and slid onto his buttocks with a thud. He laughed even louder, as if drunk and amused by his own ineptitude.

"Hello, Americans!" a stubby-legged woman shouted, waving her rosy-pink scarf in the air. Her husband – hairy and wet with perspiration – took off for shelter, leaving her to stand alone, waving at the flock of bombers. "Hollywood! New York, New York," she called, showing off the only English words she knew.

As more of the shoppers began to stop, heads poked out from behind stone columns and arched doorways, catching whiff of a few breaths of freedom from fear and routine humiliation.

"Run, you stupid Krauts!" a gray-bearded man screamed, cupping his hand over his mouth, and limping away as quickly as his cane would let him. He made it to the entrance of the Tylovo Theatre basement as the first bomb was dropped from the belly of the *Chicago Lady*.

The ground thundered, buckling cobblestones throughout the street, although they were at least a half-kilometer away from detonation. Rankled by this hard reminder that freedom would come with a price, most of the shoppers stopped welcoming the Allies, and fell away like snow shaken from a boot with one, heavy stomp.

In the corner by the flour stall, a child sat huddled next to the podium where Tadeas had done his business just moments before. His mother seized his hand, yanking him up off the cobblestones and propelling his bag of marbles out of his pocket. They scattered haphazardly, bouncing and zigzagging over the uneven ground, until a big blue one rolled under Magdalena's foot as she started to run for cover. Her heel set down on the marble, sending her feet flying in the air. She landed hard on the cold, uneven stones.

"Goddamnit!" Dasa cried.

She scanned the nearly empty marketplace and spotted a dark-haired man throwing eggs at an abandoned police sedan. His wire-rimmed glasses were hanging off one ear and he kept nudging them straight. The young intellectual was aiming at the driver's side window yelling *"Bullshit!"* each time he hit his target.

"Help me," Dasa pleaded from behind the bread stall.

Antonin Melan was oblivious to her. He looked up at the American planes and then back at the sedan, and was struck with sudden horror by his own hunger and waste. He leapt to the automobile and licked every globule of the snotty yolk off the window as another bomb rumbled near the castle.

Dasa threw a turnip at him, hitting his temple. "Help me, you Goddamn nut, she's hurt."

Antonin looked down at the woman who was lying semiconscious on the ground. Her full lips were parted and her wig had come undone, revealing a head of hair the color of coffee grounds and thick with glossy waves.

For a moment he lost his breath. She was the most beautiful woman he had ever seen.

CHAPTER TWENTY
ROZNOV POD RADHOSTEM,
CZECHOSLOVAKIA: SAME DAY

R oznov pod Radhostem hardly looked any different than it did on an engraving from 1436 that now hung in a gift shop that had once been a granary. The village had grown a bit, expanding out of the thick mane of pine forest it was nestled in, and into the clover-carpeted valley that lay at the foot of Mt. Radhost. Yet the stone and wood homes – like fairy cottages – were mostly the same, and the people who lived in them had been there for generations.

Beekeepers kept bees, and old women made wafers in hot iron presses, sprinkling them with sugar and nuts and selling them to the tourists who came by for a taste of fifteenth-century country life.

The costumes they wore – Slavic lace and ankle-length, woolen skirts for the women, and lederhosen, wide-buckled shoes, and heavy, tweed jackets for the men, not to mention the hats – gave the village an unnatural, theatrical flair that was on its best days quaint and on its worst, silly. This was underscored by the fact that most of the villagers didn't work in the village at all, but in the factories of larger, industrial towns like Frýdek-Místek or as maids in the ski resorts of the Tatra Mountains.

Lower-ranking German officers often came down from their ski vacations for the day, and bought lace or wooden hair ornaments for their ladies, acting as if this had been the backward state of Czechoslovakia before they'd come to take things over.

It was enough to make Pepík want to sear their eye balls with the pointed tip of his hot poker. Instead, he would scratch his head – hairless and ruddy, like a baked apple – and invite them into his salon of weaponry.

"*Danke, Danke,*" he would ape as they complimented him on the gilded hafts of his signature Falchions, each sword handle shaped in the profile of a conqueror: William, Charlemagne, Napoleon, Alexander. There was one, hidden behind his tool cabinet, he'd fashioned with the head of the gypsy Srut. But that one was for his own, private play.

Pepík spent nearly every weekend in Roznov regardless of the season – away from the nagging visits from his ex-wife, the fog and pollution of the winter air or the revolting litter of dog excrement in summer. And away from the bachelor's apartment building, where every day since Henrik's arrest had felt like quicksand.

He was thrilled to get a request, from Svoboda no less, to pack up and go to the country for awhile – two to three weeks perhaps – and host the young athlete that Srut had brought into the fold. He even fashioned a lucky horseshoe engraved with a profile of FDR as a gift for his coming guest, and laid it like a pillow mint over the folded edge of his best, gray-checked bedspread.

Over the coming days, he would be charged with making sure no one in his village was suspicious of his visitor – just a distant cousin making his way from Prague to Bratislava. Pepík decided that he would not elaborate further. If he mentioned that his visitor was a hockey player for the national team, his neighbors would find all sorts of excuses to come by. Even if he was recognized, as Svoboda pointed out could happen, Pepík could dismiss such nonsense. "A hockey player? In my family?" he could say. Given Pepík's size and physical comportment, it did seem rather ridiculous.

"Why didn't you bring your guitar?" Pepík asked his guest as he met him at the train station. Felix answered correctly.

When they arrived at his pension, Pepík offered his guest some tea, serving it in one of his decorative pewter steins. They were too hot to touch once the boiling water was poured inside and he apologized to "Mr. Felix," as he had settled on calling him.

Felix smiled and held the pewter stein in his hands, with the sleeves of his shirt pulled up over his palms. For Pepík, who was used to working with fire, the steins had never been a problem.

"We're part of a living museum here," Pepík chuckled, adjusting his round-framed glasses.

Felix drummed his fingers over an elephant footstool. "It's beautiful. Just like my grandfather's place."

"My mother died three years ago and it's all mine now," Pepík said, his belt disappearing under a belly fold as he sat down. "Of course, I'm only a weekend hotelier. This was a hunting lodge for almost four hundred years, you know."

The Pension pod Radhostem was decorated with pine furniture that was trimmed with deer antlers and moose horns, and carved with familiar, Moravian adages about the health and social benefits of beer and wine. Boar heads and bear skins, the mounted scalps of antelopes, zebra pelts from Africa somewhere, monkey carcasses serving as doilies on the worn, pigskin sofa, as well as posed, lifelike trophies of squirrels and beavers stared with willful disinterest from walls, corners, and floors as if they were at a bad party.

Pepík hadn't hunted any of these animals himself, but had bought most of them from a local group of naturalists who lived off the land near Karlový Vary. He also scoured regional flea markets, occasionally finding a real gem – like the zebra pelt – discarded by a country gentleman who had liked to go on safari. Travelers raved about the ambience of his hotel, admiring its eccentricity and his apparent skill with a rifle.

On most days Pepík was proud of his pension, but not today. He knew that Felix, a famous athlete from Prague, saw his home for what it was; a stone box crammed with trophies Pepík hadn't earned and furniture and trinkets that catered to a certain kind of tourist – the kind who lived in cities and had some money, but lacked any real sophistication.

"Want to see my receiver?"

Felix shrugged.

Pepík knew he was behaving like an eleven-year-old country boy trying to impress his city cousin, but this was the one thing he had that didn't humble him and set him apart from the local yucks who used to pelt him with snowballs.

"Can you send messages, too?" Felix asked.

"Yes," Pepík told him. "It's my job."

He uncrossed his legs and stood up, teetering for a moment on his bad knee. He then brought Felix up the narrow staircase that led to the second floor, where all the guest bedrooms were located.

"We are the only ones here, aren't we?" Felix asked.

"Oh, I got them out. I told a man this morning I was getting scarlet fever and he ran out of here like he was on fire. That's what we always tell people around here when we want them out of our hair."

The truth was that Pepík was the only one who'd used this excuse more than once. His neighbor had used it on a lodger, but then, he really did have scarlet fever and died of it. In that moment, Pepík noticed a faint tickle in his throat and remembered that he'd overslept that morning – which he never did. It occurred to him that he might be getting scarlet fever after all, maybe as punishment for the series of lies he'd been telling since he started work in the Resistance, and maybe for a few he'd told before that. But in God's eyes, he asked himself, what is the greater sin? Lying in order to help his country, or truthfully doing nothing?

The tickle in his throat faded away as he allowed himself this moral victory, and Pepík was able to get back to the task at hand. He took a finger-sized iron key shaped like a small pilliwinks and slid it into his bedroom keyhole, performing a series of jerks and turns.

"No one gets into this room but me. I made the key and lock myself," he boasted.

At first glance it was a regular bedroom with an iron bed frame positioned in the center, a plain, but well-crafted chest of drawers, a washing basin, and a night table. But in the right corner, invisible unless you fully entered the room and had a good look around, was a staircase that led to an apartment. It was neither hidden, nor questionable, as the owner of a pension needs his private space away from guests, but not obvious to travelers who thought their host was sleeping only a few feet away.

"I designed it from a book on Houdini. He could put a whole lady into the bottom and you could open it up and never know – unless you tried to carry it." Pepík dragged what looked like an old shoe trunk from under a day bed. He lifted the false bottom from the interior of the trunk, revealing a suitcase. It was reddish-brown, compact, and straightforward, much like Pepík himself.

Felix patted Pepík's back, admiring the clever construction and bent to open the suitcase containing the device, but Pepík put his hand out in front of Felix's chest as if he were directing traffic to stop. He then opened up the case himself, revealing a metal box with several black-handled switches, a stamp-sized, raised square that sat under a tapping lever, a couple of knobs, and what looked like the speaker on a radio, though smaller.

"This is how to turn it on," he pointed at a switch and a knob. "And here's where I get my messages." He tapped on the lever three times.

"And you send messages that way, too?" Felix asked, stroking the old leather of the suitcase handle.

"I don't send messages unless asked." Pepík's role as a receiver of orders and information meant a great deal to him. He thought of himself as a bank. When the instructions came, he deposited them and executed them to the exact word without inference or improvisation. "Besides, there's a code. It's like Morse code, but it's a secret, and I've sworn to protect that code with my life."

Pepík took one more look at his receiver and then closed the suitcase, locking it with two small padlocks that he produced from his desk drawer. "And if I ever told you the code, I would be putting you in danger."

"Yes, of course," Felix said, watching Pepík as he put the keys to the padlocks into his inner vest pocket.

"And I don't ask you about what you're doing."

"No, no," Felix said.

"And I know it's something big."

"You're very discreet."

Pepík nodded, pride tainting only the curl of his upper lip.

"I've got a surprise for dinner tonight," Pepík said, putting his index finger to his lips as if Felix was going to broadcast this piece of news throughout the village. "I caught a rabbit behind the house. He was sitting there like he was waiting for me."

Vladimir the Rabbit, a red-eyed, white-furred ball of a thing, was a welcome guest that Pepík had invited in, and who it was a pleasure to care for and watch get fatter. Had his neighbors known that Vladimir lay nestled in a cage cushioned with hay, and was being well fed with a percentage of Pepík's daily rations, they would've surely broken into his cellar and taken the meat for themselves. They were already resentful of his money.

"This is Vladimir," Pepík said, presenting the rabbit to Felix before taking him out of his cage and holding him under his arm like a newspaper. Tragically dumb, the creature stared ahead, blissfully unaware of its fate, even as Pepík tied him upside down by his hind legs and hung him from a copper pipe that ran across the low, cellar ceiling. Pepík then took an old, baton-sized piece of leaded pipe from behind Vladimir's cage and whacked the rabbit twice on the head, rendering him unconscious with the first whack, and dead with the second. To be sure, Pepík felt for the rabbit's heartbeat and put his ear to the animal's chest.

"He's gone," the bachelor said, running one of Vladimir's ears between his thumb and forefinger.

Pepík reached up into his pant leg, pulling out a small hunter's knife with a handle in the shape of Artemis. He then slit the creature's throat and stood back to let the blood dribble into a metal bucket he held under its head.

The blood drained quickly, allowing Pepík to continue with the cleaning, slicing right down the rabbit's middle, opening up the chest and abdominal cavities and exposing the organs. He placed the creature's urine-soaked kidneys in their own bowl so that their strong taste and odor wouldn't contaminate the rest of the innards.

"Will you hold his legs?" Pepík asked, as he cut in a circle around the delicate bone that grew out from the animal's padded foot.

Felix grabbed what was left of Vladimir by the feet, and held on as Pepík wrenched the skin and fur away from muscle and bone. When he was done, and the rabbit's fur had been peeled off as if it were a tight sweater, Pepík set the pelt aside onto an old, wooden tray.

"I have to let the meat relax; otherwise it'll be as tough as rubber." Pepík informed him, taking the undressed rabbit and laying it in his icebox on a porcelain oval.

It wasn't that Felix was impressed with Pepík's skill with a knife or his ability to kill and clean a rabbit. These were skills any man acquired after spending some time in the country. But it was the way in which Pepík had cared for the animal, killing him with a quick hand and soft heart, and never allowing his pet to overcome him with sentimentality. Pepík may have been a lonely orphan of a man, but he understood his priorities. And he made a delicious rabbit in sour cream sauce, which they ate for their supper the next day.

As they sat in Pepík's kitchen hutch, spooning the last puddles of milky-white gravy into their mouths, Felix spied one of his host's neighbors. She was a rotund woman about the age of someone expecting her first grandchild, and the

sun shone through her daisy-flecked housedress as she wad-
dled up to the pension. She waved a coral handkerchief
above her head.

"Air raid," she cried. "Prague has been destroyed!"

CHAPTER TWENTY-ONE
PRAGUE: MARCH 23

The number nine tram deposited Justus Svoboda at the base of the Charles Bridge on the Old Town side. From there, he went on foot, crossing over the bridge and looking out onto the dense clusters of Gothic, Renaissance, and Baroque buildings built by Charlemagnes, Premysls, and Hapsburgs. A scant sheet of black smoke, like a widow's veil, hung low over the city's spires – fed mostly by the one smoldering pile of rubble in the city's center.

Svoboda descended the stairs to Kampa Island and entered an old apartment building. The first two floors remained under the cover of the Charles Bridge, but the top floor peaked out over its side. The building belonged to Svoboda, although it was registered under the name of a retarded cousin and filled with the unregistered dead.

Mrs. Kameny, a heavy-set woman who'd suffered a fatal, early heart attack three years earlier, lived on the first floor. She had no family except for an aunt somewhere in Olomouc, so Svoboda gave her a decent burial. With the help of a friend who worked at the morgue, he buried the record of her death as well.

The new Mrs. Kameny – a namesake cousin if anyone asked – looked considerably younger than the forty-three years her birth records contended. She had dark, Jewish features, although friends from the town of Aš, where it was documented she was born, would remember her as a blue-eyed blonde. Blonde she was, thanks to a bottle of peroxide she kept wrapped in rags underneath her bathroom sink. But the blue eyes described in her personal documents had to be painstakingly amended to brown with a good eraser, rubber glue, and perfectly matched crepe paper.

The second floor apartment had recently been vacated by one Josef Belous, a victim of kidney failure or stroke, depending on the certificate. He'd left two weeks before in a steamer trunk bound for England, taking with him only a picture of his late mother and his expensive cologne. It was a relief, as Belous had been a consummate ladies' man who made a habit of luring young stenographers into his apartment and making an awful racket.

The third floor apartment, a former attic now renovated into a lovely flat, had recently been rented by a well-known hockey player. It was said he spent most of his time in Bratislava.

"Good morning, Mrs. Kameny," Svoboda called, knowing his tenant's ear was pressed firmly to her door.

Svoboda squinted up into several cobwebs that marred the ceiling of an otherwise immaculate foyer, and unlocked the third floor mailbox. From there, he retrieved a single, perfumed envelope made of thick paper, and embossed with the initials L.B. Envelope in hand, he shuffled up the stairs humming, "Who's Got Trouble?"

"Jesus, Mary, and Joseph," he gasped.

Felix was standing in the living room of the third-floor flat. "Where the hell is everybody? I went to your house – nobody there. I heard Prague had burned to the ground!

185

Thank God your friend Pepík had a car and some petrol. Not even the trains were running."

"As you can see," Svoboda swept his hand out towards the city view from his window, "our capital was spared everything but a few bruises."

"I had to see Magdalena was alright." Felix sat down. "I can go if you want, but not until I see her."

Justus Svoboda nodded and smiled at him, his eyes crinkling in the corners.

"Magdalena is fine," he said. "And of course you can see her. If you really think it's prudent."

"Of course it's prudent," Felix said, but he didn't feel the courage of his convictions. Magdalena would beg to go with him. She'd ask him to wait for her until her papers were secure. And Felix knew he would oblige her. "Unless you think my presence could draw unwanted attention."

Svoboda emptied his pockets of the tea he'd brought, putting it in a cupboard above the kitchen sink. He held up the invitation he'd retrieved from the mailbox and slid it across the kitchen counter to Felix, who pulled the ivory linen paper out of its envelope, and centered it on the table.

"She took the bait." Svoboda smacked his palms on the counter. He'd been checking the third floor mailbox every day hoping that the fickle Miss Baarová wouldn't forget to invite her newly reacquainted old friend Felix to her party.

Felix looked down at the square of paper – so perfect, elegant – and was reminded of Pepík's reverence for the receiver in his shoe trunk. Like Pepík, Felix was aware of the way an inanimate object could change the course of his life. He thought of his first pair of skates, his father's Infant of Prague figurine, and the lucky charm Magdalena had pinched from Benito the pig.

"April 18th. My father's birthday," he whispered. "And so soon."

Felix ran his fingers over the loopy calligraphy. It felt as if the party could've been on no other date.

"A perfect day for an assassination." Svoboda appeared very satisfied with himself. "And two days before the Fuhrer's birthday."

"I saw Srut at the train station before I left," Felix said. "He claimed the gypsies were taken away by the Gestapo."

Svoboda inhaled deeply. "Tragic, but a matter of time, wasn't it?" He took Felix's hand and gripped it. "Let's concentrate on those we can help and not waste tears on the ones already gone. And we're helping so many. This is not a cut we're planning, but an amputation."

Svoboda sat down at the dining table, unrolling a map of Kutna Hora and a blueprint of the mansion where Lída Baarová was having her birthday party. "The place sits across the square from the Bone Church," he said. "It's a popular destination for religious tourists."

Felix had never been there, but Magdalena's Aunt Sarah had referred to it as "the most ghastly place she'd ever visited." She used to make up ghost stories about it, reciting them with a lantern held under her chin.

It had once been a regular cathedral, lorded over by a monk who devised a most macabre solution to the considerable problem of storing the dead. Years of plagues and wars had presented the parish with an overabundance of corpses. With the fever of a mad visionary, the monk commissioned a carpenter to ornament the interior of his church entirely with human bone.

Some called it the devil's art, but most Czechs saw the monk's work as a clever solution to a sensitive dilemma. Church teachings, after all, forbade cremation.

"Legend has it that if you enter the Church of Bones with malevolence in your heart, you will remain there with the dead forever," Felix recalled.

"But it's getting out that's going to be a problem." Svoboda chuckled to himself, smoothing the curling map with his hands and forearms. "Of Miss Baarová's party, that is. The ballroom is on the top floor, where it connects to a large balcony. We'll have four floors to run down if we take the conventional route."

Svoboda's reading glasses sat at the tip of his nose, magnifying a tiny set of scars on his cheek that were the result of flying battle debris. Remnants from the First World War.

"Is there a back stairway, or a way to come down from the balcony?"

"I don't know about the balcony, but there is a back stairway." Svoboda's finger traced down the stairs and out a service entrance in the back. He took a pencil from behind his ear, then circled a small courtyard space behind the mansion and looked closer at the property boundaries.

"You'll probably have to scale a wall back here, since this area should be pretty well locked up. From there it's only a few hundred yards to the safe house."

The safe house was an outhouse behind an old manor at the edge of town. A perch had been built beneath the toilet hole. Felix tried not to think about hiding inside that toilet, while farm workers – unaware of his presence – pissed and shat.

"What will you do?" Felix asked.

"Me? I'll have to jump from the balcony onto the next rooftop. It's shorter by a floor, but a manageable leap if we're to trust these drawings."

Svoboda sat back against his chair, yawning. The teakettle whistled and Felix dropped several tea bags into the hot water, letting it draw until it was as dark as coffee.

"And Monsignor Merillini?" Felix asked.

Svoboda had avoided the subject every time Felix had tried to bring him up, but the Italian had been on his mind all week. His aquamarine eyes, red and swollen in the corners as if he spent too much time reading under a dim light, had appeared to him in his dreams.

"The Monsignor has given us a reason to sleep well at night."

Felix cocked his head.

"I told you, my boy. I don't give much more than cuts and bruises anymore. It's a matter of resources really, of how difficult it is to connect with other branches of the Underground – Paris, Amsterdam and their like. After Heydrich's assassination, Hitler all but destroyed the Prague Underground." Svoboda took his tea in his hands, sipping carefully. "The Monsignor is much cleverer than I am and has tremendous resources at his fingertips. He has strong ties with individual parishes throughout Europe and knows how to cull the assistance of likeminded friends."

Felix considered Monsignor Merillini for a moment, remembering his most striking feature – a voice with the perpetual scratch of early morning.

"He's arranged for you to be loaded into a coffin," Svoboda went on. "The kind used for transporting high Church officials who've died while away from the Vatican. You'll be taken through Austria into Italy."

"How will I get to London from there?"

Svoboda paused. "You won't."

He raised his finger, holding it tall and straight at attention. "You'll live out the rest of the war in Crespano Del Grappa. It's a tiny Alpine town close to the Austrian border. The Monsignor was born there and has family throughout the region."

Felix hated the way Svoboda manipulated him with changes at the last minute. He also hated that the strategy was effective, keeping the plan fluid and insuring that there was never any one person – except Svoboda – who knew exactly how the mission was to unfold.

"And Magdalena?"

Svoboda took Felix's face in his hands – the way he had at his house on the night he and Srut had encountered him after the fire.

"Everything else will remain the same," he said. "The Monsignor will personally escort Magdalena to Slovakia, where she'll join Dasa. God willing, they'll get to London within the month."

God willing, Felix thought. He stared down into his tea.

"The war is winding down, don't you feel it?" Svoboda's voice was nearly rapturous. "But believe me the march to the end will be long and bitter. It's desperate and brutal and far more dangerous than all the zeal of the beginning. I've seen it before. And you and your wife are far more likely to live to see each other again if you remain patient."

"And apart."

Svoboda nodded.

Felix had always understood that their uncertain situation would ultimately dictate any plan, but he'd remained hopeful about London. If truth be told – at least until that moment – any prolonged separation from Magdalena had only been an abstraction. Something that happened to unlucky people. And Felix, excepting recent events, had always been very lucky.

"Everything's always worked out for you, son," his father had said in their final conversation. He must have known his own death was imminent. Even as he pushed a pair of tickets to Bratislava into Felix's hands – insuring that luck would once again find him.

Felix ran his palm over the hard lump at his breast. He removed the Infant of Prague figurine from his pocket and put it on the table, wiping off the smudges that had formed on its nose and cheeks. He kissed the Infant's crown the way his father would have and laid it into Svoboda's hand.

"Can you give this to her?"

Svoboda nodded. He got up and went to the window, looking out onto the tops of the hatted heads that bobbled across the cobblestones, and rolled the Infant of Prague figurine in his palm. "I think its best she not know you won't be seeing each other as soon as we'd originally hoped. The anticipation of long absences can complicate things, impair judgment."

Felix hated lying to her again, but didn't protest. Magdalena would never agree to go with Dasa if she knew. Just as she would never stand for his involvement in an assassination. Felix had told her that he was merely helping Svoboda secure a permanent hiding place for Srut's gypsy kin – who Magdalena liked considerably more than Srut himself.

"I can make it back to Roznov before curfew tonight," Felix said. "And you won't see me again until Kutna Hora."

The words stung and felt final. For a moment, Felix hated Justus Svoboda as much as Srut did.

CHAPTER TWENTY-TWO
VATICAN CITY: APRIL 1

G regorio Barbarigo had finally heard the sweet, compelling words he'd been waiting to hear since his mother
had told him the story of his ancestors on the day he started
primary school. Within the year, he would be named Bishop
of Verona, the way Giovanni Barbarigo and the Blessed
Gregorio Barbarigo, after whom he was named, were in centuries past.

It had been a long road that hadn't been a foregone
conclusion for a man like Barbarigo, despite his impressive
lineage. Though an obedient cleric with a passion for the
Church that rivaled any of his colleagues', he lacked the
intellect of the men who rose into the Pope's inner circle
and were given vast responsibilities. While by no means an
ignorant man, he was short of creativity and confidence, the
very elements that transformed a good apprentice into an
effective master. The very elements that Monsignor Carlo
Merillini had in abundance.

When Carlo Merillini was brought under him he thought
at first a great compliment had been paid him. Merillni had
been whispered about at the Vatican for some time, having
distinguished himself as a great fine arts restorer and then

as an excellent lawyer. But it wasn't long after Merillini had come to him that Barbarigo realized there was a serpent in his garden.

Though he was always dutiful and deferential, Merillini had a way of making Barbarigo appear slow-witted and weak by his mere existence – his gymnastic knowledge of Church doctrine, his dry, sophisticated wit and assured manner, even around the Holy Father himself. What Barbarigo found most galling about Merillini wasn't merely his ability to shine in front of superiors, but the fact that his ideas were truly dangerous, often conflicting with the very policies the Holy Father had decreed.

"We must stand firm against the bullying fist of fascism," Merillini had peristed. "We must lead the moral world or else be devoured like Poland."

No, thought Barbarigo, we must *preserve* the moral world or else be devoured like Poland.

With prayer his only defense against Merillini's skillful rhetoric and way of currying favor, Barbarigo had prayed for two days and nights, taking only water as nourishment. In his meditations, God questioned his motives and pointed out his past failures – for it had been Barbarigo who had arranged for Merillini's "promotion" to Czechoslovakia, where he was to guard the Infant of Prague, one of the most important religious relics in all of Christendom. He'd wanted Merillini as far away from the main current of power as possible. But the plan had backfired. From Prague, Merillini was free to report on the horrors of the Nazi regime first hand, underscoring his conviction that Hitler's aim was every bit as pernicious as Stalin's – to destroy the Catholic Church.

When prayers yielded no clear answers, Gregorio Barbarigo picked himself up off the floor of the chapel, bathed, drank sugar water and returned to his office. He was at his desk less than fifteen minutes when God finally intervened.

"What!" Barbarigo said, when his nephew, an assistant to the Holy Father's highest secretary, informed him that the Monsignor had gotten involved with the Prague Underground.

"Yes," his nephew continued. "He's actually arranged for the safe passage of a group of assassins!" His hand shaking, the young man retrieved a letter from his vestment pocket and handed it to the future Bishop of Verona.

Barbarigo examined the one-page document, skimming the neat script. It outlined Merillini's dangerous exploits in a detailed, though hesitant hand. There was no signature.

"Has anyone else seen this?"

His nephew shook his head.

Barbarigo's abhorrence soon gave way to the realization that God had presented him with an opportunity. In the boldest act of his career, Gregorio Barbarigo requested an audience with his superior and pled his case on his knees, detailing Merillini's treachery as if he were confessing his own, and praying for leniency on the Monsignor's behalf.

CHAPTER TWENTY-THREE
KUTNA HORA,
CZECHOSLOVAKIA: APRIL 17

Kutna Hora reminded Felix of a miniature Prague. A "Royal City" and mint after the discovery of silver there in the 14th century, it had the same elegant, weary bones. Coal-stained stone monoliths festooned with squatting gargoyles stood shoulder to shoulder alongside once-similar buildings that had been renovated in the Baroque style and by comparison looked like Easter eggs. The passage of time was evident layer upon layer in the city's architecture like a doorframe scratched with lines marking the growth of a child.

"Enjoy the evening," Svoboda crooned, placing his small, firm hand on Felix's shoulder. "We're here for Lída's birthday party and we need to look festive. Besides, we might as well have a good time tonight as tomorrow will be work."

Svoboda, with his untold supply of ration coupons and insider information, bought them dinner at a small, converted wine cellar beneath the mint. A swanky little club known for wild game, it was officially closed to anyone but those who were on a list kept by Leopold, the ancient Maitre'd.

The vast majorities of names on any given evening were German, and tonight was no exception. The name Justus Svoboda stood out on Leopold's piece of light blue stationary as if it were a Chinese face in a Slovak country village. His staff stared with canine intensity at Felix and Svoboda, and it wasn't until a bus boy told a cigarette girl they had a Czech National Hockey Team member in their midst that the Czechs in service were put at ease. Most would never admit they felt a twinge of pride that a Czech could break into the upper ranks of their occupiers. At the same time, they felt betrayed at the acceptance of such favors. Only Leopold kept his head throughout the debate that raged amongst his staff, as he was long accustomed to the changing tides of higher society and immune to its particulars.

"Preserved wild cherries," Svoboda groaned, studying the dessert menu.

His peculiar good nature made Felix smile, despite their circumstances. The sculptor's faith in powers higher than himself was total. He believed in God. He believed in country. He believed in destiny. Felix believed in God and country, but had never quite been able to give himself over to destiny.

"Tokaji?"

The server waited for a nod before pouring the wine into Svoboda's cordials glass. Felix, bloated from French Bordeaux on top of wild boar and pheasant liver, declined his glass. He'd eaten not out of delight, but need. The exquisite food could've been made from rotting thorn weed and he would've chewed and swallowed it the same way. Svoboda, on the other hand, reveled in every last drop of gravy, which he soaked up with a soft, fresh piece of rye bread.

"We're wasting time."

"Living is never a waste of time." Svoboda touched his glass to Felix's knuckle and took an almost imperceptible sip of the Tokaji. "You have to ask yourself this: if the world ended tomorrow, would you be satisfied that you spent your last remaining hours staring at a manor house that you'll see soon enough anyway?"

Felix's boyish impatience amused Svoboda. The grin that crept across his face was the same grin that came over him whenever he happened upon a picture of himself as a young man in his first army uniform.

"Very well, then." Svoboda motioned to the waiter and slipped several Deutsche marks into the man's outer breast pocket. The waiter bowed to the table, thanking Felix and telling him what an honor it was to have served the man who scored the winning goal against the Canadians the year before.

As Felix and Svoboda left the restaurant amidst the gossip of its staff, a German man looked up from his newspaper. He was no longer wearing the bandage that had been taped to his forehead at the Art Nouveau Café, and there was an unmistakable, triangular scar in its place. He fingered that scar and then scratched at a piece of dill that was sticking to his gold tooth, sucking it off his finger as his eyes followed the men to the coat room. When the athlete and the sculptor were out of his field of vision, he stood up and left the restaurant through a back exit hidden behind the kitchen's giant icebox.

"It's enormous," Felix said.

He stood back and took in the manor house where Lída would be celebrating her birthday. The house itself was almost as big as the Bone Church, which sat directly opposite it on the square, disguising its legendary interior with a simple, Gothic exterior the color of mustard sauce.

"Yes, it is, but a lucid design." Svoboda seemed bored and restless. "Let's go to the church. It's quite a spectacle, you know, and I'd like to say a prayer for our endeavors."

Felix followed him across the square to what was officially called the Church of All Saints, though no one used its formal moniker. The skull and crossbones of a Jolly Roger sat at the top of the church's tower in place of the Christian cross, and absorbed them with its hollow eyes. It occurred to Felix quite suddenly that he wanted nothing to do with the place.

"I'll stay out here."

"You're not one of those tiresome young atheists, are you?"

Felix looked over to the cemetery sitting adjacent to the church. Its tombstones, too, glowed white like bones in the moonlight.

"I don't want to be with the dead tonight."

"Suit yourself."

Svoboda turned and walked up the stairs to the entrance of the church. As he creaked open the door, the warm light of beeswax candles enveloped him, trickling down over the first couple of stairs like honey. When the door closed, Felix felt completely alone. He thought briefly about running, getting as far away as possible. He could get Magdalena and take her somewhere – anywhere – surviving like they had before they'd ever encountered Justus Svoboda.

But Vera Ruza was never too far behind him. He didn't hear her breath this time or feel her eyes upon him, but he felt her presence as surely as if she were about to place her fine hand on his shoulder. The way she had so often done to

his father. Vera had loved him. Somehow Felix hadn't realized that –not until right then. And his father had loved her.

"Vera," he whispered.

But she was gone.

No wind blew, carrying with it Vera's smoky voice. "The
voice of a temptress," his father used to say. "Yet the heart
of an angel."

The night had become suddenly plain. The Bone
Church stood before him as any other local parish and its
tombstones were little more than slabs of rock jutting out
from the ground like crooked teeth. There was no mystery
to the sky, its only shroud being a thin sheath of clouds that
wrapped around the moon like white muslin.

Chapter Twenty-Four
Prague: Same Day

Magdalena waited at the bottom of Karlovo Square for her tram, fidgeting with her coat buttons and unfolding her collar to her ears. Rain started to fall, not torrentially at first, but enough to send the people of Prague scampering for cover. The sky, the blue-gray color of murky water, lay low as if it were balancing on the city's spires. Despite having new bona-fide false papers in her handbag, Magdalena – or rather "Anna Nork" – took comfort from the empty streets, not relishing the prospect of having to look passersby in the eye. Even cold and wet to the skin, she was grateful for the storm and thought that maybe, after all this time, she and Felix were finally getting a real break – not just one more stepping stone across a wild, wide river.

Now, if all went well, Felix would help Mr. Svoboda with hiding Srut's gypsies and join her in Slovakia, as Dasa had promised. Despite the inherent dangers involved, Magdalena thrilled at the thought of getting to London, where she could live in the open and marry Felix using her real name and documents, rather than a list of assembled facts that had been lifted from various old death certificates.

"Maria?"

Magdalena spun around. It was the young intellectual from the marketplace. The one who'd bandaged her elbow with a strip from his expensive shirt.

"Hello," she said, breathing hard. He'd scared her.

"Antonin." He put out his hand. "Antonin Melan. Don't feel bad. I'm terrible at names myself and you were a bit out of it that day. It's good to see you looking so well."

Magdalena smiled. "Just a few cuts and scrapes."

"We were all lucky that day," he said.

Magdalena nodded, looking out the window.

"And I'm lucky again today. Seeing you, I mean." Antonin Melan took off his glasses and wiped them free of condensation. He started to put them on again, but folded them instead, tucking them into his coat pocket.

"Yes, lucky," Magdalena repeated.

Thunder cracked and the sky blazed white, flickering over Magdalena's face like the flash of a camera. She turned her head, hoping she didn't appear too anxious. With considerable effort, she resisted the temptation to concoct a lie about where she was going and what she was doing out on a night like this.

"Would you like to share a glass with me?" Antonin Melan asked. "There's a wine bar very close – on Riční. Just across the street from where I live. They have several good Moravian vintages."

The tram turned onto Újezd Street and Magdalena stood on her toes. A yellow street lamp illuminated her face as the tram slowed and Antonin Melan drank in her features. She was even lovlier than he'd remembered, with eyes that conveyed a sense of romantic purity. They were eyes that understood love.

Antonin blushed, conjuring the fantasies he'd allowed himself over the past few weeks. Of taking her to the theater;

of reading to her from his fine translation of *The Waste Land*; and yes, even of slipping his grandmother's blue-toned diamond ring on her delicate finger. They were silly, he knew, but her eyes had at least gone some way towards justifying them.

"I'm sorry," she said. "This is my stop."

"Oh." He tried his best at a casual smile.

Magdalena took his hand and shook it, hating herself for being so rude. This man had been awfully helpful to her and Dasa in the marketplace on the day of the bombing. He'd carried her to safety and even offered his coat. This on top of destroying what was undoubtedly one of his best pieces of clothing. Stepping down off the tram, Magdalena waited for it to pull away, watching Antonin Melan's face in the window as he raised his hand to wave goodbye. She forced herself to wave back at him.

The Church of Our Lady the Victorious stood before her, looking smaller than she'd remembered it. Of course, she hadn't been there since she was a child.

Magdalena ran around its side to the rectory, banging her fists on the wood and iron doors as hard as the rain was now pounding onto her head and shoulders.

"Hello!" she shouted, looking around quickly and then lowering her voice. "I'm sorry; I'm a few minutes early."

She'd been told to come promptly at six and it was barely half past five. It seemed to her like it shouldn't matter – especially since the Monsignor was taking her to meet Dasa at the Svoboda's country house straight away. Tomorrow, the real journey would begin, but she couldn't bear to think about that now. It was too exciting a prospect. And too dangerous.

Magdalena slapped her palms on the door and called the Monsignor's name.

Still, no one came, so she tried the handle and it opened, letting her into a tiny hallway that led to another door – one as heavy as the first. This second door, however, was locked tight.

"Hello, I said." She knocked again, this time with her knuckle. "I got here faster than I expected."

Inside, a dark-robed figure shuffled past the gold cherub sculptures that fluttered around the Infant of Prague. Staring straight ahead from behind its glass case, the Infant's hand was raised in a gesture of peace, and its blue eyes – so moist and lifelike – appeared to follow the old nun wherever she went. She made the Sign of the Cross as she passed the holy relic, dipping her knee, but not fully genuflecting.

"Go away," she hissed through the rectory door. The sister clenched her teeth until she chipped a tiny fragment off her molar.

Magdalena knocked harder and started to explain that she hadn't meant to come so early.

"Go away, I tell you, and don't ever come back here. Plans have changed, so go back from where you came."

Magdalena started to pound on the door now, shouting that she had no intention of going away. Monsignor Merillini was waiting for her.

"The Monsignor isn't here and he's not coming back. Now go away before I call the police. Jew! Jew!"

The knocking stopped abruptly and the nun heard Magdalena's heals clicking, and the outer rectory door slamming behind her. All was quiet again. The nun slipped into the hallway to lock the outer door, but first cracked it open and peered into the street. She'd left her monocle in the parish office, but could still make out a blur of a figure running towards Riční Street. *Thank God,* she thought.

As she closed the door and stepped backwards, something cracked beneath the ball of her foot. She looked down to see an Infant of Prague figurine, with its head now detached from its body. The nun sank down to pick it up, balancing its white head – the paint worn off except for a few gold flecks at the crown – on its tiny neck. It was still warm from the Jewish woman's hands.

"That wasn't necessary," the raspy voice said from behind the altar. The nun dropped the figurine, shattering it further, and spun around.

"I'm sorry, Monsignor, I didn't know what else to say. She wouldn't be quiet and she wasn't about to leave even after I told her."

Monsignor Merillini looked over at Svoboda's startling copy of the Infant of Prague, housed in its glass case and standing on a pedestal engraved with crystals. He closed his eyes, but he could still see the divine child – his body of wax, ivory, and bronze looking life-like in his mind's eye. Svoboda's likeness was so faithful that Merillini often had to remind himself that he wasn't in the presence of the real Infant.

"Why don't you go home, Sister? I must go back to my residence and pack my things. I'll be leaving in the morning for my new assignment in Buenos Aires."

The nun bowed her head and tears stung her cloudy brown eyes. She loved the Monsignor and hated to see him go. She thought it terribly unfair that he was being punished so harshly and for a moment felt guilty about having been the one who had informed the Vatican – anonymously, of course – about the Monsignor's involvement in sheltering a group of would-be assassins.

The nun looked once more at the shattered Infant figurine and saw a small roll of dark fabric sticking out from where its feet used to be. She bent down and pulled at the cloth, unrolling it like a scroll. On the black cotton was printed a white skull and crossbones – the scull head grinning as if he were mocking her. The nun struggled for her breath and wanted to drop the evil little banner, but her fingers wouldn't let go of it – making her stare into its horrid death face as if she were looking at her own end.

CHAPTER TWENTY-FIVE
KUTNA HORA-SEDLEC: APRIL 18

F elix and Svoboda rode through the city in a glossy, pistachio Mercedes-Benz offered by their host and hostess. The setting sun burned orange against a backdrop of blackened buildings and the spires of Kutna Hora rose, pointing to the heavens as if they were stalagmites in a cavern of fire and oil paint.

Felix took this to be a good sign and made a silent appeal for Magdalena's safety, for the success of Justus Svoboda's daring plans, and for the deaths of Ivo Krev and Joseph Goebbels. Like many Catholics, Felix's God was an Old Testament God – one of justice and bold, decisive action. Jesus, His even-tempered Son, may sit at His right hand whispering pleas of mercy, but ultimately, even He would find justice in the destruction of men like Goebbels and Krev.

"*Wilkommen*," the driver said in Czech-accented German as they pulled up to the Baroque Manor house – ironically nicknamed "America" in the last century. It looked different than the night before. More like a handsome matron in the amber light of dusk, than the young woman who'd sat in the moonlight like a beauty in a cocktail lounge. Lída, who interpreted every passing year as an affront to her woman-hood, would've been aghast at the comparison. Especially as she faced her thirtieth birthday.

Felix put his simple, black mask to his face and handed his invitation to a fellow at the door, while a high-cheekboned Czech girl presented them with a tray full of champagne flutes. Felix and Svoboda each took one and the girl curtseyed away as if she were a bit player in a musical.

A German officer – fully uniformed – frisked them before pronouncing them "*Nichts*" to his superior.

Svoboda had timed their entrance perfectly by asking the driver to take the scenic route. They came well after the first wave of guests, but still had plenty of time to wander the house unmolested by overeager waiters who hadn't enough to keep them busy. Neither of them knew what they were looking for – another escape route, perhaps, if the plan went awry – so they roamed from room to room as if admiring a fine, old mansion.

And fine it was.

Looping arches dripped gold chandeliers that were large enough to take out a small party were they to fall. Plump, nude nymphs depicted in large, gold-framed ovals played lutes, ate grapes, and were otherwise admired by lecherous but well-dressed seventeenth century gentlemen.

A giant Nazi flag hanging from ceiling to floor covered the one theological painting – dating from when the house had been owned by a prominent cleric. Felix had spotted the wounded foot of Christ, which peeped out from the side of the flag, and recognized the piece. It was by Saird Nosecky, a Czech artist who'd painted the Strahov Library and Monastery in Prague.

Felix lifted part of the flag to get a better look at the composition and came face to face with Christ, who was painted in repose. Though His eyes were closed and His body limp and bleeding, He was depicted as looking alive, with His mouth slightly open to suggest breathing and His hand holding Mary Magdalene's – to comfort her rather than the other way around.

"You there. Don't touch that!" A tuxedoed security agent was stabbing his finger at Felix, barking at him in German.

Felix apologized, explaining that his father had been a collector of Nosecky's, until he realized that the agent was referring to his touching the flag. Standing at attention, Felix begged the agent's pardon one last time and performed a short bow. If he'd made a blunder like this anywhere else, he could've been arrested. But at a party thrown by a man in Hitler's inner circle, exceptions were made.

"Felix, darling! That is you, isn't it? Well, of course it is!" Lída Baarová waved her hand a little too excitedly, making the heavy gold and emerald bracelet she was showcasing jingle like a Christmas tree being shaken at its base. The security agent stepped back to the wall, becoming nearly invisible, except for the faint vestige of a snarl on his upper lip. He didn't care for the pretty Lída Baarová and thereafter would care even less for the flag desecrater she was calling to.

"Happy birthday, Lída. You look lovely. Is that new?"

"Gorgeous, isn't it? A little birthday present." She scrunched her nose like a girl, making her peacock-feathered mask ride up and down on her brow. Rattling the bracelet one more time, she smoothed a nonexistent crease on her taffeta bodice.

"You're not here alone, are you? Didn't you get engaged or something?"

"I came with Justus Svoboda."

"Ah, yes, the painter."

"Sculptor."

"Right." Lída pouted for a moment, recalling the bust her lover had commissioned for his mother. "Won't you escort me upstairs? That's where all the real fun is."

Felix offered his elbow and led Lída to the center of the stairwell. He paused before starting to climb, wanting as many people as possible to see him with her. She didn't mind being shown off.

"Isn't it beautiful?" Lída sighed with genuine emotion as they entered the Great Ballroom.

Felix couldn't deny her that. Not only was the Great Ballroom great, but possibly the most elaborate space he'd ever laid eyes on. It had a thirty-foot ceiling ornamented with stringcourse moldings of leaves and flowers, and a colossal hearth of gold and alabaster that raged at the far end of the corridor. Giant, mirrored French doors – arched like the windows – opened onto a balcony at the other end. As if none of this were enough, Goebbels had the room decorated in Sweetbrier roses, weaving the wild, pink flowers into every chair-back, chandelier, and candelabra. The strong smell of the rose permeated the room and devoured the French perfumes that would've lingered otherwise.

Limping in from the balcony, fresh from a breath of air, was Joseph Goebbels.

He wore no mask and an oxblood suit with a chamois silk ascot dotted with tiny flecks of apricot. He clashed with the roses but was a stunning contrast to the gold and egg-shell complexion of the room.

Lída dropped Felix's elbow and walked over to her lover in long, graceful strides as if she were dancing. He remained still. A small band set up near the balcony played a birthday polka, and Lída put her hand to her mouth and motioned to say, "No, no, please stop," and then gave it to Goebbels to be kissed – kneeling as if she were greeting royalty.

Unable to dance, Goebbels had hired professionals to swing his sweetheart around the room, as he clapped and made everyone pretend to be in her thrall. After a few laps, Lída was danced back to the man she expected to marry, and he raised his glass to make a speech. The chatter in the ballroom stopped as quickly as a radio dial could be turned.

"Thank you for joining me here today to celebrate, among many things, the birthday of mine and my wife's favorite actress and friend, Lída Baarová." The guests – long used to going along – clapped and cheered.

"My wife is very sorry to miss this event," he continued. "But as always, she's at home with our children, where she prefers to be." He waited again for the inevitable applause. Lída, ever the actress, stood smiling at his side, enduring his references to his family.

"Birthdays are very nice, as we all know, and we're here tonight to celebrate another birthday, as well. It is the birthday of this great city, Kutna Hora, which was born on this day in 1144, when a sizeable assemblage of Germans settled here."

Never missing an opportunity to promote his version of events, Goebbels, for Germany, took credit for all of the good fortune that had befallen Kutna Hora, exaggerating the importance of the German laborers who'd worked in the silver mines. Even guests who weren't ignorant of the facts clapped until their hands stung. Felix, for his part also clapped, but summoned no pretend enthusiasm. The security guard with the crystal-blue eyes looked on as Felix's limp hands came together.

"And happy birthday, Fraulein Baarová. Let us hope that you will be able to delight us on the screen for many years to come. Now please – everyone – dance, eat, drink, and enjoy the finest Deutschland has to offer."

The references to "hope" and "being able" weren't lost on Lída. She and Goebbels talked through tight-lipped smiles as she escorted him to a large, high-backed chair where he could survey the party. Whatever explanation he'd given her worked, because before long, she was chatting away with her guests again, sitting at his side and showcasing the bracelet he'd given her as if it were an engagement ring.

Felix watched the two of them hold court, sorting through the worthy and unworthy as if they were picking teams for a primary school soccer game. Josef Goebbels sat or stood still during the sorting, disguising his clubfoot by making people come to him. And the people who came were exhilarated in his presence, staring at him with the vacuous joy of a beauty contestant. Goebbels could take a dry lecture about the ravages of fire ants in Central Africa and transform it into an allegory about the Thousand-year Reich without pausing to take a breath. His nervous German audience drank in his certainty – anything to keep at bay the unthinkable realization that Germany might not win the war.

At the far end of the room, standing next to the hearth, was Svoboda. Felix had been scanning the ballroom for him since he and Lída made their entrance. He waded through the crowd, elbowing gently, but by the time he got to the hearth, Svoboda was gone. Standing in his place, with his prominent pink scar complimenting the Sweetbrier roses and his gold tooth matching the Baroque accoutrements, was the German officer who'd chased him through Prague

and stared him down at the Art Nouveau Café. His mannequin stillness was upset by the slight tremble of his eyeballs
behind his orange mask.

"Ach!" an older gentleman groaned, dropping his
pillbox and scattering tiny pearls in every direction. Felix
crouched to the floor, ducking the German officer's gaze,
and picked up every little pill that landed on the embroi-
dered rug, moving through the other guests as if they were
rows of corn.

"*Danke, danke,*" the gentleman kept repeating.

"*Bitte, bitte,*" Felix repeated back, as he followed the trail
of pills as far away from the hearth as they could lead him.

By the time he stood up and was able to look back, the
German officer, like Svoboda before him, had gone.

"Ladies and Gentlemen, may I have your attention,
please?" Goebbels' voice sent a startled hiccup through
Felix's body. He watched him stand, his arms outstretched
as if he were going to embrace a friend. "I think it's time I
let you in on a little secret."

Lída's ears perked up, and she displayed a look of naked
hope that made a fool of her.

"In classical times, it was customary to give the gift of
likeness on special occasions such as this one."

Felix started backing up through the crowd. A security
agent rolled the bust Svoboda had carved to the center of
the mock stage area where Goebbels and Lída sat like King
and Queen. It was covered by a white sheet and looked like
a tall child dressed as a ghost. Cameras flashed around the
concealed sculpture.

"Lída, as a present from myself and my wife, and from
the Reich and your many fans, I would like to present to you
this likeness as a symbol of our appreciation of your great
talent and beauty."

Goebbels tore the sheet off the bust to reveal a flattering likeness of himself – not his daughter Hilde, or Lída for that matter. A ripple of gasps circled through the Great Ballroom and Lída forced a look of gratitude over her face. Not missing a beat, she began clapping with a manic exuberance that spread throughout the party.

"He thinks he's John the Baptist to Hitler's Christ," Svoboda whispered, as he came up behind Felix. "I suppose in that case, the gift of his head is appropriate."

"Where the hell have you been?" Felix continued clapping as the bust of Goebbels was wheeled across the stage to its final resting place between the minister and his mistress.

"I think it's one of my finest, though not my most realistic. It makes the rat look like a lion." Masterfully, Svoboda had cut Goebbels cheekbones and strengthened his jaw without actually changing his features.

"We have to get out of here."

"We just got here."

"That German – the one who chased me the night of the fire – he's here again."

Svoboda took two additional glasses of champagne from a passing waiter and handed one to Felix.

"If he meant to harm you, you'd have a bullet in your head." Svoboda sipped his champagne and widened his eyes to mimic Felix's expression. "There's some information in your left breast pocket," he said.

Felix took a deep breath, feeling the crinkling of paper over his heart. He had the good sense to stop his hand from reaching inside his jacket, and instead tugged at its bottom flaps as if he were straightening his appearance. He hated himself for being such an amateur. "What is it?"

"Italian identity documents for you, among other things. A disguise awaits you at the latrine."

Felix squinted at Svoboda.

"Take one more walk around the ballroom and head down the way we came, telling the guards that you're feeling ill. I'll meet you at the latrine in twenty minutes."

"So soon? What about the note and the blackmail?"

Svoboda bit down and gripped Felix's arm.

"It's been taken care of. Your presence has been noted, you've walked the party with Lída – what more do you want?"

A great deal more, Felix wanted to say. He took a few steps into the crowd before turning back, but Svoboda had already disappeared back into the party. Avoiding eye contact with the other guests, Felix continued his lap around the room. Near the balcony, he focused on a large, wet pair of red lips that parted to reveal a mouthful of crooked teeth. His eyes met hers reflexively, and she turned away, offering a drink to a man in a German army uniform.

It was Svoboda's model – from her too short bangs, to her ample bottom and bird-like feet – the waitress from the Art Nouveau Café. He brushed by her, tapping her back with his elbow to touch her – a friend and helper.

He walked out onto the open balcony wanting to get a look at the place from where Svoboda, in ten minutes time, would be making his escape. It was a long drop for the sculptor's already weak knees to absorb, a good deal longer than Svoboda's plans had told. He wondered if the sculptor had been out on the balcony to assess the situation, and if he'd come up with an alternate plan. It was comforting to think that Svoboda, always so in control, would prevail – killing Goebbels and escaping to England to watch the remainder of the war play out with his government in exile.

But Felix knew in his heart that Svoboda had done no such thing. He sorted through his memories and wondered when he realized that this was a suicide mission for the leader of the Prague Underground. Was it when he first saw Goebbels at the Art Nouveau Café? No, it was sooner than that. It was watching Svoboda twirl his walking stick on the way to the Café. He walked and twirled as if a burden had been lifted; the burden of life and death over others, the burden of hope and defeat. He was ready to die in order to rid the world of Hitler's publicist, and deal Germany the kind of blow that he had felt on the night Hitler invaded Prague.

Felix wondered if Dasa knew. Dasa and Magdalena should already be in Slovakia, getting ready to flee into Austria then Italy then Greece then Morocco then London on documents impossible for an ordinary Czech to obtain. Merillini would be with them and they would be waiting for word that wouldn't come and have to leave by midnight, ducking through the Austrian countryside. Yes, Felix thought. Dasa had to have known – even if it was unspoken between her and her husband.

Felix walked back into the party and scanned the floor for the long mane of glossy, black hair and pair of red lips. She was easy to spot, even when bending down to offer a seated guest a thin slice of salami speared to a hard-boiled quail's egg. He didn't stop when he walked by her, but touched her back again for luck. She didn't even notice the drum of his fingers as they caressed her hipbone.

"Felix, is that you?"

Gustav Galinsky, a flashy, old Slav, who owned three posh supper clubs, pointed both his cigar and his enormous belly in Felix's face. Even in a large, Harlequin mask, Gustav was unmistakable.

"Gustav, what are you doing here?"

"Me? You know me, I go to any party – but you – since when do you hob-nob with these good people?"

"Lída is a friend."

"A friend, huh?" Gustav bent over, leaning into Felix's ear. "Lída doesn't have any friends."

"Do you?"

"Ha-ha! That's a good question."

Gustav blew a smoke ring into the air above his head and then stood under it, giving himself a halo.

"St. Gustav?"

"I am a saint for showing up for Lída – and so are you. None of her other old friends are here. Convenient that the party was out of Prague, otherwise it wouldn't be so easy to decline."

Felix looked different from the last time Gustav had seen him - at a game sometime last year or the year before that. It was his expression that had changed rather than his features. He'd become serious.

"Of course, I wouldn't miss this for the world," Gustav continued, his eyes twinkling as he smacked his lips. "I was about to pay homage to the ever-expectant Frau Goebbels. Would you like to join me?"

Felix ran his hand over his breast pocket, where his new documents lay. "I would."

Justus Svoboda may have come to Kutna Hora with his own special plans, but so had Felix. A plan, however vague, that began with Ivo Krev – on the night the boy-faced thug sat in his father's club chair summoning up the nerve to kill. Svoboda could take care of Goebbels, but it was Felix who would take care of Ivo Krev – and he knew Krev couldn't be too far away.

"After you," Felix said.

There was a waiting, fawning group of party guests that swarmed as close to Goebbels and Lída as the minister's bodyguards would let them. Gustav, with his giant proportions, was able to muscle through, waving and calling Lída's name, while the others, having tried a more subtle approach, glared at him for his insolence. Angry whispers hissed amongst the guests when Lída waved Gustav in past the guards and photographers.

"Halt!" The gatekeeper bodyguard pressed his hand flat to Felix's chest, stopping him from following Gustav into the inner circle, but Lída, who was watching out for any friendly face by this time in the evening, jumped out of her chair and scolded him.

"Felix! Felix! I thought I'd lost you." There was a desperate tone in her voice, mixed in with a few too many cocktails. "Isn't it a wonderful party? It is a wonderful party, right? Everybody's having a good time."

Felix smiled and told her 'yes' while he looked casually for Svoboda.

"It's all so marvelous. Marvelous!" She sat down again, forcing giggles between nervous pauses. She looked over to Goebbels, whose back was turned as he sat immersed in conversation with a Sudeten factory owner and a mediocre German composer heavily promoted by the Reich.

"He's good to me," she said. "No one's ever been so good to me. Did you see my bust? It's for me. It's his head."

"Svoboda did a beautiful job."

"Ah, Svoboda." Gustav chimed in. "I should've recognized."

"Have you seen him?"

"Who?" Lída asked.

"Svoboda. The man who sculpted your birthday present."

"Oh, no. No. I don't think he's here."

"I saw him a few minutes ago."

Lída stood up again and waved at a handsome, older woman with a tight, blonde bun.

"Olga!" Lída beckoned her and mouthed, "Come over" and "Good to see you," as Olga smiled and waved effusively, but didn't come.

"She's a Countess from Bremerhaven."

"I love Bremerhaven," Gustav exclaimed. He bent to pick at a tray of smoked trout.

"Svoboda had mentioned wanting to talk to you, to congratulate you personally. He's a great fan of your films."

"A fan?" Lída's eyes stopped wandering the party.

"Perhaps one of your people could watch out for him. He was so looking forward to meeting you again."

"That's right; we met once, didn't we? With you and Josef in Prague. And he's a fan?"

"Right. In Obecní Dům at the Art Nouveau Café."

"Obecní Dům. They had a party there for me after I returned from making *Barcarole*. That was lovely."

"I remember."

"I was twenty-two." Lída Baarová slumped into her chair and nuzzled her forehead in her palm.

"Lída, are you alright?"

Lída moved her head back and forth with her palm stuck to it like a hat. "Yes," she whispered. "It must be the champagne." When she looked up, she smiled brightly and tossed her hair, dabbing her fingers at the corners of her eyes. "I don't know what's wrong with me."

Felix removed a handkerchief from his trouser pocket and handed it to Lída. Her smile was grateful and sweet, like the smile of the young Lída Felix had encountered years earlier.

"Oh, hello! You there!" Lída spotted someone and stood up, waving the handkerchief in the air. "Mr. Svoboda, is that you?"

Felix spun around to see Svoboda standing in the crowd of fawners, waiting in line to request entry into the inner circle. If he was surprised or disappointed to see Felix, he didn't show it. He smiled and held a finger up as he was ushered to Lída's side by the guard, kissing her on both cheeks and looking Felix long in the eyes before giving his arm a warm squeeze.

"I see you decided to stay for the fireworks," he said.

"We can't possibly do fireworks. Air raids and all," Lída explained.

"Lovely to see you again, Miss Baarová."

"We were just talking about your work," Felix said.

"I love my bust." Lída lit up a cigarette and blew the smoke down on Josef Goebbels's sculpted, white head.

"I'm so glad. I had to create it from a photograph, and wasn't sure if I got the proportions right."

Lída studied the triumphant expression on the alabaster face. "I wish he'd do his hair more like that."

Lída looked over to Goebbels, who was now lecturing the Sudetan, the composer, Gustav, and a woman wearing too much eye shadow about the inferior nature of the Slavic race. His eyes, normally sad and a little bit hollow, were wide with outrage as he punctuated his tirade with the words, "Revenge, our virtue; hatred, our duty!" and then sat back in his chair with the satisfaction that he'd coined yet another Reich slogan.

It was a grotesque display of his gifts as an orator, and his audience stood in awe. Even the ever-cynical Gustav Galinsky took a step backwards, forgetting to breathe, until Goebbels broke the spell with a call for another round of champagne.

"Josef, don't you see who's here?" Lída, immune to his outbursts, reintroduced Felix and Svoboda, gushing over the artist and the bust that watched them from mid-chest height like a German Napoleon.

Goebbels opened his mouth wide, displaying both upper and lower teeth. "I admit, Herr Svoboda, that while you came highly recommended, I wasn't sure a Czech artist could capture the aura of a German."

Svoboda chuckled and bowed his head to accept the compliment. "Perhaps my mother's German ancestors sang into my ear as I worked."

Goebbels cocked his head and touched his index finger to his thin bottom lip. "And what, I'm curious, did they sing?"

Svoboda caressed the sculpted head of Josef Goebbels, and then picked it up, lifting the mouth to his ear. Those in the immediate vicinity gasped, and Goebbels' open expression fell away.

"They sang *I Once Had a Comrade.*"

Svoboda hummed a few bars and Goebbels' grimace softened into sentimental rhapsody. It was a song the German propaganda Minister had used an untold number of times to rally the German people in the years leading up to the war.

The sculptor looked briefly at Felix before smashing Goebbels' faux alabaster head to the floor. The shards, big and broken into triangles, revealed a handgun – a CZ 27 – that Svoboda had encased inside Goebbels' visage.

"No!" Lída howled, but neither Goebbels, nor his bodyguards had the chance to change their bearings before Svoboda swept down, scooped up the gun, and aimed it not three inches from the minister's face and pulled the trigger.

Lída hit the ground and fainted as the CZ 27 popped, but didn't fire. There were two seconds of absolute stillness and quiet until Josef Goebbels wheezed, wetting his trousers, and the security agent with the crystal-blue eyes reached into his tuxedo jacket. Felix broke his champagne glass against Lída's chair and slashed at the agent with a hard flick from his wrist – the way he used to cut down vines that overgrew on his parent's cottage. It hadn't been his intention to slit the man's throat, but he did – decimating his jugular vein. Two other bodyguards moved in on him, and Felix grabbed the bleeding agent and spun him around to shield himself. The man died instantly with the first shot to the heart and then absorbed five more bullets to the torso and groin.

Felix took the dead agent's gun, pointed it at one of the body guards and shot him in the neck, before shooting into the chandelier above them and sending a spray of shattered glass over the circle of party guests. The remaining body-guard dropped his pistol and palmed his eyes.

"Schneider!" Goebbels bawled.

The Propaganda Minister fell and tried to crawl away, but Svoboda hit him with the butt of the pistol, gripping him from behind by his shirt collar, and firing an unintended shot into the floor next to him. This time the gun went off and the Minister screamed while Svoboda took aim at the back of his head, execution style.

Svoboda wished Hitler could see this, and hoped Dasa would find another husband. His finger was squeezing the trigger as two shots rang from outside the inner circle, the first piercing Svoboda's upper back and the second the base of his skull. His gun slipped as it fired, missing Goebbels' head by a centimeter, and Svoboda slumped down on top of the minister.

Lída Baarová shrieked from behind her chair.

"He's dead! The Minister!" yelled Gustav Galinsky, who couldn't help but grin. Goebbels, however, was every bit alive. He was unhurt, unconscious, and covered in Justus Svoboda's blood and brain matter.

Felix whipped his head around to the origin of the shots and caught sight of Ivo Krev, who had darted in from the buffet table. He was in the same ill-fitting suit he'd worn at the Art Nouveau Café and his lip was bleeding. Krev had bitten it hard as he shot the leader of the Prague Underground, and bits of lamb sausage now flurried out of his mouth as he spit blood to the floor. He wasn't sweating, but was flushed red like a boy fresh out of Sokol.

Felix seized a second handgun from the bodyguard he'd shot and took aim at Krev, pointing the muzzle at his chest. He knew the head was a more definitive shot, but Felix hadn't hunted since his boyhood and needed a bigger target. His finger was pinching the trigger as a woman with a yellow bouffant hairdo fell backwards on top of him, two bullets having ravaged her face. The shots hadn't come from Krev, or from the security detail, and Felix stooped behind the dead woman to get a good look into the crowd.

The shooter was easy to spot. She stood high on the arms of a chair near the balcony, still holding her gun out from her ample bosom and puckering her thick, red-painted lips into what looked like a kiss as she took aim again – this time at Felix. The shot whizzed past his ear and Felix crouched, scrambling to the balcony. He could hear the soft thunder of elegant men's shoes as security agents ran up the stairs to the Great Ballroom. Felix rose to his feet, running hunched through the terrified crowd as guest after guest jumped to the floor and the China-haired assassin continued to fire.

He made it to the balcony doors and ducked behind the outer wall. Felix put one of his guns into his jacket pocket and turned back to the party, steadying the other gun and unloading it on the woman.

"Andrea." He remembered her name as he watched her fall from the chair with a hole in her forehead, and sprawl on the floor like an overstuffed rag-doll.

Felix fired a few more shots into the ballroom and sprinted to the edge of the balcony. There, he jumped from the rail, down to the next rooftop as Svoboda had planned to do. He was an arm's length from the roof's edge when he was sprayed with shots from the balcony. A bullet from Krev's gun pierced his calf as he grabbed the rope, sliding down and burning the palms of his hands. Seconds later, he landed on a grassy courtyard four stories below, his legs shaking so hard they could hardly support him.

His calf burned, but the bullet had penetrated muscle and not bone, so Felix could steel himself and shamble to the big, black mouth of a door that led to the street. Silence and darkness awaited him there. Felix wobbled, breathing hard, and tried to concentrate on the night air, still and tainted only by a light breeze from the North. For a moment, the only evidence that the night hadn't been a bad dream was the warm blood that flowed down Felix's leg, and the ripped skin of his hands.

The Bone Church was a seventy-yard dash from where he was standing, and he would have to run another mile or so beyond it to reach the latrine on the farmer's property. He thought about Ivo Krev, who had once again come to the aid of his employer – this time with a steady hand and without pissing himself.

Two valets, armed and on the lookout for Svoboda's accomplice, fired several rounds at Felix when they spotted him crossing the square. Felix shot one of them – he couldn't tell which – and the man fell. More rounds followed as Goebbels' security forces spilled out of Lída's party house. Orders were shouted, answered by loud, curt, "*javols.*"

"Is she one of your people?" Felix remembered asking Svoboda at the Art Nouveau Café.

"Not at all," he'd said, and Svoboda had been telling the truth. The girl with the meaty breasts who worked as a waitress and artist's model moonlighted as a Nazi agent – or was it the other way around? He wondered who had been shadowing who, but he didn't have time to deconstruct all of his mistakes and misinterpretations. He untied his bow tie, then knotted it tightly above the wound in his calf. Tucking his second gun into the waist of his trousers, Felix ran as fast as he could to the Bone Church.

CHAPTER TWENTY-SIX
SAME DAY

Felix charged into the Bone Church. He could've taken his chances out in the fields, but at least this way, he figured, he wouldn't be endangering the farmer who'd been bold enough to build a perch for him in his latrine. He owed that much to the Prague Underground after having helped orchestrate such an utter catastrophe.

The bronze church doors were heavy and medieval, and Felix closed them, able to latch the top lock, but not the more substantial one at the floor. A few good pushes by strong men would break the doors open like nutshells. He darted down the stairs into the nave, but even in his frenzy couldn't avoid being distracted by what he saw. Felix had heard descriptions of the Bone Church's eerie magnificence, but the sight of a pulpit of skulls, vertebrae, and femurs surrounded by pews constructed largely of what had once been arms and legs was enough to make any civilized person rethink the meaning of life after death.

Nearly every part of the interior gleamed like the new teeth of an infant. Bones from some 30,000 dead Christians lay configured into pyramids, light fixtures, chandeliers, pinnacles, coats of arms, an altar, and a monstrous hydra of ribs and skulls that sat atop an intact spinal column. He remembered Svoboda had stood in this very place not quite a full day earlier making his peace with God.

The doors to the church thrust open again and an eruption of gunfire from eight security agents shattered a row of femurs behind him, sending bone chips flying as he dove behind the altar. He felt the impact of another bullet as it penetrated his bad shoulder, and then another that hit him mid-torso, breaking a rib upon entry. Felix pushed himself up, his back against the base of the altar. He wrapped his arms around his ribcage. He knew he should try to tend to his bleeding, but the agony in his shoulder and his inability to take a deep breath made even small movements a struggle.

"I got him!" a rookie German guard cried out. An expert marksman, he'd been taken out of combat after only two weeks to serve as an elite bodyguard for German High Command. His comrades had seen his abilities first hand and had no reason to doubt him. They started to move in on Felix, but were stopped by a loud whistle from their commander – a man named Pfef. The tall, chiseled man, hairless after a youthful illness, signaled his men to ready their firearms. "Dying men always want company."

"Come show me your *herrenvolk* faces," Felix hollered, emphasizing the German word for master race. Bracing himself, he raised one of his guns above the altar and shot blindly in what he hoped was the direction of the Germans. They returned fire, spewing bone into the air like wood chips until their commander shouted for them to stop.

Three Nazi security agents and two guards remained hunched in the pews, silent, as another three of their comrades lay dead with gunshot wounds to the head. It was uncanny that the wounded man could've shot with such precision from behind the altar and Pfef wondered what elite force he could've come from. Perhaps he was American. As a scout earlier in the war, he'd watched the Americans out on the battlefield. They were always so maddeningly optimistic and he imagined the man behind the altar grinning like an idiot throughout his ordeal – even as he bled.

The commander grunted and raised his arm to launch another round of gun fire, and his men unloaded their weapons on the altar. The rookie aimed at the strings that supported a giant bone crucifix affixed with a full human skeleton as Christ. First one string was sliced, and then the other, sending the thing crashing down onto Felix. The crucifix broke his wounded arm, sending his gun sliding across the shiny floor.

Felix propped himself up with his good arm the best he could and removed his second gun from his coat pocket. The security agents pitter-pattered like tap dancers as they secured closer positions. They urged Felix to give himself up. Another barrage of gunfire sent more bone particles into the air, shooting the protruding feet off the skeleton depicting Christ.

At the end of that round, one more security agent lay dead in his pew and another next to him injured. He clutched his bleeding head where a bullet had grazed him, slicing off the top of his ear and leaving a straight line of a lesion that stretched to his brow.

The commander hissed at him to stop whimpering, and turned to his deputy. "We have a mouse in the kitchen."

The deputy nodded, slinking further into his pew and scanning the church for the sniper that had killed four of his comrades. Maybe there was more than one. There could be an entire unit surrounding the building by now, ready to storm this ossuary and do away with them, leaving them to die with the poor slugs who were entombed here as decorations. A short crack, like a rock falling into a glass, made him jump. He turned and pointed his gun at a pyramid of bones behind the lectern.

"There!" the deputy cried. The pyramid was showered with bullets by the four remaining agents until the hipbones ornamenting its exterior were broken into little bits. The commander grinned when he saw his men were left standing after the onslaught.

"I think we found our mouse," he gloated. Rubbing his bald brow, he signaled his deputy and rookie agent to surround the pyramid.

The young rookie hadn't even reached its base when he was felled by a shot to the back of his head, getting knocked face-first to the stone floor and losing his two front teeth. The deputy hit the floor in defense, but received his shot no more than a second later.

Commander Pfef ran and crouched behind the podium again. He knew now that the shots hadn't been coming from the pyramid at all, but higher above. He'd fallen for the oldest trick in the book – allowing himself and his men to get lured from their cover. Pfef swore to fuck the mother of this sniper as another shot fired, finishing off the bleeding agent, who'd tried to crawl, unwisely, to the transept.

"You hear me?" he growled. "I'm going to fuck your mother!"

Pfef could see he was in a bad position. The shots were coming from the interior balcony, which spanned the length of the church entrance and afforded the sniper mobility

and a plum aerial view. There was another officer outside
guarding the exit, but he couldn't chance calling him in lest
the assassins make a run for it. If they escaped, he would be
shot the next morning for his incompetence.

Right there, Commander Pfef made a pact with himself
that he would die by his own hand if he failed tonight. At
least his wife could hold her head high that way. She could
wear her widow's veil with dignity and not have to suffer
through the petty snubs and passive insults hailed at her by
other military wives. He rose, firing into the balcony and
ran to the transept, squatting under a piscina basin, which
drained waters used for ceremonial washing. Pfef splashed
his face and neck with the cool, holy waters, taking a few
gulps to wet his dry throat.

"Clever bastards," he muttered. Maybe the assassins
were British. He hated the British. Always sneaking around.

Pfef heard the sniper jump from the balcony, landing on
his feet and scurrying into a pew. He took a compact out of
his breast pocket and opened it, pulling a thin, folding bar
out of its side and elongating it into a rod. There was a small,
framed mirror inside the compact and he held it out with
the attached bar, getting a decent look into the main area of
the church. Pfef could see nothing in the aisles or the pews
except for the bodies of his men, until he held it up higher
and angled it, catching a look at the top of the sniper's head.

Seizing what could be his only chance; Pfef slipped off
his shoes and ran noiselessly out of the transept to the row
where the sniper was waiting.

"Mein Gott," he stammered, when he saw him. Pfef hesitated for a moment he would regret, allowing the sniper
to point his gun. The two men fired almost simultaneously,
Commander Pfef's belly hitting the floor only a fraction of a
second after the sniper's back.

"Pfef," the sniper whispered, trying to remain focused. He was losing blood and his body would go into shock soon, causing him to lose track of time, sequence, and even basic facts – his name, age, and hometown. He couldn't afford to forget what he was doing.

Soothed by the cool comfort of the church tiles, the sniper took a few breaths and stood up, steadying himself against the pew. He could see the inert body of Hansel Pfef, his commander, lying in the aisle, and put his hand over his own chest, applying pressure to his gushing wound. One step at a time, he made it to the altar, kneeling behind it next to Felix, and pushing the crucifix off and away from the injured man's body.

"We have to get out of here," he said.

The sniper coughed up a dribble of blood, wiping his mouth with the edge of his sleeve. He reached into his pocket for a key ring, pulling it out slowly as if he barely had the strength to hold it. He then lifted his buttocks up off his heels, sat down next to Felix, and died – his eyes wide open and his mouth poised to tell Felix once more that time was of the essence. Blood drained from the man's face and lips, leaving color only in his gold tooth and the pink, triangular scar that now seemed to glow like a beacon on his forehead. His hand fell to his side and with it, his keys, jingling as they hit the marble altar base.

Felix lifted his gun, shaking with cold sweats, and pointed it at the dead German's head.

"I'll blow your face off," he choked, vomiting some of the champagne he'd drunk onto his lapel. He was trying to focus on the blurry figure next to him, but his pain and nausea were overwhelming. Instead, he focused on his breath. The raspy in and out flow of air helped to quell his unsettled stomach, and with the reprieve of his nausea, his hearing became more acute. He heard himself swallow and picked up a low gurgle that he recognized as coming from the dead German. He heard himself exhale through his nose and his head make a swooshing sound as it slid further down the altar before thumping to the floor.

There, lying flat on his back, he could hear his lungs expanding and contracting, and his blood moving through his body – some of it leaking out of him and some of it pumping back into his heart.

Felix's pain began to lift and he thought with increasing clarity as his body stopped fighting its injuries, submitting to a leisurely march towards death. His vision became sharp and every color he saw intensified, as if it were burning. He felt stronger now; a buoyant strength that made him feel like he was swimming in warm saltwater.

Felix sat up and looked into the dead German's face and then out into the church to survey the carnage. His joints felt pliable, as if he was a boy again and just out of 5:00 a.m. practice. He stood up and tested his legs, no longer bothered by the hole in his calf, and found he could bend, pivot, and turn, despite the bullets in his shoulder and side. His broken arm was swollen and bent out of joint, but didn't cause him any trouble. He let it hang beside him like a loyal companion.

"It was you all along," he said, putting his hand on the German's head. Felix understood now and recalled the ease with which he and Srut had gotten away from the SS on the night of the fire. He smiled down at the man with the pink scar, wishing he could thank him. The German no longer looked as if he had something to say and was about to say it, but rather that he'd had something to say, but forgot it. Felix closed the man's eyes, bent over, and picked his keys up off the floor, rubbing them between his fingers like worry beads. He was about to return the keys to the man's pocket, but he noticed a small charm – a medal of St. Michael, the Archangel – dangling from the chain that held the keys together. Michael, the Receiver of Souls, was depicted as sheathing his sword just as he had appeared to Pope Gregory the Great above Hadrian's mausoleum during the plague in Rome.

Felix looked up to see Michael standing opposite him at the front of the altar. His skin was smooth and shiny – like it was wet – and his brown eyes knew Felix. The angel was holding out his hand. He had no wings and no gold vestments, but floated like a common spirit in everyday clothes, the way God took the form of man as an ordinary carpenter and not a king.

"Should I come with you?" Felix asked, and Michael smiled. It was his father's smile – with the same weary sadness that used to cling to the corners of his mouth. Felix reached out to him, but the angel drifted down to the floor and became flesh. The Infant Jesus appeared cradled in his arms and he placed the Child naked onto the altar with the tenderness a father would show his newborn son. The Infant Christ stood up and held His hand in a gesture of peace before His flesh fell away, revealing His skeleton. The bones of the Infant then collapsed into a pyramid and Felix could hear Vera Ruza's breath again – still shallow and sickly like it was in the days before her death.

His eyes searched all over the church for Vera, but it was only her breath that had made the journey. Felix turned back to the Archangel and asked him for Magdalena's protection. If he was going to die here, then he wanted God to find her a safe place. Perhaps God would even allow him to watch over Magdalena as a guardian, a whisper of a ghost that followed her on her life's voyage.

But Michael the Archangel had other plans, and he began to convey them softly, with plain language. Felix listened to Michael's gentle voice and simple instructions. He nodded to the Archangel and offered his life – if it was to be spared – in exchange for Magdalena's.

A moment later, Michael the Archangel jerked backwards and fell to the floor, his arms and legs spread apart into the shape of an X.

In one, deafening rush, Felix felt his pain return. His legs were no longer able to support him and he collapsed, but didn't fall down to the floor. Instead, he was cradled under the arms and dragged from behind the altar.

"Don't die, you fool. Don't die!" Srut chanted as he pulled Felix past the hairless, dead body of Commander Pfef. Pfef had crawled to the altar to finish Felix off, and Srut had shot him. He would've left the man alone and let him wait for a doctor, if the crazy German hadn't decided that Felix's death was worth his life.

That was something Srut couldn't understand. It's not that he didn't hate – he hated all right. He hated Svoboda for his meddling and self-righteousness and for exposing his gypsy kin to the Germans. He hated the Germans and most Czechs for that matter, and he really hated his father, whoever that was. But none of this hatred would rouse him to waste his dying breath on trying to take one of them down. Had it been he who was injured and lying on the church floor, nothing could have made him get up and drag a gun to the altar to kill a man who was half dead anyway. He was probably delirious from his injuries – like Felix, who'd been holding his arms out to the German commander like a long-lost friend.

"I wish to hell you could walk," he told Felix. His heels kept catching on the cobblestones as Srut dragged him out of the back of the church. A set of keys fell out of Felix's hand, and Srut picked them up, drawn to a little metal that depicted an angel with a sword. The doors to the Bone Church shut, startling him, and he shoved the metal into his trouser pocket.

"Cursed place," Srut muttered.

He'd been tracking Felix since his trip to Roznov and had followed him and Svoboda to the Bone Church the night before. He cursed himself for not having clocked Felix over the head then and taken him away – letting the self-appointed savior of all Czechs do his own dirty work.

But Pepík would have none of it and Srut needed his help.

Pepík, absent his stupid receiver and instructions from On High, was utterly useless, in fact. But he was one of only two Czechs that Srut trusted – the other of course, lay bleeding to all hell in his arms. Pepík, with the right motivation, was an ally and willing to do all manner of things. All Srut had to do was keep pretending that he was on a mission for the Prague Underground and not coming to save his friend from himself. It was one of the few times Srut wished he'd learned to drive. Had he done so, he could've stolen a car and wouldn't have needed Pepík to get him from here to there.

"Mr. Felix!" Pepík exclaimed. He turned over the engine of his Skoda, his hands shaking and the top of his head sprouting sweat beads.

Srut laid Felix in the back seat of Pepík's car and tightened the tie around his calf. He took off his coat and wrapped the arms around Felix's chest to slow the bleeding.

"Where's the other commander?" Pepík asked.

He could never just go with the flow, and Srut was tired of it. "How the hell should I know?"

"I'm not going anywhere without him."

"You'll go wherever I tell you to go." Srut waved the German's Luger and tapped Pepík on the head with it.

A spray of gunfire shattered the rear passenger window and pockmarked the side of Pepík's car. Srut saw a gunman in bad Czech clothes – the kind worn by low-level clerks trying to look professional – standing at the rear of the church holding his firearm at shoulder level. A fair-haired youth with plump cheeks and a silky fuzz of hair on his upper lip, he looked no older than eighteen – a point underscored by the way his suit hung on his shoulders.

As Srut looked into Ivo Krev's eyes he could see the single-minded grit of a street waif. Srut had known his type before: sly and parasitic, lonely. The kind of boy you kept your distance from when you were working the street, but kept your eye on to learn a thing or two.

"Hit the pedal! Let's go!" Srut shouted.

Srut lurched forward as another chain of bullets from Krev whipped through the car. Pepík gasped as Srut's gushing head sagged onto his shoulder – the Luger falling from his chapped fingers into Pepík's lap. He slammed his heel into the gas pedal and the car took off with a piercing whine, careening off the pavement and into the barley fields.

Pepík, a receiver of messages for the Prague Underground, would be sending a message that night.

CHAPTER TWENTY-SEVEN
DOMAZLICE, CZECHOSLOVAKIA:
MARCH 22, 1956

It was quiet for a long time after the gun shots. Magdalena dared not move or make a sound until she heard the squeal of a tire and recognized the sputtering of the beer wagon's engine.

"Friend! Mr. Friend!"

Magdalena arched her back and kicked into the dark, pounding her heel against wood and metal. Her beer barrel was lying on its side now after having been bounced from the wagon as much as an hour before, nearly breaking her neck as it rolled. The air had been getting thin since then and felt humid. Magdalena felt queasiness creeping up on her and wished she had some violet chewing gum.

"Friend? Are you out there?"

Magdalena ripped off the felt material lining at her sides, exposing all sorts of prickly staples and mysterious holes that now caught her fingers and tore at her skin. She pounded against the sides of the barrel until dozens of splinters embedded into her palms. When she stopped, she wrapped her arms around her knees as if they were Ales and rocked back and forth, sinking her barrel deeper into the soft soil of wherever they were. *They,* she thought. Maybe it was just *her* now. *No, please no.*

Was it even daylight yet? What time had it been when Friend had come for her?

It must have been deep into the middle of the night when she'd heard the keys jingling outside of her cell because the dim light bulb that had hung in the corridor and glowed through the crack under her door had been extinguished. There was hardly a sound except for heavy snoring from the Bulgarian in the cell across from hers.

"Get your shoes," he'd whispered.

Friend led her away from the cell block to the loading dock, where it had been nearly empty except for the single, remaining guard in the office cage.

"Good evening, Comrade," the guard had said.

Friend had nodded and the guard had returned to his previous state of boredom, puckering his lips and breathing inward, as if he were sucking a milkshake through a straw. He was a poor whistler.

Holding open the back flap of a beer wagon, Friend had beckoned Magdalena inside. He told her to get into a barrel – they were heading for the border. At first, she'd told him to go to hell.

"Ales is waiting," he'd insisted, taking her hand – cool to the touch and smooth, like a woman's, except for a patch of psoriasis as large as a plum that lay in the middle of his palm.

What happened next?

The air in the barrel was so hollow it could hardly carry her voice. "Please! Someone! I can't breathe!" She shouted into nothingness. The air was becoming an invisible pair of hands around her throat.

Magdalena wondered if anyone could hear her at all on the outside and then remembered the tapping and the voice back at the loading dock.

"Magdalena?" It was a man's voice – barely audible through the beer barrel, or maybe he was just trying to keep his voice low. He'd seemed to have known her.

She'd pounded back three times with her fist, but nothing more had come of the exchange. Of course she had still been groggy from the ether then.

Ether. That bastard. She remembered now. No wonder she was so out of sorts.

She wouldn't get into the barrel without Ales – no matter what Friend's promises were. He smiled, as if understanding, reminding her he had a boy of his own. He'd then taken a small card from his breast pocket. It was a prayer card and featured a Baroque image of the Infant of Prague, standing on a marble pedestal, surrounded by the heavens.

"What is this supposed to mean?" she'd asked.

"It means your prayers have been granted."

And then he'd grabbed her and put his handkerchief over her mouth and nose, forcing her to breathe in the ether.

"Help me – Please – someone!"

Magdalena kicked and grasped at every part she could reach in the barrel, until her knuckle struck something that was about level with her neck.

She ran her hands over the thing. From what she could tell in the darkness, it was a tube of some sort with a hole in it. It was made of hard rubber. A cool waft of air came through the hole like breath, and Magdalena tried to put her mouth near it to fill her lungs. There wasn't enough to fill even her nostrils. Wiping her brow, and breathing in what air she had left, Magdalena eased down and began exploring behind her head, feeling for a handle, a lever, anything. Her fingers caught nothing but a hard nub the size of a small grape. Magdalena prodded the thing with her fingers, but they weren't strong enough to budge it. The nub seemed as firm as a rusted screw entombed in the hull of a boat.

Magdalena wanted to cry. After everything she'd been through, gasping for air in a beer barrel, abandoned somewhere, was no way to go. No enemy, only a slow, desperate fight for breath until she lost consciousness.

Ales appeared to her in the darkness and called to her. He was so real. It was as if his face was inches from hers and she could smell his sweet paprika skin and catch the aroma of fresh bread from his mouth.

"Don't go," she cried out to him, but his ruddy cheeks and fair, tussled hair faded away until he was only an outline – like a line drawing in a newspaper meant to depict a well-known politician.

Friend had promised her he was safe at an orphanage in Louny, having been moved from the rat-infested hole they'd been keeping him in. She now closed her eyes, trying to shut out the image of Ales alone in a cell with no cushion, no blanket and no view to the outside world. Only old, yellow bricks with scratches from former prisoners – initials, day markings, and the small symbols of hope or desperation.

I'm losing my mind, she thought. *Isn't that what happens with the denial of oxygen to the brain?*

Magdalena squeezed her fist around the rubber tube again, pulling it up and jamming it into the nub with all of her might. She pulled it back and thrust it over and over until her hands were aching and vibrating.

"Goddamn you, Friend!" she screamed, punching the nub behind her and kicking the bottom of the barrel, breaking her second toe. The pain of her toe could've been one last insult to her body were it not for the barrel top popping open, letting in the early light and morning air.

Magdalena slithered out onto the grass, gulping in the fresh farm air of Domažlice. She ran her fingers along the ground and watched a ladybug teeter along the edge of a blade of grass as she felt her head clear and her body come alive with a flood of oxygen. This might be heaven, she thought.

As the sweet high from the fresh air wore off and the blades of grass beneath her began to feel less and less like a comfortable bed, Magdalena started to move again. She lifted her head up and twisted her aching neck from side to side before pushing her chest up from the ground. Her air tube had been packed with dirt from the barrel rolling through the dense mud – it was no wonder she couldn't breathe in there. There were footprints all around her that looked to be from the same pair of men's shoes.

Something black caught her eye. It was a shoe –or more accurately – a foot with a shoe attached that was sticking out of the grass. And it wasn't black, but brown, with matching socks and a matching suit that she could see mosaic pieces of through the thick blades surrounding the man.

Magdalena got up onto her knees and crawled towards him, parting the dense grass – still fresh and springy – as she inched closer. She hoped to God it wasn't Friend, and couldn't remember what he'd been wearing earlier. It could've been brown.

She made her way past a deep, muddy row of tire tracks and around the trunk of a partially collapsed tree. That was when she saw the second man. Magdalena sat up on her heels and covered her mouth with both hands, stifling a shrill, involuntary scream. She'd seen dead bodies before, but his one – his eyes rolled all the way back into his head and his bright blue suit soaked in blood – appeared incongruent somehow, like a dead child.

She glanced over at the brown-suited man, fearing he'd suffered the same fate. He lay still, like the earth, but Magdalena kept watching him. She couldn't pull her eyes away. Minutes later – not many – his chest moved and his finger twitched. She heard him expel a shallow breath, like a sleeping dog. It was only then that she dared inch closer to look at his head.

His light chestnut hair was caked with blood, as was the side of his face. It was turned away from her. Magdalena felt a stinging sense of familiarity as she ran her eyes over the man's torso and legs, settling on the finger that had twitched moments before. It was a long, muscular finger, with a pronounced knuckle, and a flat, shiny scar the size of a pea that had once been a hard callus. She'd seen a callus like that before. Hockey players had them from the way they held their sticks.

Her breaths quivered and her throat closed in on them. Her hands began to tremble as she scooted closer to the man's hip. Magdalena rose up, kneeling, and bent over the man's face, turning it towards her.

"Oh, my God," she whispered. "Oh, my God."

Chapter Twenty-Eight
Vienna: Same Day

Krev knew it would've been faster to get to Vienna through Czechoslovakia, but he thought the whole thing reeked of over-confidence and opted for the long way. His head ached and he swallowed two more aspirin, washing them down with a piss-warm Limonada he'd bought at the train station in Passau. There, he'd installed his Gladstone bag in a brand-new locker, and waited for the number fifty-three.

"Passport, please," the attendant demanded. She took a good look at the document, studying Krev's features. He knew he looked pale and tired, but figured that worked for him rather than against. Passport photos were poor quality black and white – everyone looked sickly in them.

"You lose some weight recently, Herr Horst?" she asked him.

"You noticed," he said, smiling.

She handed the passport back to him.

Hans Liebermann had been closer to his weight, but his papers had become splattered with blood. It made much more sense to take the other identity, since Krev could cover his dyed black hair with a hat and do a quick, dry shave in the beer wagon's side mirror, shaping his goatee into a mustache. He'd tucked is own documents into Felix Andel's breast pocket in place of the ones he'd taken and drove over the border without a hitch.

"Mind the arm, please," Krev cautioned, not more than thirty seconds after he stepped off the train in the Vienna *bahnhof.* A short, stocky Italian had grabbed hold of his elbow and led him out and into the back seat of a white Mercedes-Benz limousine with a red leather bench. The fume of incense pervaded the car and fused with the smell of new glove leather.

"I was beginning to think we'd never meet." Krev extended is hand, but the courtesy wasn't returned.

Cardinal Merillini sat next to him, erect as a book spine, and ordered Primo to get them out of there.

"You bungled it," he said.

The Cardinal's voice sounded as old as he looked. The many times they'd spoken on the phone over the past year, the Czech intelligence officer had wondered if it was the Vatican phone lines that were so poor, or the phone at the State-issued flat Magdalena Melan and her son had abandoned in favor of their country shack. Clearly, what he thought had been static, was in fact, a voice box damaged from years of smoking and sermonizing. The Cardinal's face was in no better condition. It looked like a mask – pasty and dull. Even his fingers gaped out of the gold trim at his cuffs like brined sardines.

But the Cardinal didn't move like a man with one foot in the grave. He moved with the precision and ease of a healthy man of about forty, which meant that he was probably only sixty. Krev wondered why the man looked so prematurely old.

"Don't you have anything to say for yourself? I should drive you straight to the Czech Embassy and have Primo drag you inside."

Krev helped himself to some Grand Marnier from a small bar tucked into the side of the door. He drained his glass instantly, using his tongue to fish out the last driblets of the orange liqueur, then poured himself another.

"Cardinal, you couldn't be all upset over a former Nazi could you? The woman I didn't expect to leave behind, but she won't spend more than a year or two in prison. They'll be lenient if she tells them all about me – which she will."

Cardinal Merillini turned towards him, but made no overt contact with his eyes. He seemed to look through Krev, making the spy feel vaguely uncomfortable.

"You have to understand that I had no choice in the matter," Krev continued. "We had a bit of a mishap at the prison, and that Horst gentleman you sent was acting very strangely."

"Primo, take us to Czech Embassy," the Cardinal said. "On second thought, the Russian Embassy. They're so much more thorough when it comes to dealing with rubbish."

"Maybe the woman will be able to get over the border on her own somehow?" Krev offered. "I hope so. I left her with that Horst fellow and he seemed like a pretty clever type. Speaking for myself, it was a hell of a pain getting the Infant of Prague into free Europe."

The Cardinal didn't raise his voice, but let it hiss like steam. "I know all about what happened. That you saw our mission as your vehicle for defection."

Krev remained silent and let the Cardinal continue. If he let him say his piece, he would be easier to deal with later. People always wanted to be heard.

"Tell me," the Cardinal persisted. "Was there a reason you killed the German or was it for sport the way you murdered Father Duch in my bathtub?"

Krev shifted in his seat to face the Cardinal. He found the man's righteous indignation remarkable considering what he'd been willing to do for what was little more than a doll of the infant Jesus. Krev had first laid eyes on the Infant during the war, after Marek Andel had given him the key to a locker at the train station in Prague where he'd hidden it. He didn't see what was so special about it. The Infant of Prague stood about a foot and a half tall, dressed in fancy robes not unlike the Cardinal's. The thing was fussed over like a live infant and its clothes were changed for various church holy days, as if it couldn't bear to be seen in the same outfit twice.

"You're right," Krev said. "It worked very well for me that you could use my help both to free Mrs. Melan from her political situation and to smuggle the Infant into the West. If I were a man of your beliefs, I might think God intervened on my behalf."

The Cardinal looked through him again. "You seem to have a knack for making yourself indispensable, Mr. Krev – when it suits you. I suspect Mrs. Melan's recent political situation would never have so deteriorated without your assistance."

"But isn't Mrs. Melan a detail?" Krev said. "The real issue seems to be one of accounting. Wasn't it, after all, your friend Duch who discovered that you were squirreling money away from those private masses you like to give? The ones with all those wealthy men with terrible problems."

The Cardinal's eyes widened and a series of cross-hatching lines appeared on his forehead.

"Did you expect me to watch my nest egg disappear when Pius the Twelfth ships you off to some pitiable, pre-industrial country like he did last time you displeased him? It's funny, your people tolerate all sorts of things within the organization, but theft – or pardon me, a 'redirection of funds for an eminently worthy cause' – is not one of them."

Krev leaned back against the red leather and produced the prayer card of the Infant of Prague from his breast. He held it before the Cardinal, pinching the card between his fingers.

"You wanted me to bring you the Infant of Prague," he said. "And I wanted you to pay me for it so I could get on with my new life. We remain with that one mission in common."

"Where is it?"

"Safe and accessible."

The car stopped in front of the Russian Embassy, but the Cardinal gave Primo no further orders. He detested Krev, but had been dealing with people of his ilk for years, using them to hunt down so many of the religious artifacts that had been pilfered during the war and the subsequent Soviet spread. It was his ability to obtain what was thought to be lost or unobtainable – the bloodied tunic of a martyr, a black Madonna, the jeweled crucifix of Constantine – that had brought him back from his exile in Argentina and pro-pelled him into the upper ranks of the Church. He'd waited a long time for the Infant of Prague – the crown jewel of his pursuits – and Ivo Krev, if he knew what was good for him, was going to deliver.

"How do I know you have it?"

Krev reached into his back pocket and pulled out a short stack of bowed pictures. Each shot showed the Infant of Prague from a different angle – side, face-on, back, standing, lying down. The figure wasn't encased in glass and appeared to be on an old sofa. The faded, striped fabric it laid on made the Infant – costumed in a bright, teal vestment and a large gold crown – look overdressed.

"I had to make a decision," Krev said, showing each photograph to the Cardinal. "It was either the woman or the Infant. I chose in the way that most pleases you, didn't I?"

The Cardinal ripped the photographs from Krev's grasp and held them up to the light. He certainly looked like the authentic Infant. He was even dressed in the same vestments He'd been wearing when Marek Andel hid Him from Josef Goebbels's greedy hands, replacing Him with one of Justus Svoboda's copies.

"Nothing about this pleases me," he said.

The Cardinal waved Primo on to circle the block, passing several mansions belonging to the Chinese, Egyptian, and British Embassies. He narrowed his eyes and ran his thumb along the embroidery of his sleeve.

"How, Mr. Krev, do you envision the transfer of the Holy Infant of Prague taking place?"

Krev knew it was a rhetorical question, but voiced his preference anyway.

"Cash was fine for the first $50,000, but now that I'm a refugee – so to speak – I don't want to be carrying so much responsibility. You can wire the rest of my money to a Swiss account I've set up, and I can have the Infant delivered to you after I retrieve it."

"Mr. Krev, you'll get half of the remainder of your payment today as a goodwill gesture, but don't for a moment think you're getting any more until I have the Holy Infant in my hands and have had Him authenticated."

The Czech agent shrugged.

VICTORIA DOUGHERTY

The Cardinal was surprised to find Krev so reasonable, but the prospect of a fortune in cash often did that to a man.

"Is the Infant here, in Vienna?"

"It's very safe. And available at a moment's notice."

"I'd like that moment to be tomorrow. First thing in the morning."

Primo appeared at the Cardinal's window with a cognac leather briefcase. He handed it to Krev, who promptly opened and inspected it. He flipped through the stacks of hundred-dollar bills, eyeballing the contents and testing the authenticity of random bills with a pocket light and monocle.

"It's never easy coming up with this kind of money, Mr. Krev."

Krev chuckled and put the briefcase under his arm.

"I would think in a largely cash organization, like yours, that's both unregulated and untaxed, coming up with just about any amount of money would be a snap."

The Cardinal opened a small flask of Grappa.

"Tomorrow, Mr. Krev."

"Tomorrow it is," Krev said. "But you needn't send your driver around."

Krev drew an Infant figurine from his pocket, dangling it before the Cardinal. The effigy was dressed in bright yellow vestments and Krev shook it by the Cardinal's ear, allowing him to hear the *ping* inside.

"What is this?" the Cardinal asked.

"It's the key to your future," Krev told him. "And to a locker in Passau where you'll find everything you've been looking for."

Krev opened the door and exited the limousine without looking back. Cardinal Merillini watched him disappear into the misty Vienna night.

"Primo, follow Mr. Krev to wherever it is he's going," he said. "I'd like my briefcase back, after all."

Chapter Twenty-Nine
Same Day

Felix woke up to a roaring pain in his right ear and dry, saliva-caked lips that stung. It was dark – early evening perhaps – but a lantern provided a tempered glow that helped his eyes adjust.

He was lying in a bed under several moth-eaten blankets, naked, and staring at a smoke-yellowed ceiling, peeling in most places. There was an unmistakable femininity to the room despite an iron-framed bed, a plain wooden night table, and a pair of army blankets substituting for curtains. Perhaps it was the prominent display of a clay ashtray, clearly sculpted by a child. The mattress creaked and he heard a deep exhale.

"Who's there?"

The heavy breather jerked awake, gasped, and then leaned in to whisper in his ear. It was a woman. Her hand – petal-skinned – touched his shoulder and squeezed it the way he imagined she might squeeze a peach at her grocer's.

"Is it really you?" Her whisper was faint and breathy, like a little girl's.

Felix ran his hand down the mattress and up onto the curve of her waist.

"We're not dead, are we?" he asked.

Felix started to laugh, but his head hurt too much. Tears stung his eyes and the room became a blur of geometric shapes and muted colors.

Magdalena put her forehead into the crook of his neck. He realized she was laughing, too.

"What, in God's name, were you doing by a gravel road in Domažlice – clothes full of stuffing, beaten to an inch of your life?"

Felix turned his head towards her slowly. It didn't seem like any time at all had passed between them. It was only when he began to study her that he saw the little differences. Her face was gaunt, but still beautiful, with only a couple of vertical lines between her brows, and two small commas at the corners of her mouth. She wore her hair in its natural state – curly and now sprouting a few silver strands at her widow's peak. Her lips appeared fuller – perhaps because of the hollowness of her cheeks. He realized that she wasn't merely thin, but had been hungry recently.

"I was looking for you," he said.

"I should say the same thing." Magdalena smoothed back his blood-stiff hair and kissed his cheekbone.

She sat up, reached over to her night table and lifted a plum brandy-soaked rag out of a chipped porcelain tea cup. Magdalena dabbed Felix's ear and skull with it.

"You're lucky to be alive," she said. "That man, the agent, must have wanted you out for a long time, or dead."

"Ivo Krev? Probably the latter," Felix told her.

The new, improved Krev, with better clothes and a better title.

"Where am I?"

"You're in Klobuky," Magdalena said. "About thirty kilometers from Prague."

Felix took a better look around and realized he was in a one-room cabin. With chipped windows and a roof that looked as if it were about to cave in, the cabin – or rather, hovel – was a place no one could survive in for very long, especially not through a bitter Czech winter.

Magdalena saw him staring at what had been her latest in a series of awful living quarters and felt embarrassed.

"Home, sweet home," she murmured.

The place was exactly the way Magdalena had left it on the day Ivo Krev had come back for her. Even the potato dumplings she'd bought at a local cafeteria sat on top of her counter feeding its remains to the maggots.

"We weren't here long," Magdalena said. She and Ales had found the cabin on a walk one weekend. They moved in without notifying the authorities – hoping, at least, for a small reprieve from the tyranny of spying neighbors. The rat-infested basement apartment they'd been living in before was no better – cold, damp, and blooming with the prospect of disease.

Magdalena felt like a wreck. Cold sweat ran down her neck and she started picking furiously at a bleeding hangnail on her thumb. Ales was still out there, as if in a void, and the Czech Secret Police was liable to come knocking at any time. She had no idea if anyone from the village had seen them arrive, but what worried her most was that all of this was some kind of trick played by the man Felix called Krev.

"Ales is at an orphanage in Louny," she said. "At least that's what that man Krev told me. He was supposed to pick him up yesterday." She glanced up at Felix before pretending to focus her attention on her hangnail again. "Ales is my son."

Felix removed a coil of hair from over Magdalena's eye. "I know about Ales. We're not going to leave without the boy."

Magdalena put her fingers to her lips. "You know?" Perhaps that's why he had come back to Czechoslovakia.

Felix nodded. "I'm so terribly sorry about his father."

Magdalena took her fingers from her lips and ran them along the edge of Felix's blanket. "Yes," she said. "So am I."

Felix smiled at her. He reached over to the bed table for the plum brandy, but the simple movement caused his head to pound. Magdalena took the cup in her hands and brought it to his lips.

"I have a friend here," Felix said.

"Friend," Magdalena groaned. "There are no friends left in this country."

Felix took a bigger sip of the plum brandy. It burned his throat and flooded him with a brief sense of well-being. "He's an *Indian*."

Magdalena shook her head.

"A true eccentric and a true friend – even if not a true Indian. But he got me out of Czechoslovakia the first time and I'm hoping he can perform the same miracle again."

Felix reached up and rubbed his hand across his cheek and mouth. He noticed his false mustache and peeled it off from corner to corner in one strip. Magdalena started to laugh, nervously at first, until her eyes filled with tears. She laid her cheek onto the warm skin of his chest.

"I thought you were dead," she whispered. She had heard rumors about him at the end of the war. Incredible stories. That he had taken over as the chief of the Prague

Underground. That he was fighting the Bolshevik invasion. It wasn't long after that Felix's name became something his former acquaintances would only whisper. And then something they stopped uttering altogether.

"I was dead," Felix told her.

He wondered, for a moment, whether he'd dreamed the last dozen years, and if he was waking up in 1944 after a strange delusion.

With the sun having set, it was starting to grow cool inside the cabin. Magdalena got up, lit another candle and retrieved a cream, wool jersey and a pair of brown, brushed cotton trousers from a cabinet, laying them next to Felix. They had been her husband Antonin's clothes – well made, good fabric – and she'd been saving them for Ales.

"Who are you?" she asked Felix, sitting on the edge of the bed and studying his face. He didn't seem like a man with children to her. A man with children wouldn't return to Czechoslovakia and risk being put away in prison when he had advice to give and food to put on the table. A good man with a wife wouldn't come looking for a former lover. Whatever he was, he wasn't a happy man.

Felix watched her as she searched him for answers and wanted to tell her everything. It was too much to say at once, so he decided to start with something simple – his name.

"Mr. Wulff." The young nurse licked her lips and fiddled with the button beneath her throat. "Do you know what date it is?"

Felix nodded. "1945. June, I think. As of today."

The nurse smiled. "And your last address?"

He took a deep breath and mouthed the single word that had been on his mind all that morning.

The nurse shook her head. "Did you say chocolate, Mr. Wulff?"

"Yes," Felix said. His mother's maiden name sounded strange on her tongue, though he'd been going by it since he'd left his sickbed in Roznov. But perhaps it sounded so because, in the slightest way, the young nurse resembled Magdalena.

"You may as well want a French chateau," she said. It was her reluctant smile that made the likeness. And perhaps the way her hair tumbled over one eye when she cocked her head. "Besides, you look frail." Her eyes fell to his chest and she blushed. "You could use a better meal than that – we've been liberated, after all."

"So we have," he said. Felix laid his head back, settling onto the mattress the Red Cross had provided. Dozens of them were lined up in the school gymnasium where he and other relatively healthy men had been given a place to sleep. It was one of the few buildings in this outlying area of Prague that had been swept for mines and other booby-traps left by the Germans as they retreated.

Despite his emaciated body and sore shoulder – still troubled by a stubborn bullet fragment – Felix wanted chocolate and nothing else. Not a strong drink, or a goose feather pillow. And not the nurse who reminded him of Magdalena – and who he often found himself staring at with a longing that she misinterpreted as lust.

Chocolate it would be.

It was the luxury he'd imagined enjoying with Magdalena in a London park – where he hoped, believed, she had arrived months before.

It was the only extravagance he'd craved as Pepík cared for his wounds following the debacle at the Bone Church. It was the only thing he wanted other than Magdalena.

After days of approaching soldier after soldier, and several black market Czars who sold indiscriminate items like butter and shoelaces, Felix finally managed to acquire a small piece of chocolate. He traded his cherished cigarettes for that tiny bit of civility.

It was time to begin acting like a man again, he thought. No longer would he sit slumped against the side of a wooden garage, trying to stave off hunger and worry by smoking his daily meal. In peacetime, a cigarette was to be enjoyed after a meal and with friends.

The man who finally traded the chocolate with Felix called himself Milan. His eyes possessed the stare of well-crafted glass eyeballs and moved quickly over each of his customers. Those eyes traveled over Felix's sunken face, and then down to his shoes. He had a mild fondness for Felix and even tried in his half-hearted way to let him know that he was making a serious error in judgment. Cigarettes were like money, and there was little practical return in chocolate – even if it was criminally expensive. In the end, however, Milan walked away whistling, his bounty hidden in his saggy trousers.

Felix pocketed the chocolate and hid behind a tall, disheveled apartment building to enjoy it. It had been at least four years since he'd last tasted chocolate and he wasn't sure his senses would remember the warm, hearty flavors of burnt nuts, honey, and bitters. They did remember, and how they remembered! Before he was able to swallow, he felt the grip of a powerful hand take him up by the collar. What was left of the chocolate square lodged itself in his throat and Felix began to choke. The same hand that had grabbed his collar slapped his back until the coin-sized piece flew from his windpipe and landed in a small puddle not far from his feet.

"What's a matter with you?" The hand's master spoke in provincial Russian.

The voice was cracked and uneven, climbing to each decibel with the shaky legs of a thirsty man. Clearly, the Russian had been up all night drinking.

He demanded that Felix follow him back to the main street, where several other Russian soldiers were rounding up able-bodied men for help with various tasks – moving heavy machinery, or items they'd stolen from Czech homes, or bodies of soldiers and civilians. This Russian moved like an old ape, waddling on his bowed legs, and using his arms for balance. He wasn't much older than twenty, but weeks of hard drinking had made him unsteady and stale-smelling. He motioned for Felix to walk closer behind him and then pushed him with the butt of his rifle.

"I could use a cognac," the commander said, pronouncing it *ko-nak*. He'd seized some from the home of a local grocer and took an instant liking to it.

He was one of two Russian regimen commanders in the area, and Felix searched the street hoping to spot the other. That commander was from Moscow; an intelligent, civilized man, whose men respected him. He used expressions like "thank you," and "would you be so kind?" The Muscovite was able to keep the rapes and thefts his men would perpetrate at a minimum.

Unfortunately, Felix had encountered the other – the one who was illiterate and enjoyed reminding anyone within earshot of his superior proletariat roots.

They walked across the street and into an old post office that was being used as a temporary hospital. It was a shabby space that had been closed even before the war and slated for demolition. For years it had been a home for the suburban village's rat population and stank of mold and fecal matter. Felix hated the smell. But at least it had a suitable roof and could accommodate a couple of dozen wounded. The soldiers could be kept dry during rain and shielded from the days' heat.

From what Felix could see, these men all needed serious attention, but were not in any immediate danger. Mostly, they required amputations or minor surgery. "Nazdar," Felix said, greeting one of the boys in Czech. That boy smiled and reached out. He asked for his mother. *Poor kid,* Felix thought. He was one of the last of the battle soldiers who'd fought an increasingly desperate German army. He'd even been part of the regimen that liberated the area.

The Russian commander pointed at his men. "They're useless."

Few of them were over eighteen, and they were frightened and in pain, asking for a cigarette, a sip of water, a kind word.

"You want a go at them?" The commander gave a hard scratch to his scalp – probably riddled with lice. "I hear you gave it pretty good to the Germans until we got here."

Felix clenched his teeth. *Don't,* he thought. *Please.*

In one smooth motion, the commander picked up his machine gun and discharged it into his wounded men. When he was finished, he threw the weapon down and turned away.

"Pile them up in a corner," he said, surveying his work before walking out and away.

Felix's clothes were splattered with blood, and the young men before him lay motionless. Some had their eyes open in shock, but most had been sleeping when they were shot, and still looked peacefully oblivious. Although he was not yet a priest, Felix knelt down at each dead soldier and gave him absolution.

He said, "None of this is your fault and God knows this. He forgives you your sins and will take you into heaven. There, your bodies will be whole, and someday you'll be reunited with your families. Until then, watch over the mothers you called for. They'll need all the comfort you can give them. Pray for your Russia, that she finds her moral compass again, and brings her people back into the arms of God."

He didn't pile the bodies on top of one another in a corner, the way the commander had ordered. He laid them next to each other, head to foot, like sardines, and crossed their arms over their chests. His father had once told him that this position was meant to protect the hearts of the dead. When he was finished, he dug down into his breast pocket and pulled out his last remaining cigarette, the one he hadn't traded for chocolate, but saved for luck, and smoked it.

"My name is Felix Andel, as you knew me," he told her. "Or Marek Wulff or Marek Andel, or any number of combinations thereof, depending on who you talk to." Felix lifted his head and eased it further up the pillow. He regarded Magdalena's eyes – the color of chocolate – and savored their attention. They bore an expression of worry and fatigue, just as they had on the morning he'd left her up in Justus Svoboda's attic. "But most of the people I know now call me 'Father.'"

Chapter Thirty
Louny, Czechoslovakia:
Next Day

"An older boy, I think. I wouldn't be good with the little ones."

The woman stared at Felix, her eyes crusted with black mascara that coated her short, blonde eyelashes and pooled in the corners of her eye-sockets. She tapped her pearl pink fingernails on the wood of her desk, scraping off a few flakes of cheap varnish.

"Mmm," she said, looking down at his adoption petition.

Felix stepped forward and presented Ivo Krev's identity papers. He wore a hat over his dense, wavy hair and a pair of cheap, gray-tinted glasses that helped to conceal the bruise under his right eye. He hoped the woman wouldn't study the papers for too long.

"It says here blue eyes and yours look green to me." Not that she could tell. But she did want to appear thorough.

"They change with what I'm wearing," Felix said.

The woman seemed to accept that explaination.

"Married. How long?"

"Ten years."

"One child."

"A playmate, we hope, for the new boy."

The woman wrote down these few bits of information and handed Krev's papers back to Felix. She stamped his petition and folded his identity documents into a neat square, as if that task itself was more important than the prospective adoption. Looking once more, good and hard, at Felix, she walked out of her office without a word and didn't return for nearly an hour.

"Come and look," she summoned, bringing a blunt-featured man with her. His orange hair was greased down, but still defied gravity at his crown, sticking up in three clusters like birthday candles.

Felix walked into the orphanage first, with the woman and orange-haired man following. The boys – some thirty of them – were lined up, each standing at the foot of their cots with their hands at their sides. Felix looked out over his glasses and scanned the children for Ales. Magdalena had described him at length, but as it turned out Felix didn't need her portrayal. Ales was unmistakably her son, and even wore her pensive facial expression. Only his fair hair distinguished him from her. Felix smiled at the boy and Ales looked down at his shoes, an old pair of leather oxfords.

The woman nudged Felix, who regarded the boys as he walked down the dormitory, faking an interest in a couple of them until he came to Magdalena's.

"What's your name?" he asked.

Ales said nothing and put his hands behind his back, fingering the bleach-stained quilt that covered his cot.

"My name is Ivo."

Magdalena's boy nodded.

"This is Ales," the woman offered without ceremony, and Ales glanced up briefly.

Felix walked around Ales, tipping his chin up and taking a long look at his face. "This boy looks like my mother. She passed away many years ago."

The woman exhaled from her nose, and the orange-haired man stepped up close behind her.

"I'd like to talk to him, please."

"Go ahead," the woman said.

"Alone. Can we have some time alone?"

The orange-haired man shook his head. Felix shrugged and squatted down, tilting his head up at Ales. "Hello, young Ales. Do you like the city? I live in a city, though I travel a lot. Maybe some day you could even come with me abroad for a holiday."

Ales remained silent, looking past Felix's ears rather than into his face.

"I have a nice home. And my wife sure could use some help around the house. She makes a wonderful tripe soup."

Ales swallowed and folded his hands at his belly, rubbing his thumbs together. He looked into Felix's eyes.

"I like him," Felix announced. "He's quiet, but I was a shy boy, too. I'd like to take him."

The woman stepped between Felix and Ales, plucking a short, sharpened pencil from behind her ear. "This isn't a general store. You'll have to fill out more paperwork. This kind of thing doesn't happen in an hour's time. It can take days or weeks. Maybe months."

The orange-haired man narrowed his eyes at Felix, as the woman continued to lecture him about adoption procedures.

"I was hoping," Felix said. "That I could take him with me at least in the mean time – while you sort through your paper work and necessary procedures. He was, after all, left here on a temporary basis."

"He was abandoned here," the woman clarified. "And he is our responsibility now."

The woman urged Felix along, guiding him back into the office. Felix looked back at Magdalena's son, who dared to look up at him before they disappeared behind the office door.

"Over there. Sit down." The orange-haired man held a handgun in his left hand. Half of his index finger was missing on his right, and he pocketed the hand when he noticed Felix studying it. The nub of the finger was still inflamed, as if it had been a recent injury. The orange-haired man motioned to a metal chair and Felix sat, while the woman picked up her phone and began dialing.

"It's busy," she said.

"Well, try again!"

The orange-haired man sat on the corner of her desk and tapped his foot in quick patters like Morse code. "Did you think you could just waltz in here, Mr. Krev, after what you've done? Did you think we wouldn't know?"

"I don't know what you mean," Felix answered.

"Where's the boy's mother?"

Felix looked into the orange-haired man's eyes and stood up slowly. The man popped up from the desk and jumped backwards, waving the handgun.

"Back, I say. Sit down right now!"

The man was an amateur, frightened by the simplest diversion from his imagined script. Felix had been aware of that from the first time he entered the office. A professional would've never entered the office the way he did – not even introducing himself and arousing all sorts of suspicion long before ever pulling his gun. Felix had his doubts that he'd even fired it at anything other than cut-outs at the shooting range. That and the fact that he was right-handed. It amazed him that the secret police would've sent such a rube to guard over Ales, but then they knew Ivo Krev very well. They didn't believe there was a chance in a million that he'd come back for the boy, and they were right. Krev didn't.

"You sit down," Felix said, pulling his own gun. The orange-haired man's hand started to shake like an old woman's.

"No. I'll shoot."

"Not if you haven't released your lock," he told him, raising his pistol to the man's forehead. The orange-haired man's gun dropped to the floor and he slumped back onto the desk. The woman sat down in her chair and Felix ordered her to put her hands on the desktop where he could see them.

"Miss?"

"Kouková," she offered.

"Miss Kouková, please take my matches and burn my papers in the trash can."

He handed her his matches and she did as she was instructed, letting every bit of paper burn into ash.

"Now sit down again please, but this time, in the chair next to your comrade here."

Felix lifted the metal chair and placed it back-to-back with the chair the orange-haired man had taken. Miss Kouková sat down. He took a spool of packing tape from her desk and made the man and Miss Kouková tie their feet to the legs of their chairs. Felix then had them raise their hands above their heads, taping their wrists and elbows together. Last, he taped their mouths shut and looked back at his handiwork the way he imagined Ivo Krev would do.

"Thank you for your help, Miss. Kouková. You're an excellent communist." He caressed the woman's cheek with the mouth of the gun. She glared up at him and grunted.

"Now, now," Felix said. "Don't feel too badly about yourself. I don't think this will land you in much trouble at all." He turned to the orange-haired man. "You, on the other hand, have a bit more to worry about. This might be a career-killer for you."

Felix took the orange-haired man's gun from the floor and tucked it into his trousers. He then closed the office door and headed straight for the dormitory.

Chapter Thirty-One
Czech-West German border:
Same Day

"**A**re you sure he'll still be there – this eccentric of yours?" Magdalena asked as they entered the outskirts of Karlový Vary. She couldn't quite refer to Felix's friend as an Indian the way he did. It seemed too absurd. And there was enough absurdity in their situation already.

Felix was driving her old Lada – doors freckled with rust, the knob on the stick shift missing. Ales was drawing a gun fight between two stick figures onto the foggy back windows and Magdalena erased it with her sleeve. He turned to her and she regretted the action, telling him, "This may be the last time you see your birth country, so take a good look."

"Hugo was born on the land in the border region," Felix said. "He's not going anywhere."

"Maybe the State has had other plans for him since you last talked?"

Felix smiled. "The State's given up on Hugo. They treat him and his people like they do the gypsies – they assign them jobs they never go to, and assign them flats they don't live in – theirs is hardly a lifestyle most Czechs are likely to adopt."

"Better than living like a robot, I'm sure," Magdalena said.

Felix silently agreed. He reached forward to change the radio station, but despite there being four channels, there was only one content provider – the State. They would have to settle for polkas and propaganda.

"Have you ever been here?" Felix asked.

Magdalena and Ales had gone quiet as they entered the town limits, watching Karlový Vary go by from the back seat. She shook her head. Felix wanted to tell her that he'd take her one day, perhaps in another lifetime, but Ales spoke up first.

"It's like a dream," he said.

Magdalena smiled down at him and petted his head. "You and your dreams."

Karlový Vary was a spa town that had once boasted kings and composers as some of the many illustrious guests that used to frequent it. Nestled in a river valley, princely villas studded the hills that surrounded its main thoroughfare. Though the buildings were still grand, the place exhibited none of its past hustle and bustle. The nightclubs had all been closed down and the restaurants – once serving haute cuisine – had been turned into State-run cafeterias that dumped bowlfuls of greasy goulash onto the tables as if it were a mess hall.

The town was now affordable to any Czech and free to anyone sick with arthritis, nerve and autoimmune diseases or gastrointestinal problems. For the State, a good spa was cheaper than providing real medical care and having to dispense real medicine. The sulfurous-tasting mineral waters from the ancient spring after which the town was named were promoted as having almost magical healing properties and lauded by the State as a secular alternative to Lourdes. Scant-haired men with calcified humps and women with thick, elephantine legs bent over the springs – often with the help of two canes and an orderly. They'd fill their cups with the hot, fizzy water, pinching their eyes shut and drinking it down quickly to avoid savoring the strange, metallic tastes, as they said a silent prayer for their recovery.

Felix pointed to a statue of Lenin at the end of the boulevard. The Soviet leader's back was to the border and his arm was raised as if he were literally conducting traffic away from West Germany.

After the Communist demagogue, there was nothing but greenery and rolling hills that grew precipitously taller.

Somewhere on that land lived Hugo Lesny.

Felix drove until a half mile before the road ended and parked. Years ago, they could've driven over the border, but the State had built a roadblock and destroyed the pavement. He looked over Magdalena's Lada one more time and thought he'd done a pretty good job on it. Having driven it several times through a muddy pasture, its license plate was well obscured as were any other potentially distinguishing marks. So far, it had attracted no attention.

With a small compass and a brandy flask filled with water, Felix, Magdalena and Ales made their way upwards into the thick brush of trees that grew over the hillsides like curly hair. They hiked uphill for nearly three hours. It was a tough trek for Magdalena, who hadn't moved with this kind of vigor in over a year, and whose muscles had wasted away around her slender bones.

"Ku-ku-roo-ku."

A bird noise echoed through the trees, seeming to come from up high.

"Ku-ku-roo-ku," Felix replied. He smiled and quickened his pace. "I think we're close."

The sun streamed down in shards, as if it had burned through the treetops. It made Magdalena's eyes tear. She put her hand up over her brow and looked ahead as Felix strode uphill, followed by Ales. She caught a glimpse of a tree trunk as it seemed to split in two, but realized the double image was that of a man coming towards them.

"*Nazdar.*" A tall, broad-shouldered man conveyed the Czech greeting.

Felix grasped the man's hand and held it tight. "Hugo."

Magdalena stepped forward and smiled.

"This is Hugo Lesny," Felix told her. "My friend."

Hugo Lesny put his arm around Felix's shoulders, dwarfing him by a full head. He moved into the light and Magdalena saw his face for the first time. His hazel eyes were set far apart and sat under a bush of a single brow, a shade lighter than his hair, which was light brown and cascaded down his shoulders in waves. His cheekbones were high and more orange than rosy, and his mouth was delicate and feminine, surrounded by deep pucker lines.

"Madam," he said, bowing his head. Magdalena returned the gesture.

Hugo Lesny's clothes suited his disposition the way a uniform suits a soldier. In the bare minute she'd known him, Magdalena already couldn't picture him wearing anything else but a long, suede overcoat, handmade and tied at the waist by a thick rope, brown tweed pants befitting an English country gentleman, and handmade suede moccasins affixed with rubber soles.

"And this is Ales."

The boy moved behind Felix and Magdalena, watching Lesny from between strips of his shaggy bangs.

"Ales is a bit bashful right now," Felix said. "He's had a harrowing month."

"A good piece of meat might make him more talkative." Lesny turned on his moccasin and moved through the tightly knit trees following a path that only he could discern. Ales trekked behind Felix, jumping easily around fallen branches and other obstacles, but his mother had a harder slog. By the time Magdalena caught the scent of roast pork in the air, she was ready to collapse.

"Ku-ku-roo-ku," Lesny called out, and a tall, blonde youth jumped down from out of a tree and jogged over to his chief. The young man was no older than sixteen and wore a black, hand-knitted angora sweater, heavy suede pants torn at the knees, and miner's boots – thick-soled and looking new. Lesny whispered something to him and he gave a terse nod. He walked over to Magdalena, pivoted, and crouched low with his back to her.

"Jump on," he said.

"No – I..."

"Jump on," he insisted, and Magdalena wrapped her arms around his neck as he reached back and clasped his hands under her buttocks. He stood up with a spring, carrying her as if she were a sack of potatoes, and whistled the rest of the way to their camp. There, the trees cleared into an area about the size of a soccer field.

"Oh," Magdalena said, as she looked out at the small, nomadic village.

At first glance, it didn't look so strange. It could've been a campsite peopled with vacationing families. But when she looked closer and saw that the tents were, in fact, teepees – much like the ones she'd seen in her American history book – and that raw animal pelts hung on clothes lines instead of bathing suits and playwear, and that every man, woman, and child was wearing a mish-mash of hand-made and factory-made clothes, she abandoned the pretense that these people were normal.

Bows and arrows hung on the backs of most of the young men and nearly everyone from age five and up carried hunting knives of various sizes, hanging along whatever served as a belt – a rope, a scarf, a piece of leather, even steel wire.

There were totem poles carved with stacked animal heads and Czech composers. A fox, a Dvořák, a bear, a Smetana. Like shishkabob. As for feather crowns, face paint, and the usual accoutrements depicted in any self-respecting cowboy movie – she saw no evidence of them.

The blonde youth carried her to a large, central teepee that sat like a circus tent in the middle of camp. Small fires roared in a half-circle around it, each with a black caldron suspended above them – the flames licking their bellies.

"Welcome!" Lesny crowed.

There was a hearth burning in the middle of the tent and the deerskin walls contained its warmth. Billows of smoke puffed from the fire's tips, disappearing through a hole in the ceiling. Mats, blankets, and pillows were stacked along the back wall and Lesny took an armful, tossing them one by one to Felix and Magdalena. They put the pillows on a woven mat that clung in a thick ring around the fire, and sat down. A girl of about ten offered them each a hot mug of tea. She called Hugo Lesny "Papa."

"Indians?" Magdalena whispered. "You were serious."

"More or less," Felix said. "Naturalists, I'd call them."

Hugo Lesny took off his suede overcoat, revealing a muscular chest tattooed with an intricate series of images telling the story of a hunt. The vivid ink patterns reminded Magdalena of the ancient paintings she'd seen in the Cave of Lascaux when she was a girl.

"They're virtually ignored by the State," Felix assured her. "And they've provided passage for more than just me over the years."

Magdalena finished her tea and the little girl scuttled over to her and refilled her cup. She smiled and bowed before running back to her father, giggling into his bare chest. A woman with a long, white braid entered the tent and the young girl ran to her, helping to carry a small cauldron smelling of roast pork.

"This is Zaba, my wife, and my daughter Fiala."

Zaba said, "Nazdar," and put the food down on the far side of the mat. She took a few small bags filled with uncooked rice and placed them around the wooden bowls. The bags were hot from laying so close to the fire and would keep the food warm.

"Pork, sauerkraut, and dumplings." Zaba announced their dinner and left with Fiala on her tail.

They ate in relative silence, except for an occasional offer of more from Lesny. When they finished, Fiala cleared their dishes but quickly returned to the tent, peeking her head in and signaling the chief with an indiscreet "pssssst." Hugo Lesny waved her in and she squealed, running over to sit behind him. She carried a toy boat that had been carved from the same wood as the totem poles and handed it to Ales, touching her chin to her shoulder. The boy murmured thanks and took the boat out of the circle to play alone, much to her disappointment.

Zaba came in again, this time holding a jar of home-made plum brandy – the plums still soaking in the liquor. Using a pair of tongs, she gently removed four plums, putting one each into their teacups.

"Opice!" Lesny called out, and the blonde young man who'd met them on the trail appeared from outside, still gnawing on a slice of pork. He sat down next to his chief, staring at the visitors as if it was the first good look he'd gotten at them. He chewed with his mouth open.

"Hugo," Felix began. "I was hoping that tomorrow…"

"Tomorrow, the two of you will go out with Opice, starting at dawn. Your boy will stay back with us and help Zaba and Fiala prepare lunch. It's very important we stick to our routine and do nothing out of the ordinary."

Fiala crinkled her nose and looked over at Ales, who pretended not to be listening. He made splashing noises as the toy boat entered rough seas.

"The three of you will make your cross starting mid-afternoon," Hugo said. "After your bellies are full, and you've become more familiar with our ways."

Hugo Lesny patted his daughter's bottom and whistled again, this time in two, loud shrieks. Zaba came back in and Lesny signaled for her to take Ales and Fiala out of the teepee.

"Come on Ales," Zaba beckoned. "There are many more toys in the children's tent. That's where you'll be sleeping tonight."

"I want to sleep here," he said, but Magdalena gave him a look.

"We're guests here," she chided. "Go with Zaba and I'll see you in the morning."

Ales picked up his boat, and shuffled over to his mother. He gave Magdalena a kiss, glancing over at Felix and Lesny for hope of a last minute reprieve. Felix nodded at the boy, making Ales feel grown up and cutting his fears with a dose of confidence. He left the teepee with Fiala bouncing after him asking, "Have you ever seen a wolf pack? I have."

Lesny waited until he could no longer hear the light step of his wife and the two children, but still spoke barely one notch above a whisper.

"You don't have much time to get to know the land here, and you're going to have to know it pretty well if you want to cross successfully. We'll give you clothes so you look like us. The snipers, if they see you, will think you're gathering food. They know our rituals, like we know theirs."

"This is lunacy," Magdalena said.

"Don't you hear that every once in a while a farmer goes mushroom picking and somehow finds himself on the other side of the border in free Germany?"

"It's a one in a thousand chance."

Felix patted his friend's shoulder. "Not with Hugo's help. Nobody knows this part of the country like Hugo does. He knows where the mushrooms grow; he knows where every rabbit and squirrel makes its home, every tree and beehive. And he knows where the border is vulnerable. I'm not saying there isn't risk, but it's the only way we'll be able to get to the other side without papers right now."

Felix took a bite of his plum, nearly choking on the sharp sting of alcohol as he swallowed. Opice grinned, handing Felix a cup of water and a napkin.

Hugo Lesny put his hand on the boy's knee. "Opice knows the forest better than any of us – from the ground and from the tops of the trees. He likes to climb."

Hugo Lesny smiled at the boy and beamed with pride. Felix now noticed the resemblance between them – it was around the mouth, a subtler trait to share than the eyes.

"We'll do whatever you say."

"In that case, get some sleep. You have a long day tomorrow."

Hugo Lesny stood up with his teacup in hand and his son put a couple of more logs on the fire. Zaba and Fiala returned, preparing beds out of mats woven of horsehair, and fluffing up some down blankets and pillows. They left with Opice and the chief.

Felix looked down at their beds and saw that Zaba had made them several feet apart. Somehow, he'd expected them to be together. "Goodnight," Magdalena whispered. She snuggled under her blanket on the other side of the fire.

"Goodnight."

Chapter Thirty-Two
Vatican City: Same Day

Cardinal Carlo Merillini was sitting alone in his office at the Vatican, tapping his pen at the edge of his desk as he waited for Dr. Tangelo, the Vatican's resident expert on post-Renaissance religious artifacts, to authenticate the Holy Infant of Prague.

He'd flown back to Rome at seven-thirty that morning, a little over an hour after learning the horrible news about Primo.

Primo had been found in an alleyway with his throat cut and his wallet missing. Gone, too, was the cognac-colored briefcase as well as any trace of Krev. *Barbarian,* he thought. Primo had been an excellent valet and he would miss his calming presence and keen skills of observation.

It troubled the Cardinal that Krev had never returned to his pension for his papers, which he would need in order to get in or out of any country. In fact, for all intents and purposes, Krev had disappeared the moment he stepped out into the Vienna night with his earnings in hand. Primo could no longer give testimony about what had happened to the Czech agent and Krev hadn't been spotted at the airport or train station or any border. Of course, a man like Krev would know when the gig was up and make a hasty exit. And the money he'd gotten was certainly a good booty, if not the full amount he'd demanded.

Yes, Krev got much more than he deserved. For all of his sins, he got to start anew as a rich man, while men like Felix Andel had to fight for their lives. There had been no word on the Jesuit, and the Cardinal prayed the quick-thinking Felix would be able to get over the border with the woman as he'd planned.

Even Liebermann deserved better for his contribution. His wife was still waiting for the release of his body, and the Czechs were dragging their feet – to make some sort of point, he assumed. And then there was Father Duch – electrocuted in his very own bath by Krev. It was an unspeakable intrusion – the thought of Ivo Krev breaking into his apartment and committing a mortal sin.

Krev certainly got much, much more than he deserved and Cardinal Merillini would make sure that the Soviet government was informed of his every move, once he got a whiff of Krev's whereabouts himself.

Francesco, the Cardinal's secretary, knocked at the door, bringing the Cardinal a cup of espresso and the news that Dr. Tangelo was done with his assessment.

"By all means, bring him in."

Francesco returned moments later with a tiny, bearded man with black, oily hair. The Cardinal motioned for the doctor to sit and the doctor did, a nervous tick twitching at his lip.

"It's very good," the doctor said. "The eyes – their coloring, the sheen of the face, and the hair – quite flawless, all of it. And the vestments, as I told you before, are perfectly authentic. They are indeed the same ones the Empress gave to the Infant in 1743."

The Cardinal sat back and took a sip of his espresso, smiling a broad, closed lip smile.

"But the figure is not as authentic as its vestments."

"What?"

"The figure," the doctor continued. "Is an excellent fake. Truly a work of art, but not the Holy Infant Himself. The artist even signed the work – on the back of the eyeball of all places. J. Svoboda. I suspect it's one of the duplicates made in order to permit transfer and thwart thievery. It was quite common to..."

"Yes, I know."

The Cardinal sank into his chair, his breath picking up pace. Dr. Tangelo could almost hear his heart beneath the green and gold embroidery of his robe.

Chapter Thirty-Three
Czech-West German border:
Next Day

The landmarks Opice had shown them had been fresh in Felix's mind less than an hour before, but were now confused in his memory as he struggled to lead them back to the cave and the rock and the path leading into free Germany. It had all seemed obvious and clear, but now Felix saw several rocks that grew out of the ground like tree stumps and more than one cave in the rock wall where Opice had said the snipers liked to hide. Nothing resembled a path until he saw two tall pines, standing together like a pair of bowed legs.

"This way," he showed them. Ales and Magdalena scuttled after him.

Felix had only a vague idea of where he was going. There was a reason he only ever used Hugo as a last resort, and a reason why he and the handful of others he'd arranged to pass the border this way had lived with Hugo and the naturalists for two weeks or more before attempting to cross. With tree cover this dark and overgrown, it was no easy task.

The border could've been no more than two kilometers away, but the uphill stepping and cold, patchy ground made it difficult to make quick progress and threatened to take as long as two hours – provided they were going the right way and didn't run into snipers or the secret police hot on Ivo Krev's trail.

As they headed into a dense stretch of pine forest, Magdalena tripped over a low coil of barbed wire. Her knee twisted, tearing her muscles as the sharp teeth of the wire dug through her pigskin trousers and bit into her lower calf.

"Take the boy and go."

"Get up!" Ales demanded.

"You can make it," Felix assured her, untangling the wire.

"I can't get up!" She clamped down on her knee, trying to contain the inevitable swelling. "I'll be fine," she said. "I'll make it back to camp and maybe I could hide for a few days. They might not come looking there, and I could cross in a couple of weeks."

Felix bent down to get a look at Magdalena's knee. He could already see the beginnings of bruising and swelling. From a loop on his leather belt, he unhooked the hunting knife Hugo had given him and stabbed it into the slushy ground, loosening icy bits of mud from the earth. He cut a wide strip from the cow pelt he'd been given to wear and wrapped it tightly around Magdalena's knee, packing the partially frozen mud between her skin and the strip. He then picked her up and threw her over his shoulder the way his coach used to make him skate, carrying his team-mates one by one around the rink in order to build his leg muscles. Ales looked up at him, awed by his strength, and Felix winked at him. The boy hadn't had a man in his life for a long time.

Slower and clumsier, they marched up a series of rocks and crunched over dead branches and decayed leaves that had only emerged from under the snow the week before. The tree trunks all looked the same, as did the budding flora, untouched by the sun and still caked with morning frost.

When they hit the thickest patch of pine trees yet – ones that blocked the sun like a heavy, velvet curtain – they stopped. Felix had seen nothing like these trees with Opice that morning and cursed himself. Perhaps the trees had been there all along, and he hadn't noticed them, or maybe he'd gone a different way entirely and was leading them into the view of several well-positioned snipers. Felix put Magdalena down, pretending to rest, and got a good look at their surroundings.

He took deep breaths that filled his lungs like cold water and examined every part of the world around them patiently, as if they had all the time in the world. He caught glimpses of the sky and compared the colors of the sprouting leaves to the ones he'd seen that morning. He looked down at the mud and moss at his feet, feeling the tiny, sharp rocks that studded the ground like diamonds, and ran his fingers along the prickly bark waiting for a memory to come. His senses were heightened and alive, but still, the images from their scouting time with Opice remained elusive.

Something whizzed by him, perhaps a dragonfly, and he heard distant thunder and the sound of cracking wood. Felix felt a strong cramp in his side, and leaned into a tree to keep from falling. Two strong hands pushed him upright from behind, their palms cupped over his shoulder blades. He rested on them – leaning back and closing his eyes for a moment.

Magdalena gasped, throwing herself onto Ales as three more bullets came at them from different directions, tearing into the pine trees and sending down a hail of splintered wood.

The hands moved up onto Felix's shoulders, gently pushing him towards the ground. Felix dropped down on one knee and drew his gun from the back of his trousers, aiming it upwards into the pines. He could see nothing but the forest around him.

"You see his foot? There – on that high branch to the right." Jura Srut squatted behind Felix and spoke into his ear, pointing up into the trees.

"Is that a foot or a squirrel?" Felix asked.

"Quit stalling and shoot."

"I can't."

"Do it!" Srut wrapped his arms around Felix from behind, reinforcing his hold on the pistol and putting his finger on the trigger with Felix's. "Don't you believe in the Angel of Death?"

Srut's finger tightened on the trigger and released the shot. A second later, a man in fatigues fell from a high branch, impaling himself on a small, young pine.

"Good," Srut mumbled, turning the Jesuit a few degrees to the left. "Can you see the reflection of a watch – near the top?"

A flash of light blinked at him and Felix pulled the trigger, jerking backwards. Srut steadied him as yet another man dropped from his perch. His collar caught a branch off a thick bough and he dangled like a hangman, his feet twitching.

Felix crouched lower, looking up into the tightly woven pines and scanning every visible branch for movement. But the forest was quiet, emitting only a faint rustle as a breath of wind blew through the tops of the trees. Felix remained in position, his right eye squinting over the barrel of the gun. Magdalena watched him whisper something and nod his head, as if he were having a conversation with someone close by.

"Are you talking to me?" Magdalena inched towards him.

"We'll die if we go there," Felix said.

"Where?"

"To Opice's clearing and rock path. It's over there." Felix pointed south.

"Felix, can you hear me?" Magdalena touched his moccasin – tentatively at first – and put her hand up his woolen trouser, rubbing the bare skin of his calf. "Opice told us which way to go."

"He's wrong."

"What do you mean?"

"Srut knows the right way," Felix said, pointing west into the small opening that led deeper into the thick brush of pines.

"Srut? What are you talking about?" Magdalena took hold of his cow pelt and started tugging on it, pulling him in the direction of Opice's path.

"We're not going that way."

"Have you lost your mind?" She stopped pulling and started slapping and punching his legs. Ales crawled away from her and stood next to Felix, gripping the man's pelt and holding it to his chest like a blanket.

Felix bent towards Magdalena and lifted her over his shoulder again, telling Ales to stay close.

"No!" she cried.

"It's okay," Ales told his mother. He walked behind them, taking hold of her hand, and nuzzling his face into Felix's side.

Ales didn't want to look too long at the litter of bodies around them and he believed Felix would lead them out of there. It was, after all, Felix and not Opice who'd shot down the snipers and seemed so sure about where they needed to go.

As Felix strode, his pelt billowed out, and Magdalena caught a glimpse of a large, red stain on his dove-gray sweater. She looked down at his feet, which were sure and stepped lightly, as if he were hardly carrying anything at all.

"Felix, you're bleeding," she said, but he wasn't listening to her. He was staring into the sky, with his ear cocked like a Vishla. It was then that she heard it, too – a deep, flapping noise getting louder by the second.

"Run to the cave!" Felix shouted to Ales.

Two helicopters came into view, hovering only a few feet above the treetops. With their long, thin tails and squared, glassed-in noses, they looked more like the American rescue helicopters Felix had seen during the liberation than Soviet-issue aircraft. Machine gun fire sprayed near his heels and Felix ducked into the cave after the boy. He set Magdalena down next to him.

"Opice said there are snipers in these caves!" Magdalena shouted.

"Not in this one," Srut said.

Magdalena took Ales in her arms, cradling him like a small child. Standing at the mouth of the cave, Felix peeked up at the craft, holding the gun close to his chest.

"He's a good shot, that one." Srut squinted up at the Czech army captain, who dangled from the side of the heli-copter. The other copter circled around, giving cover to the first with random shots into the pine forest. "I wouldn't try to shoot him down – he'll kill you first."

Felix shook his head and stepped out of the cave, hug-ging the rock wall as he readied his gun. Its chambers were half empty, and he had no more ammunition.

"Two more steps and you're in his sights," Srut said. He gripped his elbow.

Felix shook him away and raised the gun barrel. Another charge of bullets came down on them, chipping into the rock and earth, and sending a gust of pine needles into Felix's face. He shielded his eyes, coughing out the dirt and dry pine that had blown down his throat.

With Srut in tow, Felix ran to one of the dead snipers and took his rifle. He jumped up to catch a low branch of the nearest tall pine and scrambled up the trunk. The sniper's rifle hung clumsily at his side, knocking into his bloodied sweater.

"I'm not going up there," Srut said.

More bullets discharged, pattering around the gypsy's feet, but the shots were more random this time – as if the shooter had lost sight of his target.

Felix balanced on a heavy bough and shimmied his shoulders between two branches above him. They held him steady and made it easier for him to aim. The belly of the helicopter loomed above him and he could see the shooter leaning out of the craft and searching the forest below.

The helicopter not only looked like an American rescue model, it was one. The blue starred corner of an American flag peeked out from under a coat of messily applied black spray paint.

Felix aimed and fired, shooting up the tail as the helicopter dipped and lunged like a gawky insect. The shooter fell out of the cockpit and hung on at the base of the door, further wobbling the craft. Its belly brushed the treetops and its nose tilted forward. The copter tipped suddenly to the side and its blades chopped into the pines, clearing an area the size of a hotel suite. The helicopter recovered briefly – flying about a half kilometer away only to sputter and stall. The dense, tacky pine needles embedded further into its joint, stopping the blades altogether. For a moment the helicopter seemed to float, and looked as if it would keep floating, until it plunged with alarming speed, crushing the trees beneath it and exploding before it hit the ground.

"Woooo hoo!" Srut hollered, clapping his hands and whistling through his teeth. He jumped up, wiggling onto the first branch, and scaling the pine as the second helicopter made a pass over the billowing smoke.

"Aim high, my friend," Srut said. He hoisted himself next to Felix and pushed the nose of the rifle up by two centimeters. "He's taller than he looks."

Felix stared into the cockpit as the helicopter charged, but glare from the sun along with blowing smoke obscured his vision and made it impossible for him to see inside. He could ill afford to miss, as the rifle had only two shots left.

"I can't see," Felix yelled.

"Shoot!"

"I can't."

"Now!"

Felix pulled the trigger, firing once, and then twice. The third time, the trigger clicked, signaling its empty chamber. The helicopter stayed on course, barreling towards them like an oncoming train. It came at them and over them, continuing to fly straight as the co-pilot jumped out of the craft, and the pilot – a bullet hole between his eyes – sat at the helm with his hands stiffly gripping the controls. The helicopter flew in a direct line until it collided with a water tower in West Germany, some three miles away.

"You got em," Srut chuckled, pulling a cigarette from the pocket of his red clay Italian shirt.

Magdalena had heard the ground-shaking crash of the first helicopter. She'd kept Ales nestled to her breast, with her poncho wrapped around his head to muffle the sounds of gunfire.

"Felix!" she cried out.

He jumped from the tree and stood at its base for a few moments, as if he were waiting for something, and then ran towards the cave.

"There's not much time," he said, boosting her over his shoulder. Ales took his mother's hands again as he followed Felix out of the cave and deeper into the heart of the pine forest. The trees were huddled closer together there, and the sun could barely penetrate the knit of branches.

"There's a mine a few feet to your left, so walk straight." Srut took a long, last drag off his cigarette before flicking it onto the damp moss.

Felix heeded Srut's advice and stuck to a row of pines that were aligned and looked identical. The pines led to a small clearing shaped like a shark's tooth.

"Hey, guess what?" Srut said. They stepped onto a thick carpet of mushrooms. "You just crossed the border."

The gypsy stopped, letting them enter West Germany without him. He patted his clothes for another cigarette, but all he could find was a partially smoked butt that had lain crushed at the seam of his rear pocket for an indeterminable amount of time. It was one of Pepík's blends – perhaps the last one his impish friend endeavored to smoke before he died of scarlet fever on the night before D-Day. Srut lit it with Henrik's silver butane lighter, embossed with the fat man's signature *HP*, and made his way back into Czechoslovakia.

CHAPTER THIRTY-FOUR
SAME DAY

The island of Santorini, with its dramatic cliffs, red and black sand beaches, and whitewashed homes like tiny chapels - all of them - looked exactly the way it had been portrayed in the adventure books of Ivo Krev's youth. Though he'd never been to Greece, Krev had always known he wanted to live there and that Santorini would be his island of choice. The mild weather agreed with him and the landscape was startling and dry. He loathed the wetness of tropical island weather and could imagine himself reading on the beach here in comfortable clothes and well-made leather sandals. The women were pretty enough, too, though few of them spoke any of his four languages.

As he stepped out of the living room onto the enormous terrace of the villa, he knew this was the real selling point of the house. It stood atop the town of Thera and looked out across the water and onto the high, rocky cliffs that geologists speculated had been formed by an earthquake thousands of years earlier. One that tore Santorini from the side of Crete like a rib from Adam.

It was funny that a biblical metaphor had come to his mind and rather unlike him. All this business with the

Infant of Prague was still coursing through his veins. It had been a while since things had worked out for him exactly the way he planned them. He got the money he wanted in exchange for a good copy of the Infant – for the real thing he would've wanted a lot more than $75,000, and he intended to get it.

Krev looked down off his new balcony at the small boat-house at the edge of his soon-to-be property. The Infant of Prague – the real Infant he believed, and not the handsome forgery that had almost fooled Josef Goebbels and had done a good enough job of keeping the Cardinal guessing – was lying on a shelf above the fishing equipment the previous owners had left behind.

By now, of course, the Cardinal would know he'd been duped. Keeping him occupied with a little treasure hunt had given Krev enough time to pick up his new identity and slip out of the country. The Cardinal's man, Primo, had almost ruined everything for him. Uncommonly strong and as deft with his hands as some of the Orientals Krev had seen street fighting in China, Primo could've broken him if it wasn't for the switchblade Krev had hidden in his boot.

"Do you like?" The real-estate agent, Demertis, asked in his far-too-ready-to-please fashion. He'd repeated this phrase every time he entered a room in the hillside villa. The dining room, "Do you like?" The kitchen, "Do you like?" The expansive bedroom, the courtyard and swimming pool, etc.

"Yes, I like," Krev finally acknowledged, and Demertis clapped his hands.

"I go to the office and I draw in the agreement right away."

Krev knew this could mean anywhere from a week to a month. "I'll pay cash in full if you can have them drawn up by tomorrow morning. And there'll be something in it for you, too."

Demertis clapped his hands again. "Tomorrow morning is yes."

"Good. I can stay here tonight then?"

Demertis shrugged his shoulders and cocked his head, his eyes sweeping the empty villa.

"Yes, but Sir Mr. Von Gorpp, there is no furniture for to sleep or sit, only – how you say – lounge for the beach? The Americans left it here. Three or four of them. They fold so nice and small, but I don't know how comfortable."

"They'll be fine. Now, move along."

"Please?"

"I want to be alone in my new home."

Demertis collected his manila folder from the mantle and turned to Krev one more time.

"Start putting together the sale," Krev told him. A dry breeze blew through his thin hair. "I expect you here at 8:00 AM, sharp."

Demertis nodded and scrambled out the front door. He would go straight to his office and get all of this done by the evening. Not because of the money he was promised – he had plenty of money for his simple life – but because this man, Von Gorpp, had never been agreeable to him.

Halfway down the cliff side, Demertis stopped at an overlook and settled onto a stone bench for a cigarette. His age was catching up to him, as he used to be able to scale these stairs two by two and now had to rest – not only when going up, but when going down as well.

"You got one of those for me?"

Demertis tipped his face up into the sunlight to see the dark silhouette looming over him. The man's head fit like an eclipse into the round visage of the sun and his dark complexion looked nearly black with the solar halo behind it.

"Of course," Demertis said. "I always carry an extra to share with a fellow traveler."

The man took the cigarette and lit it with a silver butane lighter.

"You're not from here, are you?" Demertis asked.

The man shook his head and inhaled, then let the smoke trail out of his nostrils.

"Work," he said, gesturing at Von Gorpp's new villa.

Demertis nodded. "They need a lot of work, these fancy places. They're not nearly as good as they look, but it fools the foreigners, you know?"

The man laughed. The dark rings around his eyes reminded Demertis of his son-in-law, who was part gypsy – although he denied it.

"Just last spring," Demertis continued. "There was a villa – beautiful place – that blew up like a bomb in the middle of the night. Faulty pipes, a natural gas leak. Luckily the owners were in London. They came down maybe once, twice a year. Nice peoples."

"You don't say," the man said. He flicked his cigarette off the cliff side and stared down onto the boat house and smiled. "Yeah, these foreigners – they'll fall for just about anything."

Demertis chuckled and stood up to continue his walk to the seaside. He turned to shake the man's hand and wish him well, but he'd already gone. The stairs were empty and Demertis could hear no footsteps, but then, gypsies were always fast and light on their feet. The man was probably at the doors of Von Gorpp's villa already.

"Strange stranger," Demertis laughed to himself.

When he arrived at the seaside, Demertis looked up at the villa one more time before getting into his boat and starting his journey back to Crete. The man he'd encountered was nowhere in sight, but he could see Von Gorpp looking down onto the cliffs from his terrace and wondered why someone like him had come here, of all places. In Pericles Demertis's vivid imagination, he created a life for Mr. Von Gorpp that included spying and murder and thievery.

"Pericles, you've been living on an island too long." Von Gorpp was probably what he said he was; a retired financier escaping a bitter divorce.

Demertis pulled the engine chain three times before it started to hum again, and felt a sense of relief as his boat skipped over the tiny waves. He took out the octopus sandwich his wife had made for him, but nearly choked on one of its rubbery tentacles as the explosion erupted behind him. It caused the boat to rock perilously from side to side.

An enormous cloud of black smoke obscured the jutting cliff where Von Gorpp's villa used to be and several more pops – like giant firecrackers – spouted above the smoldering ruins. A second explosion sent what was left of the terrace wall crumbing into the sea, destroying the boathouse.

"Great Zeus, great Hera!" Demertis sputtered. It was bad luck, he feared, to have been the last person to speak to two men before they died so unexpectedly. Nobody would mourn a man like Von Gorpp, he noted, but the other man, the gypsy worker, had seemed okay. Demertis wished he had gotten his name so that he could've said a prayer for him.

CHAPTER THIRTY-FIVE
NUREMBURG, WEST GERMANY: APRIL 2

Magdalena waited in the hospital lounge for visiting hours to resume. She'd been hoping to get in early to see Felix, as she had yet another appointment with the Americans, but the hospital was strict about its rules. It was just as well – she had no further information for the Americans anyway. She'd told them everything she knew. Almost everything. She'd left out Felix's bizarre behavior near the border, attributing it to a psychosis induced by loss of blood.

"Frau Melan," the nurse called, waving her into a suite of private rooms. Magdalena walked up to her, still favoring her left leg. She felt unexpectedly nervous at the prospect of seeing Felix again, even if it had only been a few days.

"He's tired, so I don't recommend a long stay," the nurse said.

But when Magdalena entered the stark, aqua blue room, Felix looked alright. His bruises at Krev's hands had finally faded and his complexion appeared normal.

"How are you? How is Ales?" he asked. He held his hand out to her and she took it, squeezing his warm palm to hers.

"Good," she said. "He's excited about going to America. He thinks he'll get to wear cowboy hats and ride horses, but I told him that I didn't think there were many cowboys in Washington, DC."

Magdalena walked around to Felix's side and flipped through the books and stacks of magazines that sat at his bedside table.

"Will you be going after Krev once you recover here?" She didn't know what made her think of the Czech spy, but she knew he weighed heavily on Felix's mind.

"No," Felix said. He glanced down onto his view of the hospital parking lot. Krev, strangely, felt like a waste of his time now.

"I have a present for you," Magdalena said.

Magdalena reached into her leather tote and pulled out a small, old copy of a picture book titled *The Ossuary of Sedlec* or the Bone Church, as it was more commonly known. Magdalena had found the book in a little shop on Artisan's Lane, where busts of Goethe, Moliere, and Tolstoy kept guard over hundreds of antique volumes.

As she'd leafed through the book, she'd imagined her bones and Felix's bones as becoming a part of the macabre sculptures of the Bone Church and thought it somehow a fit resting place for their remains – back in the country that rejected them, in the place that tore them from each other. She found it curious that she couldn't hate the Bone Church and in fact took comfort from it – glad of its peculiar existence.

"It's just as I remember it," Felix said.

He stopped at a grainy photograph of the altar where he'd seen Michael the Archangel and the Infant Jesus. Vera Ruza's low breath had followed him there, too, and had hung in the air like a soft chorus.

Magdalena started to put her hand on Felix's shoulder, but stroked his pillow instead and straightened his sheet. "I wanted to come days ago, but I'm not a blood relative."

The truth was she'd sat by his bedside during his first two days of delirium. *Do you still love me? Do you know I never stopped loving you?* she'd asked him as he lay there unable to answer. She'd told him all of the things it would have been so easy to tell him a dozen years ago, but that left her searching for words when she was with him now.

"I knew you'd come. You don't have to explain." Felix took her hand and kissed it. She sat on the bed, nestling her head between his neck and collarbone. Felix stiffened and repositioned her; the entrance and exit wound of the bullet he'd taken was still tender.

"I'm sorry," she said.

"It's an old wound brought back to life. I don't even recall getting hit." In fact, Felix remembered nothing of crossing the border. His last image was of Magdalena falling and spraining her knee. The next one after that was of his doctor telling him that he'd taken a bullet in the same place he'd taken one before. It was one of the shots in the Bone Church, and somehow the border sniper's bullet had found the same path. It was a good path that managed to avoid his vital organs, so Felix couldn't complain too much. He would make a full recovery.

"You don't remember anything?"

He shook his head. "Do you want to fill me in?"

"No. I mean there's nothing to fill in. Opice gave us directions and there we went. You were in shock, I guess. We didn't realize you were hurt until Germany."

Magdalena couldn't look at him, so she pulled him close to her instead and kissed his forehead. "Will you come see us in America?"

Felix nodded. He took her face in his hands and kissed her forehead, cheeks, chin, and finally, her nose. He combed his fingers through her hair. "I went to you. Once. More than once. A friend found you for me in Prague and took me to see you. I was going to tell you everything then, but you'd gotten married. Imagine – a real marriage in your real name."

"Imagine," she said, touching the raised scar on the side of his head – the one she'd tended to after she'd found him on the side of the road. Despite her best efforts, she started to cry. "You could have come to me. You could have said something. Anything."

Felix looked away. "I was arrested the next day and taken to Pankrac. Maybe we shared the same suite there." He smiled. "I'm sorry."

Magdalena got up and looked out the window.

The other windows in her life came to her now, like pictures in a book: her parents' home in Vínohrady, which stared out onto the dramatic cliff that made Vyšehrad, the first seat of the Bohemian Empire, the summer cottage of her youth, surrounded by hectares of cornflowers, the miniature cellar window of her hiding place in Marek Andel's home. It had been bricked up, but still indicated a world outside. The tiny cracks in the sliding doors on the train to the work camp – Auschwitz, as it was known to her now – where she and Felix could see frozen trees, a glass menagerie made by an ice storm the night before, and of course, her apartment with Antonin.

Many nights had been spent there with friends drinking robust, black beer and dreaming about a future that seemed so ripe with possibility. They laughed and ate open-faced sandwiches, while talking passionately about the new social order. Power to the people!

Then there were the miserable leaded windows of her icebox cabin in Klobuky, where she and Ales would have died. Even those windows helped keep alight a single candle of hope against a midnight of unknown horrors.

Now she was looking out yet another window – one that looked out onto freedom, whatever that meant. She hardly knew anymore. And it felt dull.

"Appointment," she said, pointing to her watch. She wasn't ready to leave. "The Americans again."

"They want to see me, too – the Americans," he said. "And the Cardinal wants me to accompany him to New York and then to Washington."

Magdalena smiled. Her eyes flitted from the cover of the book – a skull and crucifix posed on the altar like a still life drawing of fruit – to his eyes. He thought for a moment she might kiss him, but she didn't. "I don't suppose he knows I'll be in Washington?" she said.

Felix shook his head. "I haven't the slightest idea."

She went to the door, forcing herself to jiggle the handle, but turned around.

"What is it?" he asked.

Magdalena shrugged her shoulders and glanced down at her new navy pumps – a gift from her sponsor family in Arlington. "I was wondering," she said. "What ever happened to Srut?"

Felix looked at the book on the Bone Church, running his thumb over the photo of the altar – the last place where he'd seen the gypsy. "He was killed."

She turned back to Felix, but couldn't look into his eyes.

"You called his name, you know, when we were crossing the border."

Felix took a deep breath and clutched the book close to his chest. There were times when he could feel Srut's presence beside him, but not today. "I can't imagine what made me think of him," he said.

Felix wanted to tell her that she'd been wrong about Srut and that the gypsy had saved his life at the Bone Church – he felt he owed him that. But Magdalena left, closing the door before he could get the words out. He sat listening to the fading click of her heals on the linoleum as she walked to the elevator.

It was a short walk from the Alstadt quarter to the American Consulate and Magdalena had more than an hour before she was expected there – and before Ales' minder, Gretel, would be bringing him to meet her.

Nuremberg, while only a short distance from Prague on a map, was like a different world – brighter and richer – even if it was still struggling to dig its way out of devastation. Most of Alstadt had been reduced to rubble during the war and was still in the process of being rebuilt – stone by old, worn stone. It looked good. In parts, it appeared as if nothing had happened at all. The sweet, half-timbered houses that lined the river Pegnitz had fresh flower boxes, lace curtains in the windows, and were newly painted as if they'd gone undisturbed all these years, cared for by the same, fastidious families that had lived in them for generations.

They were beautiful little homes – ones her mother would've loved. Vera had often said she could never live in a home without flower boxes and her own had always been brimming with violets.

"Oh, Mama," Magdalena whispered.

She bent over the embankment railing and wept for her mother, letting her tears fall into the river Pegnitz. For so long, grief had been a luxury she could ill afford, and in one sudden wave, stemming from one simple thought about flower boxes, Magdalena's sorrow overwhelmed her. Sorrow for her mother and for Felix's parents; sorrow for her Aunt Sarah, who died in Dachau with her infant son; sorrow for Antonin Melan who'd been such a good friend; and sorrow for the loss of her only real husband – Felix Andel, or whatever he called himself now, Ales's real father. He'd disappeared from her life for so long, and she'd almost convinced herself that she was fine without him. Magdalena had intended to tell Felix about Ales at the hospital. He was recovering well and she thought she'd summoned the nerve, but something had stopped her. The view out the window, perhaps, or the mention of Srut. The gypsy had always left them at an impasse with one another.

Magdalena shook her head and wiped the last of her tears from her cheeks. Tomorrow, she thought. She could get Ales a haircut before bringing him to the hospital. He would look good with his hair cut more like his father's.

From her pocket, she drew a copy of *"Solitudo"* by Jakub Deml, the Czech writer and former Catholic priest. She'd bought it at the same shop as the book on the Bone Church and had planned to give it to Felix as well, but forgot. It had seemed like something he would like.

Magdalena took a pen from her purse and opened the front book flap, running her fingers down the yellowing page that gave only the title. At the top of that page, she began to write. She wrote about what had happened to her after Merillini, the Monsignor, had abandoned her. How she'd gone to the wine bar Antonin Melan had told her about and found him there. How he'd let her stay with him and agreed to marry her even after he found she was pregnant with another man's child. How much Felix would have liked him.

When she ran out of room, she turned to the back cover and wrote there on the last, blank page. She wrote of Antonin's death, of Ales and how strong he'd been throughout all of it. Finally, she wrote all of the things she'd whispered to Felix at the hospital as he lay unconscious.

For the first time in what may have been years, a wide, contented smile unfolded across Magdalena's face. It could barely be contained by the look of censure a well-dressed bureaucrat shot her way. She bit down on her bottom lip and the man turned back to his own business, feeding the black swans on the river below. Felix had gone to her, he'd said. More than once. Maybe she should go to him again today, with Ales and the copy of "*Solitudo.*" After everything they'd been through together, she should at least have the courage to do that.

Magdalena looked down into the river Pegnitz and watched a fistful of violets glide under the bridge, past the swans, emerging on the other side and floating out of Nuremberg towards Hersbruck. They made her laugh out loud.

Magdalena wondered if at any point the river Pegnitz intersected the Vltava River, and if it was possible that those few perfect violets could float by the remains of the Castle Sverak and over her mother's grave.

Epilogue
The Outskirts of Prague: April 18, 1956

The Spaniard floated in the Vltava, drifting past a castle ruins that sat high on a hill top above him, and played with his wedding ring - a gift from his new bride.

"Alicia," he hummed, elongating each vowel.

He was daydreaming about a small scar on the curve of her hip that she had no recollection of getting. She swore it had to be a birthmark. As his mind's eye followed the scar and then continued on up to her navel, the unthinkable happened, and the Spaniard's wedding ring slipped over his knuckle and dropped to the bottom of the river.

"No! No!" he shouted, as he dove down into the murky water, forcing his eyes open and following the flicker of metal to the muddy riverbed. He swore he could see it, and tried to pick it up amongst the rocks and weeds of the river floor, but had to come up to the surface for another gulp of air before going down again. This time, he grabbed his shirt from the riverbank and used it to scoop up the entire area where his wedding ring had fallen, tying it off like a hobo's bag and dragging it to the surface.

When he untied his shirtsleeves and unraveled the soiled shirt, the Spaniard gasped and fell back into the river, inhaling a large gulp of water and crawling back up the river bank like a wet dog. He'd found his wedding ring, which lay burrowed into the bristles of a silver hairbrush, surrounded by a nest of finger bones and imprisoned inside an intact rib cage. The Spaniard plucked his wedding ring off the hairbrush and examined the skeleton parts, determining that they were indeed human.

Bones didn't frighten the Spaniard the way they did some people. He, infact, found them beautiful and consoling – especially ones this white that had been so thoroughly cleaned by fish and other river creatures. The Spaniard jumped once more into the Vltava and swam down to where his wedding ring had fallen, feeling for the rest of the person he'd disturbed. He found a skull, two femurs, the pelvis, and parts of the spine, bringing them up to the surface and placing them with the other bones. He knew now that it was a woman, and that she'd been buried with some ceremony – having been given such a fine hairbrush to hold. It concerned him that he'd taken this woman from her resting place, but once he'd disrupted her skeleton, there was little he could do but collect every piece he could find and try to give what remained of her body a proper place to rest. As he reassembled her, it occurred to him that finding this woman had been no accident. His twin sister had drowned in the Adriatic Sea four Christmases past and her body had never been recovered.

That afternoon, he drove to Kutna Hora with the woman neatly wrapped in brown paper and placed in his back seat with a small bunch of wildflowers tied into the twine that held the package together.

Jelena, the minder, was sitting outside the church when he pulled up. She toddled over to him, greeting him in Czech, though she knew he scarcely understood a word. The Spaniard was but one of a handful of pilgrims that still came to the Bone Church every year and she looked forward to his visits as much as she would've looked forward to her own son's had he not fled the country after the war. The Spaniard sent her postcards from Lourdes, Avila, Mount Nebo, the Sea of Galilee and other pilgrimage sites.

The Spaniard gestured to her as he took the brown package out of his car, and Jelena pulled a key out of her waistband and opened the doors to the Church of All Saints. She let the Spaniard enter first.

Like the Spaniard, Jelena wasn't particularly troubled by the sight of human bones. She sat with them all day long, and took comfort from knowing that her skull would one day stare back at the next minder of the Bone Church, the way past minders' skulls stared back at her. The last minder had only been dead a dozen years and Jelena had boiled and limed his bones herself, adding them to a garland that draped across the upper balcony and had been damaged by a gunfight within the church towards the end of the war.

"They're lovely," she remarked, caressing Vera Ruza's tibia. She picked up the silver hairbrush that lay with the bones and pulled a long, wavy black hair from its bristles.

"So nice," she said. "Like mine when I was young."

The Spaniard didn't understand her, but he motioned that the brush was hers if she wanted it and Jelena ran it through her hair and said, "Si." She hadn't seen such a fine brush in years and had never owned something so frivolous, though she'd always wanted to.

Jelena swept Vera Ruza's bones into her arms, the way she had her dog's after the poor poodle had mistakenly eaten rat poison. She carried the skeleton to the smallest pyramid of bones in all the ossuary. It lay just beyond a doorway leading to what used to be the rectory and had remained blessedly untouched by the ugliness of the gunfight. There, she arranged Vera's bones on top of the pyramid, placing her skull at the apex. If anyone other than the Spaniard had come to add a dearly departed to the Bone Church, she would have told them exactly where they could stick those bones, but she would've done just about anything for the Spanish pilgrim.

Although it was a privilege to have one's bones entombed in this ossuary at all, the Spaniard couldn't have known what a particular distinction it was for Jelena to have placed the dead woman's bones on this particular pyramid, on these particular bones. Apart from Jelena's poodle, the bones on that pyramid had come from people who were thought to be no less than saints, even if the church hadn't yet formally recognized them as such.

She'd always been adamant that only the most pious remains could protect what had been hidden at the bottom of the pyramid since her cousin, Marek Andel, had brought it there the day before he was killed. Jelena dared not say His name – even in her mind's voice – but pictured the benevolent look on the Infant of Prague's face. He lay shrouded by the true bones of Aldabert of Prague, the only official saint in the jumble.

Jelena wondered if it was time to let the church know where the real Infant was. She felt guilty that all these years, pilgrims and clergymen had gone to the Church of Our Lady the Victorious and knelt before a mere copy of the original.

Marek, however, had been convinced that the safety of the Infant was their utmost priority and that if the prayers of the faithful could reach God throughout the universe, then they could certainly reach the Infant in the short distance between Prague and Kutna Hora. Jelena agreed, and had ensured that upon her death, her son would send a certified letter to Rome detailing how she and Marek had kept the Infant safe all along.

"*Dekuju.*" The Spaniard thanked her in Czech and took her hand in his. The dead woman's skull looked good on the pyramid and when he looked deep into its hollow eye sockets, he almost felt as if it were his sister staring back at him. He kissed Jelena's thumb like a good knight and made the Bone Church's minder blush. Jelena and the Spaniard then bowed their heads, uttering a prayer in Latin – their only common language.

When they finished, the Spaniard voiced a Kaddish he'd once memorized – nearly singing its verses. He didn't know what made him say it and was surprised that he'd remembered the strange Aramaic words at all, having learned the Old Testament prayer so many years ago now.

"*Bella,*" Jelena told him. She caressed Vera Ruza's skull one last time, before closing it behind the heavy, gated door and turning the key in the lock.

The End

Acknowlegements

First, I'd like to thank my mom, dad, grandparents, and aunts and uncles for providing endless fodder for an aspiring thriller writer. Your harrowing, real-life experiences have not only informed my fiction, but the way I conduct my life. Thank you for showing me what real bravery looks like. Next, I want to kneel at my husband, Jack's, feet. I'm not kidding here. He deserves so much thanks for his tireless support and enthusiasm. I don't think a better spouse exists. Dale Eastman and Michele Kayal are great writers, terrific editors, and my best friends. Without them and our writing weekends, this story would never have evolved beyond a few pages.

Thanks also to Josh Getzler, Maddie Raffel and Danielle Burby at Hannigan Salky Getzler for editorial guidance, counsel and an occasional hand – not to mention belief in me. Kate Brauning, my terrific editor, who has pointed out so many things that I knew in my heart, but didn't have the courage to change…until she came along. Thank you, Kate. I love my cover art and have the talented Matt Roesner to thank for that. I also have so many wonderful readers who follow my blog, *Cold*, and I want to thank all of you, too. I especially appreciate your thoughtful comments about my Cold War musings. It means a lot. The writing community, both here in Charlottesville and online around my virtual watercooler have been a huge source of strength and inspiration as well as a wealth of information. Thank you for sharing and always being there with a kind word. Thanks in advance to all of my Prague friends, because I know you'll buy this book and hopefully see some of your own experiences and stories reflected in it. And finally, thanks to my kids, who not only put up with my shutting myself away in my office to write, but who talk me up to their friends and can't wait to read my books – even if they don't quite understand them.

CPSIA information can be obtained at www.ICGtesting.com
Printed in the USA
LVOW10s1639140914

404006LV00001B/56/P